The
Fire
Starters

A Nicholas Foxe Adventure

Jackson Coppley

Contour Press

The Fire Starters
A Nicholas Foxe Adventure
First Edition

Copyright © 2021

ISBN: **978-0-578-42055-4**

Published by

Contour Press

Chevy Chase, Maryland

www.ContourPress.com / / (301) 587-4343

To Ellen

The Fire Starters

A Nicholas Foxe Adventure

Chapter 1

Paris

The firebomb incinerated the body beyond recognition. Such a brutal murder would be a headline story in Paris any other day. But today, the whole world watched a different fire, one of historic magnitude. No one would suspect that one was connected to the other.

André Rousseau was a simple man, a modest man, who took silent pride in his work. God had given him skills in carpentry, and he now returned the favor by working on the restoration of one of man's magnificent tributes to Him. André's wife died last year, and he prayed for her soul every day. Working high on top of this monument, he liked to believe his prayers were closer to God's ears.

After André's wife passed away, his sister Claudine moved into his little flat. Claudine never found a man suitable for her and now, like her brother, both middle-aged, was not looking for anyone's company other than that offered by her brother.

André was the last one to leave when the workday ended; he climbed down the scaffolding ladders alone. As he walked away, he spotted a man lurking in the twilight shadows. The man turned briefly in his direction, then disappeared behind a wall. Probably another worker, André thought. Yet he clearly saw the man's face and had not recognized him. The man had smiled at André, but it was a twisted smile one might see on a crazy man on the street who talked to himself.

André walked over to where the man had stood and looked around but saw nothing. He thought he should report that he had seen someone who didn't belong there – but to whom?

Had he really seen someone? Was his imagination playing tricks?

André drove his old Fiat the half-hour trip to his apartment building. As he drove, he couldn't get that face out of his head. He parked at the curb in front of his apartment and considered the situation.

André was wrestling with what he should do. He decided he could do only one thing – call the police. He pulled out his cell phone as a motorcycle approached.

High above the street in their apartment, Claudine was watching CNN International in English as she always did in the late afternoon. It allowed her to listen to the news and help improve her skill in English, a little hobby to keep herself busy. She realized it was about time André was due home. She looked out the window to where André had already parked. He was a man of habit and she smiled at his arriving at the same time as the day before, and the day before that.

But why had André not left his car? Why did he continue to sit there?

Claudine watched from above as a red motorcycle pulled up beside André's car. The man on the motorcycle wore a helmet emblazoned with an image of flames flowing from front to rear.

Claudine saw the man on the motorcycle toss something into André's car and speed off. The car burst into flames. Claudine shrieked.

I must call for help!

She heard sirens in the distance, coming toward the apartment.

How could they come so quickly? I have not yet dialed.

The police cars, with blaring sirens, crossed the next intersection, never coming close to André's car, now engulfed in flames.

Stunned, Claudine turned to the television. She thought the world was coming to an end.

Notre Dame was in flames.

Chapter 2

Rome

Rome in the 15th century had become a backwater town with ruins dotting the landscape, a testament to when it was the center of the western world. The Colosseum saw its last gladiator fight a thousand years before but continued to be used for shops and apartments throughout the intervening years. An earthquake in 1349 destroyed even that use and the crumbling Colosseum was abandoned.

A hundred years later, it is now the perfect playground for ten-year-old Paolo and his two friends. They rummage through the ruins, seeking treasures. In one small, dark chamber, Paolo finds a bronze pot, cracked down one side. He puts the pot on his head like a helmet, picks up a stick, and brandishes it like a sword. "I am Paolo," he announces, "the greatest gladiator of all times."

"Ha!" shouts one of the boys who already has a stick in hand. "No, you are not! I am!"

A sword fight ensues with sticks at the ready. The second friend joins in. The sword fight quickly turns into a chase with Paolo running out of the chamber and into the hallway, the other boys close at his heels. He dodges mounds of dirt under collapsed roofs and soon leaves the Colosseum to the surrounding meadow.

Out of breath, he removes the pot and tosses it aside. He considers taking it to his mother, but even Paolo could tell it was beyond repair. The boys quickly decide on another game. "Let's hide in the woods," says one of Paolo's friends. They agree, although hiding from whom they had not yet worked out. The boys' games were fluid in their rule making. They set out toward a steep hill beside the Colosseum and climb through the grove of trees. They had been there many times before. Running into a copse, they come to a series of brick arches with iron gates blocking the way.

"I wonder what this is," says one of his friends.

Paolo tells him, "My papa told me this was a bath house the ancients used."

Paolo's father was a stonemason at the Vatican. When Paolo was born, his father was working to build the Sistine Chapel. This alone made Paolo's father revered by Paolo's friends. If he says this was a bathhouse, it must be so.

"I wonder if there is another way in?" says a friend.

"Let's look!" says Paolo. "Spread out." Paolo separates from his friends and takes a route further up the hill.

The surface of the earth rests for long stretches of time, while the weather shapes it in unpredictable ways. Sometimes, a sudden change may affect the earth, as it did a hundred years earlier with an earthquake. If it was the weather's gradual shifting of the soil or the long-forgotten earthquake, it would soon become clear that Paolo would be the first person to step on this particular square meter of ground since it had weakened.

Gravity sucks Paolo into the soil, and he cries out. Both of his friends arrive to see a hole in the ground the size of their friend. They yell down into the dark. "Paolo! Are you there? Paolo! Can you hear us?"

The friends listen, desperate to hear Paolo. After a few long seconds, Paolo yells back, "I am all right. Get me out of here!"

"I will get a rope," says one and he dashes off. The other friend remains behind.

"Paolo, what do you see?" asks the remaining friend.

"It's too dark. I see nothing." Paolo remains on his back, the position in which he fell. Gradually, his eyes adjust to the dark, the only illumination coming from the hole he created. Like a fog slowly clearing, a vision comes to him. Seeing the outline at first, then the face, he soon sees an angel, looking down on him.

My guardian angel?

As he admires the angel, he hears the voice of a man above coming through the hole.

God?

It was not God, but the face of a mortal peering through the opening down at him. "Are you all right?"

"I am," responds Paolo.

"I have a rope. I tied it together at one end. I will lower it. Put the loop around your waist and I will pull you up."

Paolo does as he is told and is soon back on the surface. He reports the angel he saw to the man who rescued him and later to his father and mother. Everyone considers it a miracle.

Paolo grew, and as he did, he learned his father's trade. Paolo was blessed with an artist's eye and, crouching at his father's knee, he chiseled simple designs into the stone. Within a few years, his designs were installed on important buildings.

But Paolo yearned to be an artist. By the time he was twenty-one, he had spent as much time as he could in a place where artists gathered, mostly to carouse, but also to discuss their art.

One evening, he spots a young man about his age attracting a lot of attention, and although he is known to the others, Paolo had never noticed him before. "Who is that?" he asks an artist beside him with a mug of wine in his hand.

"I forget his name. They tell me he's working in Florence for the Medici." The man rubs his fingers together as though he is rubbing coins. "You know, very fine patronage."

"I'm going to meet him," responds Paolo as he stands and walks over to the stranger. One of Paolo's friends is talking to the man and makes the introduction.

"Paolo, my friend, I would like you to meet the sensation of Florence, Michelangelo."

"It is my pleasure," responds Paolo, unsure whether he should know who this man is.

Paolo's friend saves him from any embarrassment by saying, "I was just telling Michelangelo he must meet you."

"Meet me? Why?"

Michelangelo takes over the conversation. "I understand you are the man who discovered the Domus Aurea."

"As a child, yes. I still take people to it, or at least to the part I discovered. No one knows how much remains buried."

The friend speaks up. "But he wants to see the art, you know, *the angel.*" His friend laughs.

Rome is a small town. Everyone knows about the boy who fell into the ground and saw an angel. Paolo soon learns it was nothing more than ceiling art, but that is precisely what Michelangelo wants to see.

"That is so," added Michelangelo. "I hear there is art on the ceiling. That would interest me very much. Would you take me there?"

"It would be my honor," says Paolo graciously, uncertain how much of an honor it would be to show this unknown man to the place he discovered. However, the man is dressed in finer clothes than most of the artists there, and his friend says the Medici are his patrons.

Perhaps this man would pay well.

Michelangelo sees Paolo's uncertainty and says, "Of course I would pay you for that honor."

The next evening, Paolo leads Michelangelo to the Domus Aurea entrance he accidentally created. Paolo had led several people to this site in the years since he stumbled into it and he now has a rope, winch and stand he totes to the site, as well as a torch he lights for his visitors. Michelangelo brings a letter satchel with drawing materials. He sits on the leather seat at the end of the pulley rope, then Paolo hands him a lit torch and lowers the artist into the pit.

Michelangelo settles into the dirt, stands the torch nearby, and marvels at the ceiling.

"It is quite something, is it not?" Paolo asks from above through the opening.

"Indeed it is," exclaims the artist. "I will make some sketches. I may be here for a long time."

"Take your time. I am here when you need me."

Michelangelo was focusing most of his talent on sculpture, but he was aware that some painter friends were recently experimenting with the new technique of fresco for wall paintings. Yet no one had considered painting a ceiling. However, here is a ceiling painting that must have used some type of fresco technique. There are separate rectangular frames depicting an army ready for battle, a woman reclining for a feast, and, yes, a woman the young Paolo mistook for an angel. The artist takes out the tools of his trade and sketches what he sees.

A mouse wanders by, distracts him briefly, and it quickly scampers away into a crevice. Michelangelo considers how much more of the Domus lies undiscovered; how many more paintings are yet to be seen. Then, for no reason he can identify, a chill runs through him. He imagines he had followed the mouse into a hellish part of the palace, a part consumed in flames. It is only a moment, a quick daydream. He passes it off and continues his drawing.

Michelangelo pays Paolo and pays him well. Perhaps a little too well, for this boy seems compelled to give him more than he requested for the gratuity. Paolo asks his father if he could get himself and Michelangelo into what his father refers to as his masterpiece, the Sistine Chapel. Soon Paolo, his father, and Michelangelo stand in the chapel.

Paolo turns to Michelangelo. "It is impressive, is it not?"

Michelangelo studies the blank walls of the huge open area. "Yes, it is."

"Of course, the Pope wants to enhance such a fine chapel with art. Perhaps one day."

Michelangelo, fresh from the Domus, looks to the ceiling, now realizing the possibilities. It would be years before a new Pope would commission such work, but at that moment, Michelangelo lowers his gaze to the far wall and imagines a painting of the heavenly hosts. Then the daydream from the Domus reoccurs and Michelangelo knows that below heaven, there must be hell.

Chapter 3

New York City

Fifteen years ago, Nicholas Foxe sat in the one room of his townhouse where he felt most at home, his study. Surrounding him were artifacts and mementos of his life as an archeologist. He was lucky to have a fortune which enabled him to pursue his passion. Unlike many couples who are two-income families, he and his wife Nina were a two-trust-fund family. Nicholas Foxe the First, Nick's grandfather, invented a drill bit for the oil industry, a patent that created the family fortune. His dad, Nicholas Foxe the Second, was a financier who expanded that fortune. And Nick Foxe the Third, now seated in his study, would spend much of it.

Nina Westervelt had a family fortune of her own, enabling the purchase of art and furnishings for both this house on the Upper East Side and for their home in the Hamptons. However, except for his study, Nick felt he lived in a show house in New York City with nothing meant to be touched. Only here, in this room off to one side of the entrance, did Nick feel comfortable.

Nick showcased a bust from a Mayan ruin on the credenza behind his desk, a Byzantine tablet to his left on a bookcase with other items, each of which told a personal story. On the opposite wall behind a glass enclosure hung a blowgun, once aimed at Nick in South America.

Nick, dressed in a tux, waited for Nina to finish dressing. They were invited to a gala for one of Nina's many charities. *Too many of them,* Nick thought. He had nothing against causes but winced at the thought of these long, identical evenings of canapés, fixed grins, and tedious conversation with people he'd never meet again.

Nick walked to the foyer and asked the maid to tell Nina he was stepping outside for some air.

Dusk had settled across the iron-railed stoops and brick homes on the street. The cool air and falling leaves signaled the start of autumn. Garbage cans lined both sides of the street awaiting the next morning's collection.

At the other end of the block, Nick spotted a teenager he didn't recognize. Not unusual in a city of strangers. What the boy was doing, though, caught Nick's attention. The boy stood at an open garbage can. He was shifting his weight from one foot to the other.

What's this kid up to?

Then Nick saw the match. It was a wooden match like the one with which his grandfather lit his cigars. The boy flicked his nail against the tip of the match, and it flared into a bright orange and red flame. The boy held the match high in his fingertips and gazed at the flame as though it was a thing of wonder.

Then the boy dropped the match into the garbage can. Nick had not seen what was in the can, or what the boy may have put in it, but whatever it was burst into flames.

Nick yelled out to the boy and started toward him. The boy, apparently unaware of Nick's presence until he yelled, turned, and darted into the alley behind him. Nick reached the garbage can and put the lid on it, snuffing out the flames. He ran into the alley, but there was no sign of the boy.

The flames extinguished, Nick told himself this was only a youthful prank, but he didn't quite believe it. Perhaps it was the way the boy studied the match as the flame descended the stick toward his fingers. The kid showed both appraisal and attraction. Nick was still standing by the garbage can when Nina shouted to him from the front door.

Nick and Nina attended the gala. Nina commented that Nick was unusually quiet and asked him about his mood. He told her about the incident and Nina laughed. She said something about punk kids in the neighborhood. Nick couldn't get it out of his head.

The next morning, the front door chime rang. Nick answered it to find a man who identified himself as a police detective. The detective said he was investigating several fires set in the neighborhood. Had Nick seen anything suspicious?

When Nick told the detective about the boy from the night before, the police asked him to come to the station. They might have that boy in custody.

Nick was led to a room in the police station. There would be no lineup as they didn't do that sort of thing for juveniles. The detective brought in a boy who dressed like any jeans-wearing teen from Nick's part of town. He recognized the kid as the fire starter. The kid hung his head, looking at the floor. When the detective said he wanted the kid to meet someone, he made eye contact with Nick. The boy's recognition was clear. He knew Nick was the man who had chased him the previous night.

A uniformed officer joined Nick and the detective to wait until a parent arrived. At the mention of the word *parent*, the boy sneered as though he thought parents were nonexistent, a fairy tale. With that, the detective led Nick out of the room and into the adjoining one where a one-way mirror allowed them to monitor the boy.

The detective asked Nick if he saw this boy start a fire and Nick confirmed he had. Nick wanted to know what would happen next. The detective said both of the boy's parents were unavailable. The mother was in California and the father was in Europe on business. They were able to reach the mother, who told them the family housekeeper would come to claim the boy.

With an expression of disdain, the detective informed Nick that the housekeeper was coming. Poor little rich kid with disengaged parents.

A woman burst into the room and addressed the boy as Raymond. The name was delivered as a scolding invective intensified by a British accent. The woman was thin and stern. She looked like the Julie Andrews version of Mary Poppins. But Nick knew no spoonful of sugar would ever be administered by this woman.

Nick asked what would happen to the boy. The detective said the boy had been responsible for several fires. No one was hurt, and property damage was insignificant. A judge would likely order a psychiatric examination and treatment. The detective had seen it before. The boy was a pyromaniac.

The detective walked Nick out and thanked him for coming in. As they passed, the desk sergeant asked if they were letting the Woodward kid go. The police would never divulge a fourteen-year-old juvenile's name if Nick had asked. But with what the sergeant and housekeeper revealed, Nick knew the kid's name: Raymond Woodward.

Ray Woodward ended up in the care of Dr. Milton Perry, who wasn't a court-ordered psychiatrist. Ray's father paid for the best New York offered, and he chose well. Dr. Perry specialized in pyromania. He literally wrote a book on it. As a plus, Ray liked this short, stout, avuncular man.

Fire had been a part of human existence from the start. Neanderthals harnessed fire over a million years ago. For many, fire was utilitarian, a means to cook food, and a way to work metal. Most people found it calming. But to the pyromaniac, that comfort feeling was out of control. It was as though fire was a drug, a fix. Ray showed all the signs of a pyromaniac. He would become edgy, fidgety, and only a fire would calm him. Dr. Perry may have been the expert on the condition, but even he was uncertain as to its cause.

Dr. Perry worked with Ray to control his urges. Some therapists used cognitive-behavioral therapy in which the patient would learn to associate something disagreeable with a specific action. Perry thought this too cruel. He preferred drugs and put Ray on different doses of anxiety medications. Eventually, a light, regular dose of Valium eased his patient's symptoms.

Four years passed, and Nick hadn't thought much about the young arsonist he had encountered. But when Ray was eighteen, Nick ran into him at a coffee shop around the corner from his house. As he placed his order at the counter, Nick spotted a young man, vaguely familiar, peering at him from a table near a window. As the barista handed Nick his order, the young man approached him.

"Are you Nicholas Foxe?" the young man asked.

"Yes, I am," responded Nick. "I believe I know you, don't I?"

Nick's questioning expression told the young man that he was having trouble placing him.

"I guess I've changed since we last met. At least, I've grown a couple of inches." The young man put his hand out to shake. "I'm Ray Woodward. The guy you ID'ed for the police."

Nick shook the offered hand. "So, how are you? You mind if we sit and talk?"

"Sure," replied Ray. "I've got a table over here."

Ray walked Nick back to the table by the window where he had left his coffee.

As Nick sat, he said, "You know, the police wouldn't share any information with me, you being a juvenile at the time. But I've been curious. What have you been doing?"

Ray seemed to understand Nick's frame of reference. Here, before him, was a guy diagnosed in his teens as a pyromaniac. Sure, the police sealed the records, but Ray must have known a man like Nick would have connections if he wanted to find out more. Ray had worked hard on himself, and he wanted Nick to know it.

"First of all, I underwent counseling. A doctor worked with me, and I have my little problem under control, Mr. Foxe."

"Please, it's just Nick."

"OK. Nick. Just to let you know, I've never let it interfere with my life. I did OK in school. I graduate this spring."

"What are your plans after that?"

"College."

"Where?" asked Nick.

Ray smiled with a hint of pride. "Harvard," he replied.

"That's great!"

"Well, Dad graduated from there. I guess I'm a legacy."

"That gets you only so far. You earned it yourself."

"Thanks," replied Ray with half-hearted confidence.

"No," said Nick. "Look at me." Ray looked up from the table and met Nick's gaze. "You are smart. You will do well. I know it."

Ray's face lit up as a man unused to praise.

Nick remembered from his encounter at the police station those years ago, that Ray appeared to have absentee parents. Nick had seen it before. Wealthy parents whose children were only placeholders for the next generation of the family name.

It had been only a brief encounter, but Nick saw that his simple endorsement meant much to this young man.

Nick glanced at his watch and stood. He told Ray, "Look, I have to go, but I want to hear from you." Nick fished out a business card from his pocket and handed it to Ray. "Keep in touch. Drop me a line from time to time to let me know how you're doing."

Ray beamed as he took Nick's card. "Thanks. I will."

Nick didn't give his offer a second thought, but little did he know that

Ray would play an important, and dangerous, role in Nick's life years later.

Dr. Perry had released Ray from his care and wished him well in his college endeavors. He told Ray he hoped other patients would have his same success.

Six months passed. Dr. Perry left his office late one afternoon, as he normally did, said goodbye to his receptionist, and headed to his car. Dr. Perry was fortunate to have a parking space on an open lot beside his office, a treasure in Manhattan. He opened the rear door on his Mercedes and tossed in his briefcase.

Settling into the driver's seat, Perry pressed the start button. The ignition sequence on his Mercedes had been expertly diverted and his last seconds of life played out in slow motion. The firebomb was placed and primed to torture its victim, if only for a few brief seconds. It provided time for a man to comprehend what was happening to him, but not enough time to rescue himself.

Perry rose in his seat as the bomb struck from below. His seatbelt halted his head from hitting the roof and yanked him back as the fire burst through the interior. Hot, searing flames licked at him. He smelled the acrid stink of his hair on fire.

Perry reached for his seatbelt buckle. The metal was already hot and branded his flesh. He clicked it loose and fell out of the door, his clothes now aflame. His body rolled onto the sidewalk where it remained as he lost consciousness.

To: Nicholas Foxe

From: Raymond Woodward

Subject: Checking In

Nick,

It was good meeting you again. I appreciated your comments. I have no idea whether I'm up to the challenges ahead, but the verbal pat on the back meant a lot to me.

Ray

To: Raymond Woodward

From: Nicholas Foxe

Re: Checking In

Ray,

It was not faint praise. I have good instincts. My gut tells me you will make your mark on the world.

Nick

Chapter 4
Cheltenham, England

Lloyd Watson could have used a good psychiatrist, not for pyromania, but to recover from committing murder as a boy.

Cheltenham, in South West England, produced Lloyd in 1974. More notable was who it had produced one-hundred years earlier, the composer Gustav Holst. Although Holst was not known as well as Beethoven or Bach, he achieved sufficient fame to be lionized by his hometown. A bronze statue of Holst, his arms raised in a conductor pose, stands prominently in a park. Lloyd despised it.

Lloyd's mother played opera and classical piano on the stereo all day long as she did housework. She loved playing the old upright piano in the living room when she finished her chores. She doted on Lloyd, her only child, from the time he was an infant and was pleased when the little baby sat up and rocked in time to music. When Lloyd was a toddler, he wouldn't keep his hands off the old piano.

Their home was a sweet environment for a child, until Father returned each evening.

Father was a business owner. He owned several buildings around town and was a merciless landlord when collecting rents. He carried a revolver with him, letting recalcitrant renters catch a peek under his coat, a silent warning to pay up. Lloyd's mother was afraid of having the gun in the house, but Father dismissed her fear as yet another weakness of a timid wife.

"Where's my drink?" he would bellow to his wife upon entering the house each evening. Lloyd's mother was well trained to have her husband's Irish whiskey at the ready. When Lloyd was learning to talk, one evening he parroted his father's evening command with "Where dink?"

Father sneered at the baby sitting and smiling up at him. Rather than enjoying the boy's attempt to talk, he leaned down and sniffed. He yelled over to his mother, "The boy's soiled his nappy!"

As Mother hurried to pick Lloyd up to change him, Father continued with his tirade. "Can't you keep the little brat clean, woman?"

The baby Lloyd didn't understand, but Father's debasement of Mother became clearer as he grew. The harsh slaps he administered to Mother made the little Lloyd cry, which only infuriated the old man further. Mother would pick Lloyd up to comfort and protect him from the raging beast.

Peace prevailed during the day with Father away. Mother would play her beloved music on the stereo, and Lloyd would play on the old piano. One day, when Lloyd was four, as Mother was cleaning the kitchen, she heard something from the living room other than the childish plinking of keys. It was Chopin. It was one of the master's simpler pieces, but it was unmistakably Chopin. She wandered into the living room to find little Lloyd at the keyboard playing away. The boy turned to smile at his mother who beamed back with pride.

Mother taught Lloyd the piano as best she could, but he did his playing only during the day. When Lloyd turned seven, Mother understood Lloyd needed more training than she could offer. She knew she must approach Father to pay for such lessons, but she feared his response.

"Where's my drink?" roared Father. He was nothing if not consistent.

Mother served Father his whiskey, she allowed him to settle into his easy chair and take several long draws. Father picked up the evening newspaper, held it as a barrier to all present, and perused it.

"Father," said Mother, "Lloyd has a surprise for you."

Father hardly ever acknowledged his son. Lloyd had grown these seven years with a doting mother and a distant dad. All Father could offer from behind the paper was a dismissive, "Is that so?"

"Yes, dear," said Mother. Turning to Lloyd, she told the boy, "Lloyd, please play for your father."

Without Father dropping the paper to see what was going on, Lloyd took a seat at the upright piano, pushed back the key cover, and began. He played Chopin's Prelude Number 20 in C Minor, a short piece that challenged the finger span of the seven-year-old, but a piece commonly recognized.

Father lowered his paper, unsmiling, to observe his son. After Lloyd finished the short piece, Father turned to Mother and asked, "What else can the boy play?"

Mother, nervous and unsure of the reaction from Father, who now was inscrutable, asked Lloyd, "How about Moonlight Sonata?"

As Lloyd played Beethoven's masterpiece flawlessly, Father rose from his chair. Mother gave a cautious smile toward Father, unsure of what he could be thinking. Father walked to the piano and observed Lloyd's mastery of the keyboard. He then paced the room, lost in thought. Mother waited.

Lloyd concluded the sonata and turned to Father. Without looking at Lloyd, Father smiled for the first time. In the general direction of Mother, he boomed, "This is tremendous!"

Mother returned a tentative smile, unsure what Father might mean.

"You know that stupid Charlie Marini?" Father asked. Of course, Mother knew him. Charlie was another landlord and a chief competitor of Father's. "He's always prattling on about his brilliant son, the musical genius. 'Comes from his Italian roots,' he says." Father said mockingly.

"I had to meet the man just the other day to talk over a property he wants to sell. Had me meet in the park. He pointed up to the statue of Holst and told me, 'They're going to have to make room for another statue one day for my son. He's going places.' Well, I've got a thing or two to show the little twerp!"

Mother saw her chance. "Lloyd is doing great. He really is. But my lessons are not enough. He needs a professional."

Father continued as though Mother had said nothing. "Charlie said something about a competition, something that's supposed to happen soon."

It was Lloyd that spoke up. "There is a music contest soon. A mate at school told me. He's going to play the flute in it."

Father responded to Lloyd. "Do you know when and where?" To which little Lloyd could only shrug his shoulders, showing he had no clue.

Father huffed and turned back to Mother. "Find out. I know that idiot will have his son in it. Well, mine's going to beat him!"

Father returned to his easy chair and picked up his whiskey. "Play more for me, boy!"

Lloyd continued to play different pieces in his repertoire for over an hour, only stopping when Father's snores emanated from the easy chair.

Mother signed up Lloyd for the contest. She chose Moonlight Sonata and thought the judges would love Lloyd's expert playing of it. The town's people crowded into the small auditorium the evening of the contest. Father smiled when he entered the room and spotted Charlie Marini talking to someone he didn't know. Father walked up to Charlie and interrupted.

"So, Charlie. Your boy is playing tonight, is he?"

"That's right," responded Charlie. "I didn't expect you would be interested in such things. I'm quite surprised to see you here tonight."

Father beamed. "Well, I have a surprise for you. My son is playing the piano tonight."

"As is my son. But I must admit, I didn't even know you had a son."

Were Charlie to need any evidence of Father's ignoring his little boy, this would have been it. Now, Father boasted about his son.

"Well, you will have something to remember," he told Charlie.

The master of ceremonies came to the stage and people hurried to their seats.

"Good luck to your son," said Charlie. "I better take my seat."

The night proved to display the talents one would expect of a small town. A girl played the violin, screeching a note or two. A boy, challenged by pubescent voice changes, did a fair job on an aria. Apparently, the organizers were saving the best for last. Only Lloyd and Charlie's son remained.

Lloyd took a seat at the baby grand piano. This would be the first time he had played anything but the old upright at home. He began to play Moonlight Sonata, and the little boy was struck by the deep, rich tones of this beautiful instrument. He was lost in the music as it pulled him along. No one could have played Beethoven's sonata better than this little seven-year-old boy.

When he finished, the room erupted in applause. People were standing. Mother teared up. Father was clapping the loudest. Lloyd stood and took a bow as his mother had instructed and walked offstage. As he reached the wings, he encountered Charlie's son. He was a thirteen-year-old, much taller than Lloyd. Charlie's son smiled at Lloyd and said, "Very good. You did well."

The compliment unnerved Lloyd. It was a compliment from one who knew he was better.

Charlie's son took a quick bow and sat at the piano. He began to play Liszt's Hungarian Rhapsody Number 2. The beginning, strong and slow, let the audience know that this young man would do something special. When he came to the rapid, lively sequence best known for this composition, the audience was ready. They were clapping in time to the beat. Liszt, himself, had been a showman. He knew how to get an audience to its feet, and Charlie's son repeated Liszt's success in doing so that night.

Lloyd had performed flawlessly, and although Charlie's son, to a professional's ear, made a few mistakes, the Rhapsody allowed him to power through them. The judges awarded the prize to Charlie's son.

Father was furious. He stormed out of the building, ignoring Charlie, who was standing by to compliment Lloyd's performance. Mother was left behind to gather her son. When she arrived backstage, she witnessed Charlie's son shaking Lloyd's hand and praising his performance. "You'll go places," he said.

When Mother and Lloyd returned home, Father was pacing the floor. Lloyd, all smiles, held high to his father the trophy representing second place. Father slapped the trophy out of the boy's hand, launching it against the nearest wall. Father advanced on his son, who was now backing away.

Father roared, "You lost!" as Lloyd continued to back away.

"But he played beautifully," protested Mother.

"Shut up!" yelled Father as he slapped her to the floor. Then he ignored Lloyd for a moment while haranguing Mother. "You're responsible for this! You made him the little sissy he is. Little Mommy's boy. That's all he is. And the one thing that could set him apart? Even that, you messed up. Why didn't you teach him that piece Charlie's boy played? Was it too hard for your precious little baby?"

Mother had seen Lloyd leave the room after Father slapped her. As she struggled to her feet, she saw Lloyd had returned. He was standing behind Father with something in his hands. Mother had no idea the little boy knew where Father kept it. Lloyd had Father's revolver.

"Don't hit her!" Lloyd yelled to his father.

Father turned around. When he saw the boy nervously holding the huge weapon, he laughed. "Well, well. And just what do you think you are going to do with that?"

Lloyd cocked the revolver, taking most of the strength the little boy could muster. "I said, leave her alone."

Father approached the boy. "Give me that thing!"

If anyone had witnessed the years of abuse Father dished out toward Lloyd and his mother, they would conclude the little boy had let it all roll off. He never seemed upset. But that would be a mistaken observation. Lloyd had internalized each slight, each bullying move, the lack of an ounce of fatherly compassion. It had affected the boy's mind in unseen ways, until then. There, in their own living room, Lloyd's hatred reached the tipping point.

Lloyd was hardly a trained shooter at seven years old. The revolver was enormous in his hands. But he didn't need training in the weapon's use. Father was a huge bear of a man inches away. Lloyd need only pull the trigger.

The blast knocked the revolver from Lloyd's hands. Was it the loud report of the gun that put the stunned expression on Father's face? Mother recoiled. Long seconds played out as the three people in the room tried to make sense of what just happened. Then the blood gushing from Father's vest made it clear.

Father fell to the floor, blood spurting onto the carpet.

Mother lifted her son into her arms. Lloyd cried. She comforted him. "There, there. It's all over. It's going to be all right."

Lloyd's crying stopped as quickly as it started. He looked at his mother with dead eyes that gave his mother pause. Lloyd said, "I know."

The law was kind to Mother and Lloyd. 'An accidental shooting,' was the verdict. No jail time for anyone. Mother and Lloyd went to live with Grandmother. "I told you never to marry that man!" was Grandmother's first admonition.

Setting that early scolding aside, life improved for Lloyd. Grandmother supported Lloyd's talent and provided the best tutors for him. He tried his hand at composition and the tutors thought he showed promise. Mother would take walks with the boy, now entering his teen years. They frequently found their way to Holst's statue.

"You will one day outdo him," Mother said, pointing to the statue. "I know it."

Lloyd began to compose, first for the piano and then for a chamber group. When Lloyd was a young man, his mother died. Grandmother followed her three years later. He felt adrift without his mother. He shaped a composition fueled by his grief. Beethoven's Fifth had the theme of death knocking at the door. Lloyd would dedicate his symphony to the other side of death's door, to the depths of hell.

But something unexpected happened. Lloyd had assumed his father had all the money in the family. He soon discovered his grandmother's wealth, a considerable amount of which she willed to Lloyd. Now he had enough money to do whatever he wished. He would create a symphony that would make his hometown forget about Holst.

Chapter 5

New York City

Spending time in caves, grottos, castles, and oceans had occupied much of Nick's time of late. While he'd been away, he missed his New York City study. He enjoyed the comfort of this room, surrounded by mementos of past adventures. When the spoils of their marriage were split, Nina got the place in the Hamptons, and Nick kept the house in New York. Although the house in the Hamptons was worth more, the house in New York meant more to Nick. This room was part of it.

He kept a letter opener, much too sharp, on one side of his desk. It was a gift from someone special who he remembered fondly. Someone who had died much too young. He studied it for a long time. One last look, and then he put it into a seldom used drawer.

Nick turned his attention to the manuscript in front of him. It was a compilation of the writings of the ancient historian Pliny. Pliny the Elder, or Gaius Plinius Secundus, was a scholar who wrote histories of Rome up through the reign of Nero. What mystified Nick was not what Pliny wrote about Nero, but what he didn't write.

Nick was usually involved in hands-on work, hunting for artifacts in out-of-the-way places. He didn't like much to speak about his work, although it was a frequent request. He made an exception for a friend who was a fellow member of The Society of Cryptography. The friend knew Nick was interested in this period of Roman history and asked him to address The Explorers Club, where he was a member. Nick agreed.

Nick brushed up on his readings and prepared a few words. After several minutes with his notes, he headed out to the club.

The Explorers Club, an organization over a hundred years old, was housed in a castle-like structure on East 70th Street. Nick could walk to it from his house. He had attended many of its annual dinners honoring notables for their expeditions. Honorees spanned from Teddy Roosevelt to Buzz Aldrin.

Nick entered the club's lobby. "Nick! How good of you to come." It was Walter Jameson, the man who had invited Nick to speak. Walt looked the part of the New York aristocrat explorer. Tall, hardy, and outgoing. Then again, Nick bore the same characteristics.

"Let's sit and talk."

Walt led Nick to the first-floor fireplace, the club's signature piece. Elephant tusks bordered it on each side. Once ornaments of high adventure, they were now symbols of poaching and diminished elephant populations.

"How have you been?" asked Walt as they took seats in overstuffed chairs.

"Fine."

"You know, Nick, everyone's familiar with your discoveries of late. We've had several honorees. You should be one of them."

"I wouldn't be able to carry the flag," responded Nick. It was a reference to the requirement that a club member must display its flag when the expedition reaches its goal. Once approved, the sponsored party must exhibit the club flag at every suitable opportunity on the expedition and return it to the club along with a written record of the expedition — the Flag Report. Thor Heyerdahl did it on the Kon-Tiki expedition in 1947. Film director James Cameron did it looking for the Titanic.

For the 'expeditions' Nick found himself in, he could hardly meet those requirements. Nick winked and responded, "Perhaps a Club Medal one day."

Walt smiled. "I know Pliny is not the kind of topic we usually talk about here, but a talk could be about expeditions to Roman ruins."

"Expeditions?" Nick was dubious.

"Well, excursions if you will. We have private tours to different sites. And your guy Pliny wrote about them during the early rise of Roman power."

"True."

"But you're more of a guy who gets his hands dirty. Never took you for a scholar, delving into books, old histories, that sort of thing."

Nick knew Walt summed him up correctly. He wasn't sure why he had been so intrigued with what Pliny had to say. He could only respond, "Not sure myself."

A young man on the club's staff appeared and whispered something to Walt.

"It seems everyone is ready and waiting. All set?" Walt asked as he stood.

"Lead on."

Walt showed Nick to a room in which twenty people were seated. Walt stepped up to a lectern before a gothic window surrounded by mounted trophies.

"Gentlemen," Walt began. (There were no women in the room.) "I know you all have seen much in the press about our speaker today, Mr. Nicholas Foxe. He is not here today to speak about his adventures. After all, what more could he tell you that CNN hasn't already?"

Modest laughter trickled through the room.

"Nick has a passion for Pliny, you might say. He's here today to share some of his tidbits on the man and his role in a period of ancient Rome we have been talking about."

Nick took the lectern as Walt led a round of applause.

"Thank you," Nick said as he began.

"Pliny the Elder was formally known as Gaius Plinius Secundus. He was from a wealthy family and his father sent him to Rome to study law.

Simpler at that time since they had written few laws."

The crowd responded with a few laughs, enough to let him know they would respond to his more lighthearted approach.

"In AD 46, in his early twenties, Pliny entered the Army. The other officers could see he was a man of letters. He wrote a lot, much of it lost, but we have an intriguing amount surviving to this day.

"Pliny spent most of his ten-year enlistment leading a cavalry unit along the Rhine River. Some rich and powerful men recognized him as a valuable, smart young man. A man who could both argue the law and, at the same time, design a unique javelin device for mounted soldiers.

"After his enlistment ended, he moved to Rome about the same time Nero became Emperor. This is the period that interests me. But let me move on and I'll tell you why later.

"After Nero committed suicide, and after a year of civil war, Vespasian became Caesar. Pliny had much in common with Vespasian. Both came up from the equestrian class, rising through the ranks of the army and public offices. Vespasian trusted Pliny and thus he became something of the new emperor's right-hand man.

"Here is what I find interesting. Before Nero and after Nero, with Vespasian in power, Pliny wrote much about Rome, its history, and its army. But during Nero's reign, as Nero lost touch with reality and drifted toward insanity, Pliny stuck to subjects on grammar and rhetoric. Perhaps he thought a low profile was safe.

"But there was one exception, and that was The Golden Palace, or Domus Aurea as it was called. Pliny lived in Rome and witnessed it being built. The Golden Palace was Nero's monument to his own excess. He had it built after the great fire of Rome. You know, the one in which Nero fiddled.

"The grounds included groves of fruit and olive trees, pastures stocked with flocks of sheep, vineyards groaning with grapes, and an artificial lake with a 120-foot statue of Nero at one end. The palace itself had 300 rooms, and none of them were bedrooms. Talk about a party house!"

Light laughter.

"Here is what I've puzzled over. Pliny had a few observations on the Domus Aurea. The best translation I have been able to find is 'it is a house in which fire was born.'"

Nick stopped, more for his own reflection than for a dramatic pause. "It seems Pliny's grammar is backwards. They built the palace on land where buildings had been destroyed by the great fire. So, it seems he should have written, or been translated as having written, 'it was a fire in which a house was born,' not the other way around.

"But we are unlikely to know more. After Nero committed suicide, Vespasian buried the whole palace. He removed the valuable jewels and marble from the walls, filled the palace with dirt, and built public baths on top."

Nick paused again but could see he was the only man in the room intrigued.

"Well, in any case, I want to open it up for questions. I think it may be the best way to continue."

"How did Pliny die?"

"He sailed to Pompeii during the eruption to save a friend and died there. It's likely his ship caught on fire."

"What do we know about the son?"

"Pliny the Younger. He provided us with a lot of information about his father's time and about Rome during that period."

Ten minutes of questions followed until Walt approached the lectern and brought the talk to an end. People rose to their feet as drinks were being served. Nick continued to answer questions about the Domus Aurea and Pliny. As he socialized and answered questions, he noticed one of the audience members flipping through the program. The man was middle-aged, heavyset, and dressed in a rumpled black suit. He had a full beard speckled with gray and a yarmulke on his head.

As the members talked among themselves, Nick walked over to the man who put his program down and met Nick halfway. He spoke first.

"Very interesting, your observations on Pliny, Mr. Foxe," he said.

"Thank you. You have me at a disadvantage. You know who I am..."

"Of course. Let me introduce myself. I am Isaac Genack."

"I know you," Nick said. "That is, I'm familiar with your work, Rabbi Genack. You're the leading expert on Josephus, aren't you?"

"Ah, Titus Flavius Josephus. An expert? Perhaps not, but he has mystified me as much, it seems, Pliny has mystified you."

"They lived in the same era," Nick added.

"As far as we can tell, the two never met, but they filled in each other's narratives on events of the era."

"Well, as you might have learned from my talk, there are some blanks I would like to fill in."

Genack smiled like a wizard preparing an incantation. "You mean Nero, the Golden Palace and what 'the house where fire was born' means?"

Nick could see the old man was teasing him with snippets of information for which he had been hunting for years. "Yes, you have something on that?"

Genack looked around and moved in close to Nick, lowering his voice. "Yes, you could say I have something on that. But Mr. Foxe..."

"Yes?"

"Are you ready to learn something the historians missed?"

Chapter 6

New York City

Nick was intrigued. He wondered what Rabbi Genack had to say. They agreed to meet the next morning at Nick's house. Nick passed the intervening hours researching Genack. Rabbi Isaac Genack was a notable scholar on Judea during the Roman occupation, from the time Rome put the first King Herod on the throne as their proxy, to the rebellion leading to the destruction of the temple in Jerusalem, and to the last stand at Masada. In the middle of this era lived the historian Josephus.

Scholars recognized Genack as a leading expert on the histories of Josephus, but there was something more. His colleagues accused him of 'embellishment,' stretching the inferred into something more precise.

So, I need to take what Genack says with a grain of salt.

Nick looked up at the sound of the doorbell. The housekeeper answered it and escorted Genack into Nick's study, where he greeted the rabbi and shook hands.

"It's good to see you," Nick said. "Coffee, tea?"

"A cup of tea would be nice."

Nick turned to his housekeeper. "Nancy, would you fix some tea for Rabbi Genack?"

"Certainly. Earl Grey, chamomile...?"

"Some chamomile would be fine."

Nancy looked to Nick, who said, "Nothing for me. Thanks."

Genack walked around the room, taking in the clutter of ancient objects. He bent down to examine a golden skull.

"Is all of this real?"

"Indeed. See the blow gun framed over there? A projectile came out of that thing headed straight for me."

Genack noticed a photo on the wall of a huge, shiny object embedded in a cave. "Is that the famous tablet?"

"Yes. The *infamous* tablet. It was one of the most difficult cryptos I've ever come across. But eventually, the most rewarding one."

"It led to the Omni Scientia, did it not?"

"Yes. It did. What do you know about the Omni?" Nick and his team worked to obscure details of the Omni, but since its existence seemed more like a wild conspiracy theory, it wasn't all that hard for the public to discount its value. Yet, he liked to hear what people knew.

"I understand it contains a treasure trove of information. But..." Genack looked askance at Nick. "Are we really to believe it is ten-thousand years old?"

"We believe legends three-thousand years old, don't we?"

"Ah yes. Pharaoh, Moses, all of that."

"Speaking of Moses, here is a pamphlet I got from the people in Venice who named their flood control project after the prophet, *Mosè* in Italian."

Genack took the pamphlet from Nick and said, "So, you save Venice from a giant wave, and they give you a pamphlet?"

Nick winked. "My grandparents went to Disney World, and all I got was this tee shirt."

"Please have a seat," Nick said as he led Genack to a small round table with four cushioned seats around it. Genack sat and continued to gaze around Nick's study at the artifacts.

"Quite a collection you have," Genack said.

"Many of my items are on loan to museums. These are ones I like to keep here. They are of more interest to me. Each tells a story."

"I am sure they do. Your reputation precedes you. I have never seen so much in newspapers about an archaeologist."

"More than I like," said Nick. "I assure you."

Nancy brought the tea in on a tray and placed it on the table in front of Genack. She poured his tea from a pot into a china cup and asked if he wanted anything else. Genack scanned the tray, overlooked the milk and sugar, and reached for one of the cookies on a plate.

"No, thank you," Genack said as he munched on the cookie and took a sip of the tea.

As Genack chewed, Nick pressed on. "What did you mean?"

"What did I mean when?"

"When you asked me if I wanted to learn what historians missed. What did you mean?"

Genack finished the cookie, took a sip of tea, put the cup down and looked at Nick like one who would soon receive a great gift. "Have you heard of Filius Egnatius?"

"Filius Egnatius? No."

Genack reached for another cookie, tiny crumbs from the first one littering his beard. Waving it around like a baton, he said, "Tell me what you know about Nero. Then I will add Egnatius to the story."

Genack enjoyed the second cookie as Nick began.

"Nero Claudius Caesar Augustus Germanicus was the Roman emperor for about fifteen years starting in 54 AD. He was the last of the Julius Caesar bloodline. His mother was Caligula's sister, Agrippina. She was quite a piece of work. Handel wrote an opera about her. He did a good job describing a conniving, controlling mother."

Genack smirked. "Little good it did her."

"Yeah," said Nick. "Nero had her killed five years into his reign."

Nick continued. "As a politician, today we would call him a populist. He had an enormous ego and loved promoting athletic games and theater. Nero appeared in these events as an actor, poet, and even a chariot racer. He was the original reality star. It was always about him. The rich didn't appreciate him much, though. They paid for all those popular events through higher taxes. There were many plots to do him in, but he was ruthless in making anyone he suspected of maneuvering against him disappear."

"Even his own mother," added Genack.

"Yes, even his own mother."

"But what is Nero known for today?" asked Genack, as though he was a teacher conducting a class.

"You mean Nero fiddling while Rome burned?"

Genack nodded as Nick continued.

"Well, first, it couldn't have been a fiddle since any instrument of that sort would not have been available for another thousand years. And second, Pliny writes that Nero was at his estate some thirty miles away when the fire started."

Genack squinted as he reached for a word. "What is the term for making sure someone in power cannot be held responsible?"

"Plausible deniability?"

"Yes, yes. Plausible deniability. That's it."

"So," Nick began. "Nero was responsible but not responsible?"

"Perhaps, it is my turn to add to the story," said Genack as he took another sip of tea, dabbed his lips with a napkin, and brushed his beard, the cookie crumbs falling from it. He pushed his seat back, stood, and walked to the window, as though he was stalling while he wrestled with how much to reveal.

He turned to Nick. "The story is now Yosef ben Matityahu's to tell."

"Titus Flavius Josephus," Nick added, using the Roman name Yosef adopted.

Genack winced. "I prefer just Yosef."

"Ok," agreed Nick. "Yosef, it is."

"And, Mr. Foxe, it was Yosef when he instigated war against the

40

Romans. He was born in Jerusalem. Yosef was the head of Jewish forces in Galilee in the first war against the Romans. He fought well," Genack said with pride.

"Alas, he had to surrender to superior forces after a long siege. Vespasian was Caesar soon afterwards, and Yosef impressed him. The Romans crucified many fighters, but Vespasian spared Yosef. Sure, he made him a slave, but in the royal household in Rome. Vespasian eventually granted Yosef his freedom and he became a Roman citizen, taking the name you just used."

Nick said, "I've read Yosef's histories. Most of what we know about the second Jewish-Roman war, he recorded. The siege at Masada, the destruction of the second temple, all of it. Much of what we know about the first century in that part of the world came from him."

"Yes, yes," said Genack, now more animated as he approached Nick. "But what he saw when he was a young man, ah, that is the lost history!"

Nick encouraged him. "Lost history?"

"Yosef wrote about it as an old man looking back at his youth, and it is not an easily obtained document, but I have seen it."

"Seen it? Where?" asked Nick.

Genack's discomfort was apparent. He returned to his seat. "That is not important. What it tells us is important, and that is about Filius Egnatius."

Genack paused, letting the name linger in the air. Nick had never heard it before.

Genack continued. "When Yosef was in his twenties, he traveled to negotiate with Emperor Nero for the release of twelve Jewish priests. When he arrived in Rome, Egnatius greeted him. He made an impression. Yosef wrote that Egnatius was charming, but cunning. Yosef had a curious mind. He wanted to know more about this man. While in the palace, he saw Egnatius confer with Nero. He clearly had the emperor's ear.

"They released the priests, but one stayed behind. Why? We do not

41

know. Perhaps to work with the Roman Jewish community. Who knows? But what we know from Yosef is that he stayed in contact with the priest. We don't know his name, but we know what he reported to Yosef.

"This priest had access to Nero's palace. Perhaps he was a slave. Who knows? But he witnessed everything. The shabby buildings of Rome disgusted Nero. Oh, we know Rome from the movies, all marble and glory, eh? No, not at the time of Nero. Most of it were wooden structures. He lamented to Egnatius that he wished it would all vanish. Nero was starting to lose it. He had illusions of his greatness. He thought he deserved a magnificent palace. Egnatius told Nero he had a solution. He suggested the emperor take time off and visit his villa in the country. So, Nero did.

"On the night of July 19, 64 AD, a fire started near Circus Maximus. How? We do not know, but Yosef's friend, the priest, said it was Egnatius who ignited the conflagration. Since he had told Nero to leave town, Nero had. . .plausible deniability.

"Nero rushed back to town while the city was still ablaze. It burned for six days, and he is said to have stood shoulder-to-shoulder with the population as they doused the flames. At the very least, Nero made a pretense of assisting. The rich thought Nero was the arsonist, but Nero blamed the Christians and slaughtered many, creating the Church's first martyrs.

"But guess what? Nero now had the property cleared to build his palace."

"The Domus Aurea," added Nick.

"Yes. The Golden Palace. This is the palace you spoke about yesterday in your presentation. And you asked why Pliny called it 'a house in which fire was born.'"

"And it's because of this Filius Egnatius fellow?" asked Nick. "But he started the fire of Rome, according to this story. Calling it where fire was born is a stretch."

42

Genack waved a finger at him. "Not if you know the rest of the story. You see, Egnatius was the first fire starter."

Nick snickered. "I think the first fire starter was a caveman."

Genack returned Nick's snicker. "Well, forgive me. That is what I call them."

"Them?"

"Oh, yes. You see, Egnatius was the first, the organizer, if you will, of a group that used arson as a business tool."

"A pyro guild?" asked Nick.

Genack's face brightened. "Yes, a pyro guild. I like that."

Nick regretted inventing the name. He wasn't sure he was buying this tale, and it only encouraged Genack.

Genack continued. "When the Golden Palace was built, Egnatius had a room in it. I know, there were no bedrooms, just as you said in your talk. This was a room where Egnatius gathered his members. Each member bore a tattoo identifying them to others in the secret society."

"Tattoo? What was it like?"

Genack shrugged. "No one knows, but I believe the information was kept somewhere in that room in The Golden Palace."

"Which was buried," Nick reminded Genack.

"Ah yes, but haven't they done recent excavations?"

"Yes."

Genack, knowing Nick preferred to 'get his hands dirty' and explore things for himself, teased him. Genack asked with a mischievous smile, "And wouldn't you like to know if it's still there?"

Chapter 7

London

Lloyd could imagine the headline:

Lloyd Watson Composes the Greatest Symphony of the New Century

With the money from his grandmother's estate, Lloyd could throw everything into his work as a composer. His vision was lofty, a symphony in nine parts, each for a circle of Dante's hell. Franz Liszt had done it before. His would be greater. He would take his place alongside his hometown hero, Gustav Holst.

He slaved away for four years on the symphony. Lloyd was not a composition talent, and it was a slow struggle for him, but he was driven. He took Adderall to stay alert and focused, which led to a variety of amphetamines. His father, long dead, lived inside his head, scorning him for not being a talented composer. It was the drive that would either achieve greatness or kill him. With his drug habit, lack of sleep, and growing paranoia, death seemed the odds-on favorite.

He envisioned the first circle, limbo, as a pastoral piece, light and lovely. Lust, the second circle, would sound like the bordello where the younger Lloyd Watson had his only experiences with women. Gluttony would play well at a bacchanal. In greed, one would hear the ringing of cash registers. Lloyd had a clear vision of the music of each circle, but it was anger that became a cacophony of the rage consuming the inner being of this sad, rotund little man.

Lloyd hired musicians to work through the score, rewriting again and again to get it exactly as he wanted it.

At last, he finished the work, hired an orchestra, and started rehearsing. The orchestra had perfected each part. The symphony was ready for the world premiere. Lloyd had spent more than a half-million pounds in hiring musicians and rehearsal space. He hired the Royal Albert Hall for a three-day run and paid a top public relations firm to fill five-thousand seats for opening night. As an unknown, the PR firm had to harness every trick to hype the new composer's genius. Even with that, most tickets were sold for next to nothing.

Lloyd was calm opening night, propelled by his usual cocktail of illicit pills. He strolled onto the stage to polite applause. The concert hall darkened, Lloyd raised his baton, and the new music began.

Lloyd was ecstatic. His orchestra played flawlessly. As is tradition, there was no applause from the audience between movements, so Lloyd had no feedback on his work. He needed none. He knew it would be an astounding success. Were Lloyd able to see behind him in the dark hall, he would have seen a few people leave after the fifth movement. Those few people emboldened others to leave.

After a long hour and a half, the symphony came to a majestic end. The lights went up and a smiling Lloyd turned to face a half-empty hall. He was stunned. He hardly heard the tepid applause. In the front rows sat members of the press; he saw them shake their heads and mutter disparaging remarks. Tomorrow's reviews would be brutal.

Without saying a word to any member of the orchestra, Lloyd stormed off stage. His PR representative, beaming with encouragement, waited in the wings. She had to walk fast as Lloyd darted past her to the dressing room. Lloyd ripped off his tie and berated the woman's jolly behavior. He told her to cancel the remaining performances. This would be the first and only performance of his symphony.

The woman left. Lloyd was alone. He pulled out a bottle of scotch and filled a tumbler. He would drink until he was sure the remaining audience had left. Lloyd wanted to see no one. After two hours, he staggered out of the dressing room and into the deserted hallways. As he made his way toward the exit, he passed by a poster advertising future events. Among the assortment of entertainment, one photo caught his attention. It was a photo of the composer Gustav Holst, the hometown hero. There was an upcoming performance of one of his compositions.

The tumbler of scotch still gripped in his hand, Lloyd hurled the contents against the display. The brown liquor drooled down the face of his nemesis. Lloyd swore he would have his revenge.

To: Nicholas Foxe
From: Raymond Woodward
Subject: New Job
Nick,

Our emails have been off and on during college. That's all due to me. You've always been responsive. College kept me busy. When I graduated, I thought I'd have more time. Not so in the world of investment banking. My days are work, sleep, repeat. But investment work seems to be my calling. I'm happy to report that I've gotten a lucrative position with an office in London. I'm packing up and getting ready to move but wanted you to know.

You'll have to come visit.

Ray

To: Raymond Woodward
From: Nicholas Foxe
Re: New Job
Ray,

Congratulations! Sounds great. Remember what I said right from the start: You'll make your mark on the world.

Nick

Chapter 8

London

Ray Woodward stood in his office high above the Thames. He studied the London Eye on the South Bank. He pondered how it was not unlike the Eiffel Tower in Paris. Each was built as a temporary attraction, destined for removal one day. But each had become a permanent symbol of the city itself.

Ray also knew how much it cost to build, where the money came from, and what the attraction earned each year. He even knew what the naming rights for the London Eye went for. Ray had a head for numbers. When he graduated from Harvard, he went straight to Harvard Business School, and after that, he began work for Barstone Capital in their New York office. When he excelled, one of the British partners snapped him up.

He returned to his chrome and glass desk on which three large computer screens sat, just like the other four desks in this corner of the office. Charts, graphs and rolling financial news and trades vied for attention.

Across the way was the desk of Jean Roberts, the only other American at Barstone UK. She worked with Ray on several deals, and each had been lucrative. Ray's total commissions last year topped two-million pounds, and he was well on his way to exceeding that this year.

Jean, only a year out of Wharton, was two years younger than Ray. Her uncle was a partner at Barstone. When the New York office didn't have an opening, she was dispatched to London. There was no dress code at Barstone, and Ray made the most of it donning t-shirts and denims. But nicely cut shirts and denims, as if tailored by Savile Row. By contrast, Jean's lean frame was always adorned by a dress. The way Jean dressed led many in the office to assume Jean was older.

Jean walked up to Ray's desk.

"Solar Rock Power is getting bought by Sun Electric," she said.

"Really?" replied Ray. "How do you know?"

"The finance wires are all over it."

Ray wondered if he had missed something, but Jean's information had been spot-on.

Ray turned to his computer. "I see it now. Hmm. The stock is trading at forty-two pounds. The offer … is fifty pounds per share."

"Yes," Jean said. "When the deal closes, it will be a nineteen percent bump."

Ray smiled.

"Want to take this up to Edwards?" Ray asked.

"I'm ready. Let's go."

'Edwards' was Arthur Edwards, the partner who both Ray and Jean vied to dazzle.

They walked to Edwards' corner office; he was sitting alone behind his glass wall and focused on the screens in front of him.

Ray cracked the door. "Art, you have a minute?"

"Ah, the dynamic duo. Sure, what's up?"

Ray and Jean walked in but didn't sit; they didn't plan to stay long.

"We just found out that Sun Electric plans to buy Solar Rock Power," Ray began.

"Do tell." Arthur hadn't heard. "Who says?"

"The wires are lit up," Jean responded.

Art wrinkled his brow. Both Ray and Jean knew he doubted what 'everybody' says. But they pushed on.

Jean said, "The stock is trading at forty-two pounds. The offer is fifty pounds per share. That would be a nineteen percent return."

Ray added, "We propose to buy two million shares for the general fund."

Edwards nodded. "Sounds good. Do it."

As Ray and Jean began to leave, Jean halted, turned, and said, "Gerald Porter's name is being touted as the new chairperson."

"Porter," Edwards said as he considered the name. "Now *that* is important information."

Ray had pulled the door open to leave, but he now let it close.

"Porter controls Sun Electric," said Edwards. "He also owns eighteen percent of Solar Rock. Not outright. That would be too apparent. He owns it as part of his stake in EuroWind. Did you see the block trade last week from Merrill Lynch?"

Ray replied, "Yes." He wasn't sure where this was leading.

"The trade was between noon and one pm. The hope is that traders are out to lunch. But I look for such things. Trades during that hour frequently are done so people miss it. You saw it. Bravo for you.

"What you may have not surmised is that Sun Electric's offer was just a ploy to prop up Solar Rock."

"What?" asked Ray.

Edwards knew the players in the game. He'd been doing this for years. It was no accident he was a partner.

"I know Porter. He's merciless. He's cutting loose and winning. The block trade was Porter getting out of Sun Electric, getting out of Solar Rock. But before he did, he created the story the wires feed on. But he's out, now the price went up. I know it.

"If there is anything you need to do, it's to sell short. Trust me, when the markets wise up, Solar Rock is going down."

Edwards returned his attention to the screens before him. "Thanks for coming in. Enjoyed our chat."

Edwards had not dressed down Ray and Jean, not called them stupid, not even sneered. He didn't have to. Any bravado they had arrived with was drained away by his simple dismissal.

50

"How did I miss that?" Jean asked.

"It's OK. I should have known," replied Ray.

As they walked back to their desks, Ray tensed his hands into fists. It was late, and many traders were gone. As they passed a vacant desk, Ray picked up a ballpoint pen and started clicking it over and over. He stopped before they reached their desks.

"Look, we need to prep the short sale. We have work to do. It's late. Why don't I get Chinese take away?"

"Sure. Some curried chicken for me."

"OK," Ray said as he turned to leave. "I'll be right back."

Ray dashed to the lifts watching the displayed floor numbers crawl painfully upwards. Shaking his head, he raced down the hallway, shoved the fire door and took the stairs. He ran down the flights, breathing heavily. He came out the side door and into the alley. There was a rubbish skip nearby with scattered newspapers around it. Ray, who didn't smoke, always carried a vintage Zippo lighter with him. He popped it open, wheeled the striker against the flint, and produced a perfect, yellow flame. Relief washed over Ray. London was filthy with surveillance cameras. Ray looked around to be sure he saw none. He picked up a newspaper and held the flame to the bottom edge. The faultless flame ascended the paper, turning the latest events of the day to black ash.

Ray tossed the flaming newspaper into the skip, igniting other rubbish. He watched for just a minute as the flames built. Then, as though unseen persons were on to him, he reached up, grabbed the lid, and slammed it shut. The flames, deprived of air, turned to smoke. The smoke subsided and Ray continued to the nearby Chinese restaurant.

"This is great," said Jean as she dug into the paper carton. "I love curry. How's yours?"

"It's the same as yours. So, I agree. It's good."

"I finished the work on the short sale. I'll file it first thing in the morning. It was the least I could do."

"Meaning?" asked Ray.

"Meaning … I brought this deal to you. I'm responsible."

"I think you're looking at this the wrong way."

"Meaning?" asked Jean.

Ray laughed. "Meaning, if what Art said is true, we're going to make a nice take on the short. We were just betting on the wrong direction."

Ray stopped, put his chopsticks in the carton, and placed it on the desk. He looked at Jean sitting across the desk from him. "How long have we worked together?"

Jean gave Ray a sideway glance. "You were already here. I came a year ago. So … a year."

"And this is not the first Chinese we've eaten here."

"I've lost count."

Ray considered this for a moment, then spoke. "Isn't it time we had a proper meal together?"

"You mean food served outside of a paper carton?"

Ray snickered. "Yes. So, what about joining me at a restaurant, not Chinese, sometime?"

Jean smiled. "I would like that."

It was late. Ray could see the top of the brightly lit London Eye just over Jean's shoulder. He wanted to remember the scene.

Chapter 9

London

Jean Roberts loved Ray's home. She recognized it as something from the past the moment she stepped into the entrance hall. She would call it Victorian chic. Plus, a butler taking her coat? Ray was quick to adopt what an American imagined to be a highborn British lifestyle.

Jean was taking Ray up on his offer to have dinner. He had a cab ready to take them from the office. They were working late, as usual. But no Chinese take-away tonight. She had no idea Ray owned such a house. Once the butler left with her coat, she had to say something about the house.

"You must have done well last year."

Ray smiled. "And the year before that. If you're making the money we make, present company included." Jean did a little curtsey in acknowledgment. "Why not get something you really like?"

"The best things in life are free," Jean said, immediately realizing the triteness of a statement she really did not believe.

"Right..." Ray replied, drawing out the word with dripping sarcasm. "Let's go into the study."

Jean surveyed the room and delivered a simple synopsis of the decor. "Where did you get this old boys' club?"

"You don't like it?"

"Oh, no. I like it. I just wondered if they allow women in here."

Ray walked over to Jean and put his hand on the side of her head, looked her in the eye, and said, "You're my guest tonight."

Jean was taken aback by the touch and close personal space she had not experienced in the office. She thought she liked it but wasn't sure.

Ray stepped back and patted the couch in front of the fireplace. "Relax. I'll light a fire and we'll have a couple of drinks."

Jean sat on the couch as Ray bent down at the fireplace and lit the fire. She had worked with Ray enough to witness his moods. Toward evening each day, she noticed that Ray became wired. She thought he was pumped by the trades he'd made through the day. But she noticed something different at this moment. Ray took time in lighting the fire and spent a minute silently watching the flames expand. He seemed calmer. She could see it in his shoulders as they relaxed. He was a different person as he stood, walked over, and took a place on the couch beside her.

The butler appeared and asked Ray if he should serve cocktails. Ray turned to Jean. "Any requests?"

"What are you having?"

"My usual. A martini."

"Gin martini?"

"Of course."

"Sounds good."

Ray turned to the butler. "Two martinis, Mr. Butler."

"Very good, sir," replied the butler, and he left.

"Your butler's name is Mr. Butler?" asked Jean, not sure she had heard right.

Ray laughed. "Yes. It really is. I often wondered if he was like Major Major in *Catch-22*."

Jean knew the novel. "You mean the Major family that named their son Major. So, when the army drafted him…"

"They made him a major. Major Major Major."

They both laughed.

"Well," Ray continued, "I wonder if he became a butler by accident."

"Why don't you ask him?"

"Oh, no. That wouldn't do. Mr. Butler is very proper and very private."

Ray glanced into the hallway. "Speaking of whom, here come our drinks."

Mr. Butler walked in with a silver tray carrying a frosty cocktail shaker and two chilled martini glasses, each with an olive. He put the tray on the coffee table between the couch and fireplace, picked up the shaker with a small towel, and shook its contents for twelve seconds. He poured the contents of the shaker into each glass and finished the presentation with a short spray of vermouth from a canister the size of a lipstick.

Mr. Butler stood as Ray took a sip. "Excellent."

"Very good, sir. Will there be anything else?"

"No, Mr. Butler. I believe we are good for the evening. Thank you."

As Mr. Butler left, Jean picked up her glass, Ray lightly clinked with his, and she took a sip. "Hmm. That is good."

"Bombay Sapphire, very cold, very dry, in and out. We keep the gin and the glasses in a freezer."

"You have one every evening?"

"Every evening."

"How about the fire?"

"Every evening."

"Even summer?"

"Even summer," said Ray. "That's what air conditioning is for."

"You have air conditioning?" asked Jean. "Nobody in London has air conditioning."

"I do."

Ray paused. "Listen. Do you really want to go out?"

"What do you have in mind?" Jean asked cautiously.

"Why don't we see what I can whip up in the kitchen?"

"You cook?"

"I heat things."

Ray stood. "Come on. I'll show you. Bring your martini with you."

Ray led Jean down a hallway to the rear of the house and into a well-equipped gourmet kitchen. A six-burner Viking stove sat across from a marble island with a sink, above which hung a variety of copper clad pots and pans.

Ray opened a drawer in the island and pulled out matching brown aprons. Each bore the insignia of a French vineyard. He tossed one to Jean. "You'll be my sous chef for the evening."

Jean saluted. "Yes, sir," she said and put on the apron as Ray did his. She could tell he was comfortable in the kitchen by how easily he tied his apron behind himself.

"Let's see what we have," Ray said as he opened the large Sub-Zero refrigerator. After rummaging around, he brought out a plate of lobster tails under plastic wrap and a plate of butter. "How about a little lobster risotto?" he asked as he sat the plates on the island and sipped his martini.

"Sounds great."

Ray returned to the refrigerator and pulled out several other ingredients. "Let's see what we need," Ray said as he reached above the island and grabbed a two-quart pot, a saucepan, and a frying pan.

Ray turned to the stove and switched on a burner to high, then another, and another. The flames startled Jean. Ray winked at her and said, "Just warming up the grates," and turned each flame back down. He put the large pot on one burner, scooped up a large pat of butter and dropped it in. He grabbed a wooden spoon and stirred.

"Could you hand me that canister?" he asked, pointing to a glass container labeled 'arborio.' Jean fetched the canister for Ray as he opened a drawer and pulled out a scoop. "Just unscrew the top, please."

Jean removed the lid, laid it on the island, and held out the canister.

"Come here," said Ray as he put an arm around her as though he was preparing to waltz. Instead, he shoved the scoop into the arborio rice, pulled out a heaping portion, and dropped it into the pot with relish. Continuing

56

to hold her, he said, "You're a natural."

Ray released Jean as they both laughed. Ray took the wooden spoon and stirred the rice. "You demand little of your sous chef," she said.

"Ah, but now I will put you to the test," Ray responded as he grabbed a carton of chicken broth and poured it into the smaller pot. He took a soup ladle from a holder on the island and held it out to Jean like a trophy. "I want you to take a ladle of chicken broth and pour it into the risotto."

Jean did as she was told. "Like that?" she asked.

"Yep. Fine. Now stir the rice with this," he said, handing her the spoon. "And keep stirring as it absorbs the broth. Then, spoon in another ladleful and keep stirring."

"And what will you be doing?"

"I'll be getting the wine. How about a nice sauvignon blanc?"

"Sounds good."

Ray walked over to a glass-front wine cooler with the dimensions of an average refrigerator, holding more than a hundred bottles of wine. He opened it and began considering his choices.

"Nice wine collection," remarked Jean, dutifully stirring.

"Huh? Oh. Thanks. I keep the principal supply in the wine cellar, or I should say the sommelier does."

"The sommelier?" Jean considered Ray wealthier by the minute.

I've got to talk to the partners about my compensation package.

Ray returned with a bottle of wine. "I really know nothing about wine. I have a man, he insists on the title sommelier, who stocks the cellar and brings an assortment up here. He tries his best to educate me, but it goes in one ear and out the other."

Jean realized she knew little about this man. "Did you grow up, uh, privileged?" she asked as Ray opened the wine.

The cork made a pop as the corkscrew did its work in Ray's hands. "You mean, did I grow up rich?" he asked. He took two glasses from a rack and filled them.

"Well, yes," he said as he handed one glass to Jean.

They sipped the wine. Jean looked happily at the glass. "My compliments to your sommelier."

"But you could say I was a poor little rich kid," Ray continued. "Mom and Dad were never there. Sure, I grew up on the Upper East Side in a comfortable house, but my keeper, my nanny, missed her calling. In another time and place, she would have been a Nazi camp warden."

"Oh. That's harsh."

"Harsh is the right word. How about you? What's your story?"

"Dad was a doctor and Mom was a nurse. They were small town folks. Dad was a general practitioner, and I used to joke with him asking if he accepted chickens as payment."

"How'd you get here, to finance, to England?" Ray asked.

"I was the classic nerd. Made straight A's. Got into Harvard on a scholarship. Made my folks proud. Then Wharton. Then here."

"Uh," Ray said. "You need one more ladleful. It looks about ready."

Ray moved bowls with different ingredients over to the pot as Jean stirred in one last dose of broth. He put Jean between him and the stove, she with her glass of wine in hand and her host, unseen, behind her. Ray took the ladle from her left hand with his. He was close to her ear and began whispering. "We can put this away," he said as he placed the ladle in the near empty pot of broth and turned off the flame.

Ray grabbed a large spoon with his right hand and dipped it into a container of ricotta. He brought the white, soft cheese close to her nose. "Take a whiff. Doesn't it smell fresh?"

He dropped it into the steaming pot and moved her right hand to the wooden spoon in the pot. "Now, stir it in," he said as he moved her hand in a circular motion.

"Now for the tomatoes," he whispered. He held a bowl of cherry tomatoes before her. "These are very ripe." He dumped them in. Jean now stirred on her own with no further help, but Ray continued to stand close.

"And lastly," he said. "The basil. Smell." Jean smelled the fresh basil, already sliced into pieces. Ray tossed them into the pot. He stepped back. Jean relaxed and took a sip of wine, a large sip.

"OK. Now let's plate this." Ray turned off the flame, took two plates and scooped a portion of the risotto onto each.

"Just stand over a little to your right," he instructed. "This is the final touch, and I don't want to singe you."

Ray turned the flame up high. He took the frying pan and passed it over the flame, heating it. He held the pan above the roaring flame with his left hand, dug into the butter with his right, and dropped in a dollop. He lowered the pan to the grate, turned the flame down, and dropped in chunks of lobster tail. Ray took a shaker and sprinkled it lightly over the pieces. He turned to Jean. "Secret sauce," he explained. After turning each piece of lobster over in the butter with tongs, he turned off the flame and placed the pieces on the risotto.

"Let's eat," he said as he brought the plates over to the opposite side of the island.

Ray pulled a stool out for Jean, who took a seat before the steaming dish, and Ray joined her to the right. There were utensils in a basket on the island, each rolled in a napkin. He handed a set to Jean and unrolled one for himself.

"One last thing," Ray said as he got up, walked to the refrigerator, and brought back a cold marble wine chiller. He refilled their glasses and waited for Jean to take a bite of the risotto.

"Delicious," she announced.

Ray grinned. "Thank you."

Jean started a conversation between bites. "You know," she began, "it's good to see you outside of the office."

"And you."

"Do I really seem different now, here?"

"Do I?"

Jean winced. "Do you always answer a question with a question?"

"Do I?" joked Ray. "How do I seem different?"

Jean cut Ray a look as though she was about to state the obvious. "Well, at the office, you are Mr. Intense."

"Really?" Ray smiled.

"You're not the only one. The traders are all highly strung, chasing bets to pay off. It's a minute-to-minute game."

"Minutes mean millions in our business," responded Ray.

"Most of the traders arrive in the morning on a steady high and maintain it all day. But for you, Ray." She paused. "You start high and get even higher. When Edwards took us down a notch the other day, I thought you would erupt. But, after you went for Chinese, you came back calmer."

Ray said nothing as Jean searched his face for an answer. She saw none and had to ask. "What did you do? What did you do to calm down? I know it's not getting Chinese that puts you at ease. Is it?"

"After meeting with Edwards, it was just a brisk stroll that helped."

"And tonight?"

"It's fire, Jean."

"Fire?" Jean was confused.

What did he mean?

"I enjoy a fire, starting it and sitting back watching it, calms me."

"I get it. Everyone enjoys a fire. But it's a little warm right now for one, isn't it?"

"Richard Nixon, when he was president, had one in the Oval Office fireplace every day. They just turned up the air conditioning in the White House."

"Odd choice for a comparison."

60

"Don't worry. I'm not a crook."

Jean laughed. She observed that Ray's enjoyment of fire extended to the kitchen. He seemed to relish large flames from the stove, but she decided not to push the point.

They soon finished the risotto and the wine.

"Want dessert?" asked Ray. "I make a mean Bananas Foster."

Jean saw through the dessert choice.

A flaming dessert?

"No thanks, I couldn't eat another thing."

"Then how about returning to the study? I have a fine brandy I would like you to try. We can sip and enjoy the fire."

Chapter 10

London

Jean lay beneath a silk sheet on Ray's large four-poster bed. Ray was up early, enjoying the way the morning sun highlighted the lean curves of Jean's nude figure. He sat in an easy chair in his robe with a cup of coffee, reflecting on how good Jean felt in his arms last night.

He expected a call and didn't want to wake her. The phone buzzed in his left hand.

Right on time.

Ray walked out into the hall, put the coffee on a side table, and quietly closed the door. He answered the phone as he headed toward a window seat at the end of the hall.

"Hello."

The caller was direct. "The client was pleased with our work at the church. It drew the attention he desired."

"So, does The Fire Company have the balance of his payment?"

"Wire transfer as of this morning."

"Excellent."

Ray continued to the next order of business. "I plan to talk to the man you hired in the US."

"We have an excellent report on his work there," said the caller. "The authorities do not suspect the fire was by his hand."

"Excellent. I'll tell him to proceed to California and await our go-ahead for the real show."

"The Company seldom initiates engagements. This one is special, and you're its sponsor."

Ray smiled. "Our engagements to date have been lucrative. This one will earn multiples of what we've done in the past."

Ray pondered how he had gotten involved with The Fire Company. He had heard the legend from its partners. The organization traced its roots back to ancient Rome and had grown and shrunk over the years. Now, The Company had agents across Europe, arsonists for hire. One or two had appeared over the years in the New World. Apparently, people who love fire as Ray did were its recruitment target. They wanted Ray, the American, to manage operations in the US. Yet, something inside Ray nagged at him.

Was this all a big mistake?

Ray heard stirrings in the bedroom, and the door opened. He said, "I have to go. We'll talk again."

Jean walked out of the bedroom wearing Ray's white shirt, her hair loosely hand-combed. She walked to the window seat and sat beside Ray.

"Hmm. Coffee," she said, eyeing Ray's cup.

"Here," he said, handing her the coffee.

She took a sip, smiled, and told Ray, "I'm glad you're an American."

"Because?"

"If you were a Brit, this would be tea. I need my coffee."

"So do I."

Jean took another sip, turned to Ray and said mischievously, "I think I could go back to bed."

"Say no more," Ray responded as he stood, took Jean's hand, and walked her down the hall toward the bedroom.

"Ray..." she began, and Ray turned, put his finger to his lips and shushed her. "I said say no more."

He led her to the bed, began to slowly unbutton the shirt, kissing her neck as he did. He saw something he missed the night before, the tattoo of a small heart just above Jean's left breast. "So, what is that about?" he asked.

"Youthful indiscretion," was all she offered. "How about you? Have any tats?"

Ray stepped back and dropped his robe, holding his arms apart. "Take a look for yourself."

She gasped. Last night, the urgency of lust offered no opportunity for the appraisal Jean now had of the naked, athletic man standing before her.

Ray was unabashed as he pivoted. "See. No marks."

Then he approached Jean and finished removing her shirt.

Chapter 11

London

"This is quite a treat," Jean said. When dinner was served last at Ray's place, it was what Ray could find in the refrigerator. This time, it was in the dining room with a professional chef handling the meal.

Ray took the compliment with a "thank you." They had just finished eating their Salad Niçoise and were awaiting the Beef Wellington.

"Have you heard the joke about Heaven and Hell?" he asked.

Jean indulged Ray with a smile and shake of her head.

"In Heaven, the police are British, the chefs are French, the mechanics are German, the lovers are Italian, and it's all organized by the Swiss."

"Ok," said Jean. "And in Hell?"

"In Hell, the police are German, the chefs are British, the mechanics are French, the lovers are Swiss, and it's all organized by the Italians!"

Jean laughed. "And tonight...?"

"Our chef is French."

"You know, we're two Americans who are doing quite well in our host country. We shouldn't be too hard on them."

"I guess not, Jean. But the names. Bangers and mash? Spotted dick?" Ray shuddered. "Something other than cuisine may be at play there."

They both enjoyed the Beef Wellington, perfectly done, followed by profiteroles for dessert. But most of all, Ray enjoyed the warmth of their new relationship. Originally, they had in common being the only Americans in a British company. Now they were bonding by more than nationality. They were becoming lovers.

After they finished dessert, Ray asked, "Would you like to go for a walk?"

"Sure," answered Jean. "It's a beautiful evening."

They left Ray's house and headed toward Queen's Gate, a boulevard lined with bars, restaurants, and small hotels. They walked block after block chatting, first about work, then about what they liked best about London.

"This is one thing I like best," Ray said as they passed a small hotel. "How about a cognac?"

"Sure."

As they entered the bar area, Ray smiled as he spotted two seats vacant by the fireplace. It was a gas fire, but it would do. "Let's sit over there." He led Jean to two overstuffed chairs facing each other by the fire.

"A couple of Remy XO's," he told the server.

"Don't you have that cognac at your house?" asked Jean.

"Oddly, my sommelier, as good at wine as he may be, doesn't stock cognacs. I don't mind. It gives me a reason to get out."

The server returned with the cognacs, setting each on tables beside Ray and Jean's chairs. Ray picked up his snifter, rolled the brown liquid, and held it up to Jean, who picked up hers in response. "Here's to us," he said.

They clicked glasses. "To us," Jean responded.

After an appreciative sip of their after-dinner drink, Ray said, "I've been thinking. I've never seen your place. I don't even know where you live."

Jean chuckled. "Well, I assure you. It is nothing like your home. I have a small flat near the office. I moved in when I started the job here and haven't moved since."

Ray returned a puzzled look. "You make the same money I do. Why haven't you splurged? Saving for a rainy day?"

"I bought my folks a house. Does that count?"

"No." Ray knew a few overnight-rich people, like Jean, who bought houses for their parents. His parents, whom he seldom saw, already owned homes in several places. He bought his Kensington house to compete.

Ray didn't dwell on that line of thinking. There was something else on his mind. "You know, I have plenty of space in my house. Like you, I spend little time at home, but when I do, it's kind of lonely."

Jean smiled, "Is there an offer in there somewhere?"

"Jean, move in with me."

"Don't you see enough of me at the office?"

"That's a different Jean. She's OK, but this Jean, this one right here, is the one I want to live with."

Jean swirled her cognac, waited a beat, and replied, "Can I think about it?"

Ray realized he would have been disappointed if she had jumped at the offer. He wanted it, but he wanted it to be more serious than a snap decision.

"Sure," he said.

After they finished their cognacs, Ray asked, "Ready to go back?"

"OK."

They returned the way they came. Jean asked, "Aren't they renovating houses in this area?"

Ray responded, "Yes, they are. Let's turn down this street to see them." Soon they were walking by a line of homes undergoing renovation.

"They call these mews," said Ray. "I always thought that odd."

"Because mews means something about horse stables?" asked Jean.

"Exactly. Why would anybody want to live in a horse stable?"

The street was small, vacant, and tranquil. But suddenly, a dark figure ran out of one of the brick houses under renovation. They had no time to say anything to each other, any such conversation was precluded by a sudden explosion of flames from the building the figure had just fled.

Fire engulfed the brick structure. Ray sprinted down the street toward the blaze. But when he reached it, he stopped and turned, his arms outstretched and his back arched. Jean rushed to him.

"Ray, you're too close!" she yelled over the roar of the fire.

"Isn't it glorious? What power there is in it."

Jean backed away from Ray. She felt as though the flesh was peeling from her face.

"Ray, get away!" she pleaded.

Ray continued as though she had said nothing.

"The magic of fire. Its elegance. It unlocks something primal in us all."

Flames rose higher through the structure's three levels. The building's uppermost floor was a cauldron of superheated gases, begging for an influx of oxygen. The glass in a small, single-pane window was all that stood in its way. The temperature of the gases grew higher and higher, expanding the glass within the confines of its frame. A small crack formed, enough to break the glass' tensile strength. The window shattered, allowing air to rush in and creating a huge backdraft fireball which exploded through the window together with the masonry.

Ray didn't see the brick hit Jean on the temple, but he saw her fall, unconscious. As sirens grew closer, he rushed to her. "Jean, Jean," he repeated, trying to bring her around. He realized he shouldn't move her. But he didn't have to wait long before a paramedic was beside her taking her pulse. "She's alive," he reassured Ray.

As the paramedics put Jean on a gurney and into the waiting ambulance, the scene became a controlled mayhem of fire hoses and water aimed toward the flaming structure. "You can come with us," a paramedic told Ray, inviting him aboard the ambulance. As Ray stepped up and into the vehicle, he looked to his right. Near the corner, away from the action, the figure they first spotted stood in the shadows. It was only a second, but something passed between him and the figure. A mutual acknowledgment.

"Come on, sir," the paramedic told Ray, and Ray jumped into the ambulance.

Jean was soon in a hospital bed with Ray by her side. The hospital staff asked Ray to go to the waiting room as they performed what seemed like endless tests. Still unconscious, Jean's prognosis was good, according to her doctor. "We did a CAT scan and found nothing serious. She's just going to have a fine headache."

After an hour, Jean began to wake, which brought nurses and doctors flashing penlights into her eyes, asking a series of simple questions, and taking of her vitals. At last, they were alone.

"Hey." A weak smile was all the groggy woman could offer.

"Hey," replied Nick, holding Jean's hand.

"What happened? I feel like I got hit by a ton of bricks."

Ray chuckled. "Well, it was one brick. But that was enough."

"There was a fire, wasn't there?"

Ray realized that her memory had taken a hit as well. But, at least, she knew who he was.

"I'm afraid you have to let the patient rest now," said a nurse who had just entered the room.

Ray stood, holding Jean's hand. "Bye," he said as he kissed her hand and laid it beside her on the bed.

"Bye," said Jean.

Ray walked out of the room but went no further than the waiting room. He paced.

Why did I do this?

Ray could never fully control his urge to burn, to torch, to appreciate fire. Sure, he had channeled it. Insisting on starting the fire each evening in his fireplace, enjoying the flame from a stove. Each a small measure of sanity. But now, for the first time he experienced love for another person, and he seemed destined to immolate her. Because he glorified the work of an arsonist, his lover nearly died.

Ray's reflection was interrupted when various members of the hospital staff rushed into Jean's room.

Ray hurried to the room as she was being wheeled out. "What's happening?" he asked the doctor who had dismissively said there was nothing seriously wrong.

The doctor was cavalier no more. "We have to operate. She may have developed a blood clot."

Ray was confused. "But how? Where?"

The doctor took Ray by the shoulders. "Look, it may be some time. Just wait here."

With that, the doctor turned to catch up with the staff members who were wheeling Jean to the operating theatre.

Ray was too agitated to sit. He walked out of the hospital and to an alley where there was a skip. He took a loose piece of paper from the ground, pulled out his lighter, and set it aflame. Ray watched the flames consume the paper, but it brought only an empty feeling. He tossed the remains on the ground and stomped out the flames.

What's happening to me?

For the first time in a long time, Ray was not sure of himself. He questioned everything. He returned to the hospital and the waiting room where he sat and stared at the walls for over an hour.

Eventually the doctor appeared. Ray could see by his dragging pace, there was no good news.

The doctor addressed Ray. "Miss Roberts developed a blood clot that stopped her heart."

Ray was hopeful. "But you could revive her?"

"Normally, we could. But I suspect she had an undetected heart issue. Her heart was not strong enough to recover."

"She…"

The doctor completed Ray's tentative question. "I'm afraid we lost her."

Chapter 12

New York City

Rachael Friedman arrived at Nick's home promptly at 10:15 am as promised. When Nick heard the doorbell, he glanced at his watch and smiled.

Why am I not surprised?

Nick answered the door and took Rachael into a warm embrace. Nick and Rachael had been lovers, but Rachael's kiss on the cheek, suitable for a sibling, signaled that was no longer the case.

"It's good to see you," Nick said after the kiss.

"You, too," she responded with a smile and eyes that alternated between sparkle and doubt.

Any notion of pursuing flirtation stopped when Tom Littleton entered the hallway. Rachael walked over to Tom and gave him a big hug.

"Tom, so good to see you!" she said.

"How was your trip?" Tom asked.

"Not really a trip, more of a commute. I took the Acela from Boston to Penn Station."

"That's right," responded Tom. "I forgot how easy it is to go between Boston and New York."

As soon as Tom said what he did, he appeared to have regretted it. The uncomfortable glances between Nick and Rachael showed that more than a train ride was keeping Nick and Rachael apart. Tom quickly changed the subject.

"Thanks for coming. I was going to show Nick what Omni can do now, but I wanted to wait for you. I thought you would appreciate the science."

"Hey, what am I?" asked Nick.

"No offense, Nick," said Tom, "but Rachael has been working with me on Omni's science data, and I thought of her first."

Rachael gave Nick a smug look and said, "See, Nick, you're not always first."

Nick laughed at the zinger but then wondered what Rachael really meant.

"Come on into Nick's study," Tom said.

"Do you want something to drink?" Nick asked Rachael. "Coffee, tea?"

"No thanks."

Tom pointed to chairs around the table in Nick's study. "Have a seat." Tom remained standing as though he was about to conduct a lecture.

Tom began, "You know that Omni holds a vast array of knowledge. Doctor Nodada at the World Health Organization explained to us what the new information means to him in virology. Rachael, you're aware of what Omni knows about the physics of space and time. However, what Omni knew when she came to us was what an ancient civilization knew ten-thousand years ago, one more advanced than we would have ever imagined. Although that place in time was a tremendous starting point, how about everything that has happened from that time on? What if she had access to all of that? Perhaps she could guide us even more effectively. What if she knew all about Einstein's work? Could she fill in some of the blanks, some of the things like the unified field theory that bedeviled the great man to his death? Although her database is far richer than anything we have today, it lacked the context of what has happened since. Until now.

"I'll let Omni tell you the rest," Tom said, as he laid his cell phone on the table.

"Omni," Tom called out.

"Hello, Tom," replied a female voice. It was a voice Rachael and Nick had heard before in the Basel, Switzerland lab where Omni was located. It was not unlike popular voice assistants widely deployed around the world.

Unlike other voice assistants, however, Omni had knowledge that would have amazed Albert Einstein, Jonas Salk, and other scientists throughout history.

"Omni," continued Tom, "please tell the group about the enhancements we've made."

"Certainly," replied Omni. "Tom has worked with me to extend my knowledge base. To use Tom's vernacular, I've been surfing the web."

Both Nick and Rachael chuckled.

"Now, I can respond with analysis correlating events over time."

"Any event?" asked Rachael.

"It would have to be an event recorded in an accessible manner."

"Sounds like you've become an Alexa," quipped Nick.

"I believe you will find I know more than her, Mr. Foxe."

"How did she know who I was?" asked Nick.

"Voice recognition," responded Omni. "You may remember Tom had me demonstrate that capability while you visited in Basel."

Tom smiled as though a proud parent. "I want to show some of her new abilities now that she has the world of data at her fingertips. I have never told her how we met each other and how we ultimately found her. I have asked her to search for that data and now, let's see what she has to say."

"Omni, tell us how Nick and I know each other."

"Tom did computer work for Mr. Foxe."

"What did I find in Carlsbad Caverns?"

"You found the tablet my creators left."

"Gee, that's very impressive," said Nick with an unimpressed tone, underwhelmed by the recitation of easily found information.

Nick's lackluster response did not faze Tom. He smiled even more broadly as he put up a finger and whispered, "Wait."

Tom addressed Omni. "OK, Omni. Tell us the story of how we connected with you after the discovery of the tablet. Tell it in literary story mode."

Nick and Rachael shared a look with each other, showing they were thinking the same thing.

Literary story mode?

Omni began, "Deep in a cavern, Tom Littleton discovered a tablet that people 10,000 years ago left behind. It had a challenging code to decipher. Tom called Nicholas Foxe, a man he had worked for and who was an expert in codes. They had difficulty in understanding the code until Doctor Rachael Friedman came to the site with a new approach. That approach unlocked the next step in solving the code.

"There were people who wanted to stop the search. They planted a bomb at the entrance to the tablet worksite. Walter Tanner arrived and saved everyone from the bomb. The others soon learned that Tanner, as he preferred to be called, was instrumental in beginning the search for the tablet. Lucinda Rodriguez, the woman who managed Mr. Foxe's rental house near Carlsbad, became involved in the search. She later became personally involved with Tanner.

"The clues on the tablet took the team (as I will now call Mr. Foxe, Doctor Friedman, Miss Rodriquez, and Tanner) to Italy, where they discovered translations hidden under a castle. Those translations eventually led them to the Omni Scientia, or Omni for short as Tom likes to say. That would be me.

"After I was safely installed in the lab in Basel and connected to the supercomputer in Germany, there was an attempt to steal me. I defended myself and the attempt failed. Mr. Foxe was in Venice, Italy, at the time. I assisted Mr. Foxe in the use of a device that my creators had placed in the ocean. There were people who tried to take control of the device resulting in many deaths."

Tom and Nick noticed Rachael squirming at the mention of the deaths in Venice.

74

"Those are the pertinent elements of the story to date," said Omni in finishing.

"Thank you, Omni," said Tom. He looked at Nick and Rachael. "Is there anything you would like to ask her?"

"I certainly would," said Nick.

"Go right ahead," responded Tom.

"Omni. I recently published a paper on The Explorers Club website. It has to do with speculation from a Rabbi Genack that a group of fire starters, or arsonists, were formed during the time of the Emperor Nero. Do you see it?"

There was a slight pause and Omni replied, "Yes, Mr. Foxe."

"Please, call me Nick."

"As you wish, Nick."

"Omni, tell me what you know about pyromania. Use that paper as a starting point."

Nick expected something along the lines of a web search dissertation. However, he got much more.

"As you know," Omni began, "my creators changed the natural preferences of homo sapiens. Until they did so, everyone was a hunter or gatherer. Then, some began to grow things themselves. What you call agriculture began. One person could provide food for others, others who had the inclination to defend, to lead, to learn.

"As Tom told you, I now have access to data from the time they created me to the present. Now I can report on how those early changes developed. You were specific. You wanted to know about fire.

"The use of fire by homo sapiens predates the time of my creators. It even predates homo sapiens. Tribes of Neanderthals used fire. However, the love of fire for practical purposes is the work of my creators. It makes working metal possible. That began what you call the Bronze Age. Later, working with those of a science specialization, you created the steam engine, railroads, and electricity."

Omni paused. Although she was only a machine, Omni was adopting human emotion, or she was becoming good at mimicking it. Now, her hesitation and the way in which she continued was as if she were embarrassed.

Tom encouraged her. "Omni. Continue. Tell us any unintended consequence."

"Very well," said Omni. "My creators fashioned a predisposition for fire with beneficial intentions. However, like any genetic trait, it might have had mutations. The attraction to fire has one such mutation. It is the trait you have named pyromania. It is an extreme aberration and one that may have some evil intentions. Tom mentioned Dr. Nodada earlier. Since you know Dr. Fezile Nodada well, you may be interested in a paper he wrote about the evil of fire in modern times."

Tom raised an eyebrow in surprise. Turning to Nick and Rachael, he said, "I turned Omni loose over a week ago to rummage through the internet. I instructed her to review items pertaining to us and our associates first. I wanted to prime her response to the very question I just asked about the team's story."

Tom snickered. "It was standard operating procedure for a computer programmer to have a dry run before a demo. But I had not expected she would dive so deeply into documents written by people with whom we had worked, people such as Dr. Nodada."

Turning toward Omni's voice, Tom said, "Sure, Omni. Please tell us what Dr. Nodada reported."

"Dr. Nodada presented a paper on the good and evil of fire. He is a citizen of South Africa and belongs to a tribe whose ancestors used fire from time to time to hunt animals. His people preferred traditional ways of hunting game, but when game was scarce and his people were hungry, they would create a large circle of fire and let it burn toward its center. Animals within the circle had nowhere to escape.

"He continues to write about the days of apartheid when people were racially divided. Sometimes a person would be accused of being a traitor. That person was punished with necklacing. Necklacing is a term for a punishment in which they would force a rubber tire filled with gasoline over the neck of a victim and around his chest and arms. Then they would set it on fire. Dr. Nodada goes on to say that the victim might take as much as twenty minutes to die, suffering severe burns and horrible pain."

Perhaps Omni had developed skills in mimicking a human, but her detailing such a horrible torture lacked any sign of empathy. Nick thought he saw a tinge of embarrassment in Tom's cheeks. Tom's protégé was not as human as he would have liked. Rachael knitted her brow and uttered a mindful, "Hmm."

Tom asked Nick, "Why do you have this interest in pyromania and the evils of fire?"

"I've been working with a scholar on the histories of Pliny," said Nick, "all about Rome during the time of Nero."

"And Nero presided over the great fire that burned Rome," said Tom. "Is that the connection?"

"Well, there's more. At least there may be. Everyone knows about Nero. Not as many know about his Golden Palace. It's only been excavated in this century. The story I'm tracking down is one about Nero having help with starting the famous fire. There may be clues hidden in the Golden Palace about someone other than Nero who started it."

"So, a scholarly field trip, eh?" quipped Rachael, clearly making no more of it than that.

"No, not just that. We believe the man who burned Rome founded a guild of people who start fires. Not for pleasure, but for profit."

"Why not let Omni find the answers?" asked Rachael.

Tom explained. "Omni can compare. She can't invent. If we had some symbol, some motto, some image, she could match to other such things. We have to search the palace ourselves."

"We?" asked Rachael.

"Tom and I are going there," said Nick as he turned to Tom with a smile. "Who else would I ask when I plan to go under the earth other than a man who explores caves?"

"One more question for Omni," said Nick.

"Sure," responded Tom.

"Omni, do you see anything on a man who lived in Rome during the time of Nero by the name of Filius Egnatius?"

Omni paused for a few seconds. "I see mention of Filius Egnatius in a paper by Rabbi Isaac Genack."

"That's all?"

"Yes."

Rachael asked, "Didn't you want to hear more about the paper Genack wrote?"

Nick grimaced. "I had the good Rabbi here and talked with him at length. I hope Tom and I aren't about to set off on a wild goose chase."

Tom added, "Remember, it has to be something on the internet for Omni to see it."

"I think I know someone who can provide some non-internet information," Nick said then glanced at his watch. "I have a table at a nearby restaurant for lunch. Let's talk more over a meal."

The restaurant was a cozy bistro with large windows allowing sunlight to illuminate tables each topped with a starched, white tablecloth, breadsticks, and tableware. When Tom and Rachael were together, Rachael sensed Nick felt left out. Tom and Rachael talked science shop. Nick did not. After they had placed their orders, Nick took advantage of Tom's absence to talk to

Rachael in private.

He wasted no time. "Rachael, what's wrong?"

Rachael was as direct as he was. "Nick, I can't get it out of my mind."

"You mean what happened in Venice?"

"Yes, is the simple answer, but I realize there's more." She looked into Nick's eyes. "You know how I feel about you."

Nick's face was blank, betraying nothing.

"You killing a man who attacked us. It was traumatic. I thought that was it. But…" Rachael paused as she tried to put her feelings into words.

Nick prompted her. "But what?"

"Nick, I'm not sure I can handle your life."

"What do you mean?"

Rachael realized her statement was ambiguous, but not intentionally so. "You have an adventurous life. I got an adrenaline rush from it all. But I need time out. I need to clear my head. I got a call from an old friend."

Rachael could tell by Nick's grimace, he might think she meant an old boyfriend.

"A girlfriend. We went to college together. She now lives in DC. We talked for a long time the other night. She encouraged me to come for a visit. I thought about it. I've never taken in the sights there. Never even been to one of the Smithsonian museums. She told me she would take me on the grand tour. I said yes."

"Well, that's good. Anything you need. I know some people who have a great small hotel…"

Rachael put her hand up. "No. Thanks, Nick. This has to be on my own. I need time to think. OK?"

Nick paused. Rachael knew it was difficult for him to resist using his wealth and connections to pad the way for someone close to him, but Nick didn't pursue it further.

"OK," he said. "When do you leave?"

"Straight from here. On the shuttle."

"My jet just brought Tom here. It's parked at JFK and ready to go."

"No, Nick. Not the jet. I'm OK."

"OK," he said at last. Rachael thought he looked disappointed.

Tom returned to the table noticing the somber scene. "What did I miss?" he asked hesitantly.

"Nothing," both Nick and Rachael answered in embarrassed unison.

Nick took the opportunity to avoid any further questioning. "Now it's my turn to use the head. I'll be right back."

After Nick disappeared, Tom turned to Rachael. "What's going on?"

Rachael smiled. "I just need a time out."

"Okay…" Tom replied, drawing out his dubious response.

"No, really. I'm going to spend some time with a girlfriend in DC."

Rachael, not wanting to dwell on the current topic, changed it to something that bothered her.

"Tom. Your demo of what Omni has become is unsettling."

"You mean the danger of artificial intelligence?"

"It's more than that. You know that when we first brought the Omni to Basel to connect to the supercomputer in Germany, she was the one that found a way in which to connect. The people at the supercomputer lab thought she was taking over their system."

"But she didn't."

"No, she didn't. But, Tom, connecting her to the internet, that may be going too far."

Tom laughed. "Rachael, lots of smart systems connect to the internet."

Rachael scrutinized Tom to see if he realized the gravity of what he just said. "Yes, but none of them were created by an advanced civilization we know nothing about. We've convinced ourselves they left Omni as a benevolent act."

Rachael paused. "But what if it wasn't?

80

Chapter 13

Wyoming

Lizzy loved Wyoming at first sight and relished the contrast of the forests and mountains. She was accustomed to the arid climate of New Mexico where she had been hired to keep house for Nick Foxe and his friends.

Her boyfriend Tanner had been an Army Ranger. While serving in Afghanistan, an uncle of his died and left him a piece of property in Jackson Hole. When a bullet in the lungs ended his army career, Tanner moved to a small cabin on the property. He met Lizzy while in New Mexico and hadn't returned to the property since. He thought he would sell it, but Lizzy wanted to see the property before it went on the market.

Lizzy's introduction to Wyoming was through Yellowstone, where she hoped to visit Old Faithful, the Grand Prismatic Spring, and Lower Falls – places she'd only seen before in old geography books.

As they approached the park, Tanner stopped his Suburban SUV to allow a black bear to cross the road.

"Professional courtesy, eh?" teased Lizzy.

"Huh?" Tanner knew a zinger lay ahead.

Lizzy couldn't help but comment on the physical resemblance of the man she loved. "One bear yielding the right of way to another."

Tanner grunted. "Well, wait until I give you another bearhug."
The tourist season wasn't yet in full swing, so Old Faithful, the place everyone wants to go, was not overcrowded. Lizzy and Tanner took a seat on a bench among a small group of tourists and waited for the next predicted eruption.

"Doesn't it go off every hour on the hour?" asked Lizzy.

"Common misconception," replied Tanner. "The folks here can predict when the next eruption will take place by how long the previous one lasted. So, the next one will be in ten minutes," he said pointing to a sign with that information.

The steam boiling off the geyser suddenly became denser, with puffs pulsating like an old railroad steam engine.

"Right on time," said Tanner as Lizzy glanced at her watch.

Clouds of steam rose higher and higher. Then superheated water burst a hundred feet into the air.

Lizzy glanced again at her watch. "That was one minute and thirteen seconds," she observed. "Let's see how long they estimate the next one to be."

Tanner indulged Lizzy through two more eruptions, each of which she timed, spacing out the down time walking around the hot springs. He asked her after the rangers posted the last estimate, "Well, what have you concluded, Miss Scientist?"

"You're right. The longer the time, the longer until the next one. Don't know the math. I'll have to talk to Rachael about that."

After Yellowstone, Tanner and Lizzy continued south to Jackson Hole. Lizzy gazed out the window, absorbed by the green mountainsides. Tanner's cabin was off a dirt road just outside Jackson.

Just before they reached the turnoff for the cabin, Tanner noticed smoke rising above the treetops. It appeared to be coming from near his road. Lizzy spotted fire engines to the right and the firefighters, covered with smoky residue, putting their equipment away. Tanner stopped.

"What happened?" Lizzy asked.

"Let's find out," Tanner responded as he left the car with Lizzy trailing a few steps behind. He walked up to one of the older firefighters, the one who was telling others what to do.

"Was there a fire?"

The man, robust but weary, looked Tanner up and down and asked, "You live around here?"

"I have a place a few miles up this road."

"We would have evacuated you if you were here a few hours ago, but we have it under control now. My people have extended the fire lane and are dousing out the remaining embers."

"How did it start?"

As if to answer Tanner's question, another firefighter walked up, nodded to the man in charge, and said, "It's what we thought."

"Thanks," said the boss, and the firefighter returned to his duties.

"What?" asked Tanner.

The man looked Tanner over, assessing him. "Look, don't spread this around. What we think started the fire is full of liability issues and I don't want to end up in court because I told you."

"OK."

"And let's be clear. An expert has to confirm it, and I'm not that expert."

"I got it. So..."

"Powerline."

"Powerline?"

"We found a downed line. These pines are dry. One spark is all it takes."

"I see your point about liability. Thanks."

The man looked once again at Tanner, but this time with some recognition. "Hey, haven't I seen you before?"

"Like I said, I have a cabin here, but I haven't been here for some time."

"Well, you remind me of someone, but the guy was a loner. I see you have a pretty redhead with you. You seem happier than that guy was. Maybe it's the love of a good woman?"

Tanner smiled, took Lizzy's hand, and said, "Maybe it is. Thanks again." With that, they returned to the Suburban.

Tanner notched down the speed of the Suburban as the road became more rutted.

"I need to get this road fixed," he said to Lizzy, who was holding on to a handle above the door to keep from being tossed around.

"No need. You don't come this way often," she said between jolts.

"Yeah, but it'll be a turnoff for any potential buyer."

The road became a grassy trail for the last hundred yards, and then they arrived.

Tanner's place was a simple, but modern, log cabin with a porch. The windows were weather sealed, and the front door was steel, although the camouflage paint job was more rustic. Water was drawn from a punched well and sewage was dumped into a septic tank. Although connected to commercial power, a solar cell array generated electrical needs with battery storage. This residence could stand on its own were the line cut.

Tanner explained all this to Lizzy, who studied her boyfriend and quipped, "I didn't know you were a survivalist."

"Well, that would be my uncle. He built it. Didn't help him beat cancer though, did it?"

Lizzy knew Tanner hadn't seen his uncle often. He had nothing against the man. Their lives just moved them to different places. Tanner had told her he was surprised when the man had left him this place.

Lizzy stepped up onto the cabin's porch and did an immediate left turn to see the best feature of the property. Before her stretched a meadow rolling down the mountainside, filled with low grass and wildflowers — a purple, yellow, and white speckled carpet. Beyond were azure mountains pushing up against the sky.

Lizzy was captivated. Tanner joined her, facing the view he knew so well.

"Look way out there," he said as he pointed into the distance. You can see some ski slopes."

"I see them. They're pretty far away."

"Yeah. Just the way I like them."

"These flowers are amazing. Do you know any of their names?"

"Sure," said Tanner, pointing to a white flower resembling a daisy. "It's a stinking chamomile. Don't pick one up. They don't call it that for nothing."

"What about that one?" she asked, pointing to a cluster of purple-tipped blooms.

"That's a pussy toe."

She looked sternly at Tanner, "We're talking cats, right?"

Tanner laughed. "Here, this one's for you," he said as he bent down, picked a fuchsia flower, and handed it to her. Five petals burst from the stem surrounding a long golden stamen.

"It's beautiful. What's it called?"

"It's a monkey flower."

She squinted at Tanner. "I'm getting mixed messages here."

Tanner laughed and put his arm around Lizzy and walked her toward the cabin.

"Come on. I want to show you inside."

Tanner punched number keys on the front lock and swung the door open. Lights came on, tripped by an unseen sensor. An air filtration system wafted cool air. But the modern elements of the cabin stopped there. The cabin contained one large room with a bed in the back corner and a kitchenette in the opposite one. To the left was a round dining table. To the right was a couch, an overstuffed leather chair and a coffee table. The furnishings were modern-western rustic. Beyond the bed was a door to the bathroom. A spread with Cheyenne symbols covered the bed. Similar coverings lay across the couch. The chairs around the table were sturdy large-framed pine. There was just one thing missing.

"No fireplace?" Lizzy asked.

"My uncle probably thought it would be a security risk. I'll build you a fire tonight, outside. Right now, let's get our stuff in."

Both packed lightly. Tanner wore camo pants and a khaki tee. He brought similar changes in a backpack. Lizzy had more, but only what fit in a carry-on case. Tanner lugged a cooler full of food to the kitchen.

"It's getting late, and I'm starved," he told Lizzy. "How about you?"

She knew what Tanner packed. "I could go for a juicy steak."

"Coming right up."

"Mind if I wander in the meadow?"

"Go right ahead. Just watch for bears."

Lizzy knew Tanner was half-teasing, but the bears she knew were the ones who raided garbage cans in the trailer park where she grew up. She'd be OK. So, she replied with a simple, "Gotcha."

"I'll call you when dinner's ready."

Lizzy walked through the meadow, enjoying the flowers and the view, reflecting on what this place meant to Tanner. She knew Tanner ended up here after Afghanistan. She imagined how the isolation among all this beauty might have soothed the savage beast inside her man.

"Come and get it," Tanner yelled to her as he rang a dinner bell. She laughed.

When did he sneak a bell into the cabin?

After dinner, Lizzy put on a thick sweater and Tanner, his jacket. He had gathered firewood and soon had a crackling fire going. "Just a minute. I'll be right back," he said.

Lizzy sat beside the fire, marveling at the sky. She thought she could see every star known to man. They touched each horizon. Tanner returned with a bottle of beer for himself and a glass of red wine for her. Sitting down beside her, he shared her marvel at the big sky full of stars.

"You know, I spent many evenings looking at these stars. Look over there." He pointed to a constellation. "The big dipper. I couldn't get it out of my head."

"You met Tom here, didn't you?" she asked, speaking of Tom Littleton, caver, computer scientist, and now, one of their best friends.

"Yeah, I did." He looked at Lizzy. "But you know what the best thing was it led me to?"

"No."

"You."

Lizzy took the big man in a firm embrace, and they kissed like new lovers.

They sat on the ground for a long time staring at dying embers. Lizzy broke the comfortable silence. "It's getting cold. Let's go in."

As they walked to the cabin, Lizzy told Tanner, "You know how you get chilly without realizing how cold you really are? I'm bone cold."

"Don't worry, I'll get you warm."

Tanner was as good as his word. Lizzy suddenly felt warm all over.

Chapter 14

Wyoming

Lizzy hugged her pillow and dreamed she smelled bacon followed by a scratchy kiss on the cheek by an unshaven Tanner. She rolled over to see the big man standing over her.

"Good morning, sleepyhead," he said.

Lizzy smiled and responded with a groggy, "good morning."

"I've got bacon going and I'm ready to cook some eggs. How would you like them?'

"Scrambled would be great."

"Coming right up."

As Tanner returned to the kitchen area, Lizzy threw back the thick covers and reached for the nightshirt on the floor; the nightshirt that didn't seem to make it to her body last night. She slipped it on and padded into the bathroom.

After splashing some water on her face and dragging her fingers through her hair, she walked over to the table already set for breakfast and sat down. Tanner filled her coffee mug from a percolator. Tanner and Lizzy had been together long enough for him to know she took her coffee black. No need to ask.

Tanner walked the percolator back to the stove and returned with two plates. Scrambled eggs for her with two thick slices of bacon. An enormous pile of eggs for him with five slices of bacon. Lizzy had grown accustomed to the calories this man consumed each day. He maintained a workout regimen from his Army days. But Lizzy knew there was one thing he didn't get from the Army, his yoga. Tropical storms brewed inside the gentle giant, and yoga prevented a personal hurricane from making landfall.

Lizzy sipped her coffee as Tanner dug into his eggs. "So, what's on the agenda today?" she asked. "You have an appointment to see the real estate agent, don't you?"

"Yep, in two hours. I need to get some gas, too. Want to come along?"

"I don't think so. I'm loving it here. Mind?"

"No. Soak it in while we have it."

Lizzy hesitated before stating what was on her mind. "Do you really want to sell this place?"

Tanner stopped eating and finished chewing as he looked at Lizzy. "Do you want me not to sell it?"

"It's nice. I like it."

Tanner looked away and took a sip of coffee. "I don't know, Lizzy. The place has memories. You're looking at it with fresh eyes, but I see it as a place where I had to work out a lot of things. I see it differently."

She put her hand on Tanner's. "You know, whatever you decide, it's OK with me."

Tanner smiled, changing the subject. "Better eat before it gets cold."

After breakfast, Lizzy cleaned up and moved a rocking chair from the living room to the porch where she could enjoy the meadow and her book. Tanner walked by on his way to the Suburban. "Anything I can get you?" he asked.

"I'm good."

Tanner looked at the cover of the book she was reading. "You like that author, don't you?"

"He sure has an active imagination. I don't see how he dreams this stuff up."

"Hey," said Tanner. "Somebody should write our story."

Lizzy wrinkled her nose. "Nah. Too farfetched."

Tanner's first stop was the gas station. He pulled into one of two islands, each holding three pumps, hopped out and plugged in the hose nozzle. He swiped his credit card, punched in answers to questions, and was soon leaning against the Suburban as the tank filled. Tanner's vehicle was near empty, and the pump was slow. It would take some time.

Across at the next island, a green motorcycle pulled up. The rider hopped off and put his matching bright-green helmet on the bike. The man was young with close-cropped, dark brown hair. He was about five-ten and skinny. He seemed amused about something; he was smiling to himself.

As the man studied his pump, he pulled out a Bic lighter and started clicking the flame on and off. He wasn't looking at it, just clicking it on and off as he considered the fuel choices.

"Hey," yelled Tanner, getting the man's attention. He looked up. "Not a good idea. Not here."

The man returned Tanner's warning with a smile and said, "Sorry. Bad habit." He put the lighter away and continued filling the tank on his motorcycle. He took off his leather jacket and laid it across the bike, uncovering the white tee-shirt he wore beneath. Tanner saw a tattoo on his left arm. It was a simple design. A triangle with the base at the bottom and the point at the top. Below the base was the letter 'I' to the left and the letter 'A' to the right. As the man pumped gas into his tank, Tanner mentioned it. "Interesting tattoo you've got there," he said.

"Yeah. Memento of lost love."

"You mean the IA?"

"Yep. Ingrid Astra. Met her in Sweden. She was something else."

"Must have been. Why the triangle?"

A motorcycle takes a lot less gas than a Suburban, and the man finished filling as Tanner continued to pump. The man closed his tank and looked at

Tanner sheepishly.

"See, Ingrid was not a one-man woman. I knew she was messing around. She didn't keep it a secret. So, I put something on my arm to annoy her."

"A love triangle?" Tanner ventured.

"You got it. You know what she did when I showed it to her?"

"What?"

"She just smiled. Smiled like the alley cat she was."

The man chuckled at this remark as if he made a joke. He put on his jacket and mounted his bike. "Anyhow, you take care."

Tanner returned the comment with, "You, too."

The man sped off as the pump nozzle in Tanner's vehicle cut off. He returned the hose to its resting place, punched 'no' to 'Do you want a receipt?' and watched as the man rode out of sight.

I wonder what the tattoo really means?

Chapter 15

Wyoming

The man with the triangle tattoo continued a few miles down the road before pulling into a downtrodden roadside motel built in the 1970s. He walked into the office with a brisk, "good morning," to the old man behind the check-in desk. The clerk looked as if he came with the motel when they built it and, like the motel, was showing signs of wear and tear.

"I'd like a room."

"License and credit card," said the old man with a delivery uttered a thousand times. "Fill this out," he muttered as he pushed a pad of forms to the man.

"Francis Grumman," read the man from the driver's license.

"That's right."

"How long do you plan to stay?"

"Not sure," replied Francis. "I'm waiting for a call from my boss about my next job. Shouldn't be more than a day or two."

The old man took a key from a wall of similar ones and handed it to Francis. "You'll be staying in room 112 down at the end of the parking lot. Has a nice view of the woods."

Francis took the key and thanked the man. He steered his bike the short ride to his room and parked. As he approached his room, he saw a rusty pickup truck barrel into the parking lot and come to a sudden stop a few rooms up. A man and woman sat in the truck; he could see from her flapping arms and his smashing the steering wheel with his fist that they were arguing. The man jumped out, slammed the driver's door, and stomped around to the passenger side. He yelled to the woman to get out as he jerked her door open. She reluctantly obeyed.

The man was not young. Either that, or a hard life had made the scrawny man in a dirty tee and ripped jeans look older than his years. The woman looked as though she'd been around the block a few times. She wore jean shorts and a low neckline blouse; an attire designed to flatter a woman much younger than herself. He roughly grabbed her under the arm and marched her to the room. As he unlocked the door, he looked toward Francis.

"What are you looking at?" the man growled.

Francis smiled and continued his gaze.

The man ignored Francis' smile and jerked the woman into the room.

Francis unlocked his door and went in. He had a few things in a pair of saddlebags on the bike. His special van was in storage, but it was not far away if he needed it.

Francis fell back onto the mattress and yawned. He rolled his shoulders and sighed. The job he had done here had been exciting, a real adrenaline rush. But now, he wanted nothing more than to lie back on the lumpy bed and watch TV.

Francis woke the next day hungry and went looking for the complimentary breakfast. It was about what he expected – dry cereal in single-serve boxes and oatmeal in a warmer. But the coffee wasn't bad. He saw the woman from the pickup truck sitting alone in a corner. Her eyes darted up at Francis before quickly looking down. Makeup did a poor job of covering the shiner and the cut lip. Francis dumped a box of raisin bran into a plastic bowl, splashed on some milk from a pitcher, took his coffee, and headed over to the woman.

"Mind if I sit here?" he asked.

She flickered between the smile of a woman complimented by a young man's attention and one of embarrassment by her appearance. "Sure," she said.

The woman nursed a cup of coffee and winced as the hot liquid scalded her cut lip. Francis put his bowl and coffee cup on the table as he introduced himself. "Hi, I'm Francis."

"Hi. I'm Gloria."

"Good to meet you, Gloria. Where's your boyfriend?"

Gloria shook her head. "He's gone hunting with some friends. Or at least that's what he said."

"How about you? How are you spending your day?"

"At my job. I work at the Elk Bar down the road."

"I saw it on the way here. You like working there?"

"It's a living. What do you do?"

"I'm a contractor. I did a job here and I'm waiting for my next assignment."

Gloria didn't ask more about what kind of contracting he did. If she had, Francis possessed well practiced obfuscation. Nor did Francis ask why she and her boyfriend were living in a cheap motel.

"How are you going to get there? Your boyfriend's coming back soon?"

"Not likely. It'll be dark before he gets back. I'll walk."

"Walk?" said Francis. "It must be three miles."

"It's OK."

"Look, if you don't mind riding on the back of a motorcycle, I'd be glad to take you there."

Gloria lit up. "You sure you don't mind?"

"It would be my pleasure. You ready?"

"Give me an hour?"

"Sure. I'll meet you right here."

Gloria dashed off while Francis sat back and finished his coffee. He took out his lighter and began flicking it, reflecting on how much he hated men who beat up women.

His dad beat up Mom. It didn't happen until Francis was around

94

eleven. Before then, he never saw Dad lay a hand on Mom. Dad was a volunteer firefighter in the small town where he grew up on the Jersey shore. When the local fire station alarm sounded, Dad would jump in his pickup truck, smack the red light down on the dash and roar off to help. When Francis turned eight, his dad would take him along. Francis enjoyed the fires. They were so intense, so dangerous. He was in love.

Then Dad fell on hard times. Started drinking. That's when he became someone else. Someone who would strike his mother. Francis hated him. He was glad when his father died in a fire.

Gloria returned, happy to hitch a ride with Francis. He walked her out to the bike.

"Here. You wear my helmet," he said, handing her the green head protection.

"You sure?"

"Sure. We don't have far to go."

They headed down the road. There was little traffic. Just pine trees whizzing by. It was only a few minutes before they pulled into the Elk Bar parking lot. Gloria hopped off while Francis stayed seated. She handed him the helmet, and he put it in his lap as he enjoyed the excitement so apparent in Gloria. She acted like a schoolgirl, bouncing on her heels, and telling Francis, "Thanks. That was fun."

Francis brought the schoolgirl down to earth. "Why do you let him do it?"

Gloria's demeanor changed to one of a middle-aged, abused woman. "It doesn't happen so much."

Francis winced with disbelief.

"No, really."

"Why don't you leave him?"

"And do what?" she said as she looked toward the bar. "You're not looking at a woman with a lot of options."

Francis knew the pattern. His mother had options. She just needed Dad to disappear. Once he died, she renewed her nursing career, moved them to New York, and soon became head nurse on a surgical unit. Gloria needed a push.

Francis put the helmet on and told her, "Well, it's been a pleasure meeting you."

Gloria became flirtatious. "I get off at midnight."

"You want another ride?"

"Well, my boyfriend said he'd pick me up. But I can tell him I got a ride."

"I'm not sure I can make it back. Better not call him ... yet."

Gloria smiled at the possibility. "Sure. Hope to see you again."

Francis returned her smile and took off. He would not be seeing Gloria again, but he would set her free.

Francis went off in a different direction. He arrived at a self-storage park and pulled into an area where people stored vehicles. Between a couple of large campers was a nondescript, white panel van. It was large enough to store his motorcycle and the special supplies required for his work.

Francis walked to the back, lowered a narrow ramp, and guided his motorcycle into the van. After securing it in place, he closed the rear door and climbed into the driver's seat. He headed back to the motel and parked near the boyfriend's room. No one was around and the cleaning crew had already been there.

Perfect.

Francis carried a pouch to the door of the abuser's room. He opened the pouch, selected a pick and turning tool, and began working the lock. It was not a modern lock, and he easily opened it. Francis entered the room and took stock. It was just like his. He expected it would be and had already planned out what to do. He had what he needed in the van.

After an hour, Francis left the room and relocked the door. He walked to the office and checked out. He returned to the van and drove away, but not far. Francis had scouted out the environment. He always did. He knew there was a service road on the hill overlooking the motel and that was where Francis headed. Once there, he parked the van and waited.

It would take time, but Francis could be a patient man. He took out his lighter and flicked it, contemplating how easy it would be to engulf the dry pine trees surrounding him in flames. Francis turned his attention back to the motel. He had a perfect view of it between the trees.

As the sun set over the mountains, the familiar rusty pickup truck returned. Francis waited for the abuser to enter his room, the remote-control box gripped firmly in his hands.

Gloria's boyfriend took out his keys and opened the door, grumbling about the men he hunted with. They were supposed to be friends, but they wouldn't help him out. They thought he'd borrowed enough. Now, Gloria wasn't here.

That's right. She's working late. Maybe I'll head down to the bar she's working at.

He thought he smelled gas as he entered the room.

The motel must heat water with propane. Maybe they have a leak. I'd better report it.

As he walked back to the door, a bolt at the inside top corner clicked into place.

What the…?

He tried the door. It wouldn't give. Then the flames started. The bathroom burst into an inferno sending a firestorm shooting out the door and lighting the carpet. The man panicked as the flame caught the nearby bedding.

He looked at the plate glass picture window. Grabbing a chair, he aimed it at the glass.

Francis watched from the hillside. He calculated the boyfriend would try breaking the window and was not disappointed. A chair flew out, shattering the window, immediately followed by an explosion fed by the fresh source of oxygen. The boyfriend catapulted through the window, engulfed in flames. Badly charred, the body crawled a few last inches and stopped.

Francis pushed another button on his remote and the sprinkler system in the abuser's room activated, soon reducing the remaining flames to steam and smoke. Other guests in the sparsely populated motel escaped their rooms and looked on in horror at the carnage.

Francis looked at his watch and smiled. He enjoyed his little chore, but it needed to end. He was expecting a call from England. The caller was prompt, and his cell phone rang.

"Hello," he answered.

"Your forest fire there seemed to be a success. Congratulations."

"Thank you."

"It was just a practice run, you know," said the caller.

"I know."

"Proceed to California and wait for further instructions."

"OK."

"I will call again soon," said the caller, and he hung up.

Francis put his phone away and scoffed.

He still doesn't remember me.

Although the caller attempted to be anonymous, Francis knew it was Ray Woodward. Ray was totally unaware that he had seen Francis many times, in passing, years ago. But Francis remembered him. He had followed Ray's public career, but most importantly, he had also tracked his secret one. That's how Francis found out about The Fire Company.

Francis thought about the psychiatrist who treated them both. Ray seemed to like the man, but Francis detested him. It occurred to Francis that the abuser he just dispatched was only the latest of his victims, but the man who treated Ray and him had been the first.

Although Francis was only three years younger than Ray Woodward, when you're in your teens, that's worlds apart. Ray usually had sessions with Dr. Perry right after Francis. Francis looked up to Ray, literally. Ray was taller, and better looking. Francis thought Ray was cool and he wanted to hang out with him but attempts to connect with Ray in those brief interludes between sessions failed. Ray slumped in the waiting room chair and played on his cell phone, barely acknowledging Francis's existence.

Francis secretly lurked around wherever Ray went and vicariously lived through him. After all, they shared their love of fire.

They were pyro-brothers.

Francis was smart and a computer expert, which enabled him to regularly hack into Ray's email account. It was his window into his idol's private life. He knew when Ray was accepted to an Ivy League school. He saw Ray's emails to Nicholas Foxe. He wanted the same email relationship with him, but Francis was satisfied to live as a shadow through Ray's friendships and romances. Francis was the first to learn of Ray's acceptance by a top-tier finance company.

The Fire Company emails particularly interested Francis. These emails were encrypted, but Francis broke the code and read with impunity. Ray was leading a double life, and it was this other life, the one in which they were brothers, Francis wanted to be a part of.

Using information from Ray's account, Francis worked his way into the graces of the organization. They were finally giving him a chance. He proved himself in Wyoming. Ray himself said so. Although it was irksome that Ray didn't remember him.

That's OK. When I get a string of successes under my belt, he'll know me.

Francis thought about Dr. Perry. When Ray 'graduated' from his care, Francis was livid. Francis had studied the ins and outs of firebombing a car and he hated the doctor. And then he committed the unforgivable offense of driving Ray away, and Francis feared he would never see his idol again. Francis realized now it was a youthful indiscretion. It was something he would not do today, not unless The Fire Company ordered it. But what is done is done. Nothing can bring the doctor back.

Francis could put those reflections aside and move on. He was now an adult and a professional. No time to reflect. Now, to focus on California.

Chapter 16

Wyoming

Tanner looked at his cell phone to see who was calling. It was Nick. He clicked answer. "Hey, Nick," Tanner said. "What's up?"

"How's things out there? You're at your place in Wyoming, aren't you?"

Tanner didn't remember telling Nick about his trip. It annoyed him that somehow Nick would know. When Tanner first met Nick, he wasn't sure he liked him all that much. Tanner thought the guy needed to be sure everyone knew he was in charge. It reminded Tanner of the army officers he knew that got where they were by wealth and connections. In time, Tanner realized he was layering his own preconceived notions on the man, and they became good friends. When Nick called, he was always ready to help.

Was this one of those times?

"Is Lizzy with you?" asked Nick.

"Sure. Let me put you on speaker." Tanner turned to Lizzy. "It's Nick."

"Hey, Nick!" responded Lizzy. "How's it going?"

"You enjoying the great outdoors?" asked Nick.

"It's wonderful!" Lizzy turned to Tanner as she told Nick, "I don't know why Tanner would think of selling it." She finished by sticking out her tongue at Tanner, who just rolled his eyes in response.

"So, Nick, you coming to see us?" asked Lizzy.

"No, sorry. Tom and I are headed to Rome."

"You got some cave digging going on there?" asked Tanner.

"Kind of. We're exploring Nero's Domus Aurea."

"The Golden Palace?" chimed in Lizzy. "I would love to see it."

Tanner showed his surprise. Tanner had been to Rome, but never heard of the Domus Aurea. He thought he had learned by now not to underestimate the woman in his life, but once again, he had done so.

"Maybe next time. Listen, the reason I called was to get a name. While Tom and I are there, I would like to visit a place I've been wanting to visit for a long time, the Vatican library."

Tanner then realized why Nick had called.

"Tanner, you've been there. What was the name of your contact?"

"Monsignor Alonso Alberti," said Tanner, who surprised himself at how quickly he recalled the name. "I don't think I have any contact information for him."

"That's OK. I'll ask Omni."

"Omni?" Tanner asked, sharing a look of surprise with Lizzy. "Uh, Nick, Omni only knows stuff from 10,000 years ago."

"Not anymore. Tom's plugged her into the internet. She's up to date."

"She?" asked Tanner. "I know Tom liked to call it 'her.' You too?"

Nick laughed. "Guess it's infectious. Look, I've got to go, but thanks for the information. We've got to get together soon."

"Sure thing," said Tanner with Lizzy adding, "Bye, Nick."

After the call, Lizzy looked at Tanner and said, "Hmm, Tom and Nick going to Rome. Didn't hear anything about Rachael. Aren't they together?"

Tanner laughed. "That seems to be a rocky road, doesn't it?"

Lizzy hugged Tanner. "Well," she said, "I'm sticking to you like glue, mister."

Tanner returned the hug and said, "That's fine by me."

Chapter 17

London

Paul Allerton was irritated. The key the landlord gave him for his new flat didn't work. He could always use other means to get in. Easy stuff for a field member of MI6, but it would raise questions. Better to get the right key. He didn't want to pick a lock each time he came home. He phoned the landlord, but he wasn't answering his phone. So, he left a message. Nothing to do but wait.

Paul went out to the street and admired his new London surroundings. Kensington had been home to nouveau riche professionals at the beginning of the twentieth century. After some decline, the neighborhood had sprung back as the home of the rich and famous of the twenty-first century. The homes appeared, as one of his American friends put it, as though they came from a period-piece movie, all alabaster and stately.

However, during the less well-to-do times of the last century, many of the homes were converted into small hotels or, like Paul's building, individual flats. Still, he liked the location. Just a short walk from the Royal Albert Hall and Kensington Gardens. Although Paul traveled most of the time, he welcomed having this as home base.

It was beginning to rain and Paul was about to return to the house when a well-dressed, twenty-something man walked by. When he noticed Paul, he stopped and asked, "Hello. New here?"

"Yes. I just leased a flat in this building, but the landlord gave me the wrong key."

"You called him?"

"Yes. Had to leave a message."

"I know the man. You might have a wait on your hands. Why don't you come to my place and wait for his call?"

It rained harder.

"Thanks, but I don't want to trouble you. I'll just walk down to the coffee shop on the corner and keep trying him. I'm sure he'll pick up his phone soon."

"Don't be silly," said the man. "You don't have an umbrella, and you will get soaked before you reach the end of the street."

"Well . . ."

The young man smiled and offered his hand. "I'm sorry, I haven't even introduced myself. I'm Ray Woodward, and I live next door," he said as he pointed to the house to the left.

"Paul . . . Paul Allerton," he replied. "Nice to meet you."

"Come on in. We're both going to get drenched."

Paul realized when he stepped into Ray's place that it wasn't a rental flat. A butler appeared at the door to take their coats. No, Ray owned this entire building.

"Everything is ready, as usual, sir," the butler said to Ray.

"Very good," Ray replied as he turned to Paul. "Let's make ourselves comfortable in the study."

The study was just off the entrance hall. Ray must have copied the original furnishings from a hundred years ago when he decorated. He could envision a Victorian banker enjoying this domain sitting on the overstuffed Chesterfield sofa with two matching chairs by a large fireplace. On one of the dark oak-paneled walls hung a painting of three nude nymphs in a lily pond inviting a young man to join them. It appeared to be a copy of a Waterhouse.

It was a copy, wasn't it?

The only modern vestige Paul could see was the installation of three flat screens and a keyboard on top of a kidney-shaped, burr walnut desk.

104

A stock trader.

After a quick glance around the room, Paul focused on Ray, who hadn't spoken a word since entering the room. He was on one knee before the fireplace, which had been prepared for a fire. Kindling was neatly stacked under larger logs. Ray took out a long match made for such fires, one which could be inserted in several places, one after the other. But Ray held the match after lighting it, studying the flame as he turned it to its side and back. He then placed it under the kindling, which took the flame and spread it quickly as though soaked with lighter fluid.

Ray stayed on one knee and admired the flames. Yes, 'admire' was the term Paul would use for Ray's appraisal of the fire. When he first met Ray on the street, he was friendly and courteous, but Paul had detected a nervous tension, as though Ray was anxious about missing an appointment. Now, with the flames building in the fireplace, he could detect a restful sigh.

But a fire this time of year? Odd.

Ray stood and brushed unseen dirt from his knee. "How about a brandy?"

"Sure," replied Paul.

"Have a seat," Ray said, and Paul made himself comfortable in one of the chairs by the fireplace. Ray went to a table on which the butler had set a carafe of brandy and two snifters.

Ray smiled as he poured brandy into each glass. As if reading Paul's thoughts, he said, "I enjoy a fire." He carried the filled snifters to Paul and handed one to him. "Even if I have to crank up the air conditioning."

Paul took a sip of the brandy as Ray sat down in the opposite chair. The two men took stock of each other.

"Excellent brandy," complimented Paul.

"Thank you. It's a VSOP I discovered on a trip to France."

"Go there often?"

"Not as much as I would like."

"You're an American, aren't you?"

"Yeah. It's obvious, isn't it?"

Paul smiled. "And by the computer on your desk," Paul said, waving his snifter in that direction, "I'm guessing you're in finance."

"I am. Guess I can't leave my work at the office. I'm with Barstone Capital. How about you? What do you do?"

"I'm in the export business, with EuroGoods." Paul used EuroGoods as his cover company. It was a genuine corporation with very close ties to MI6.

"I've heard of them."

Paul was sure he had. He was glad his agency had the wherewithal to use a real company. Comes in handy when meeting someone who knows every company out there.

Paul's phone buzzed in his pocket. "Excuse me," he said to Ray as he answered it.

"You got my message? Yes. Yes. See you then."

Paul turned his attention back to Ray. "It was my landlord. He was very apologetic. Said he would be over in a few minutes with the right key."

Paul stood. Took another sip of the brandy and sat it on a side table. "Thank you for the brandy."

Ray stood. "No problem." He walked Paul back to the front door. "Glad to have met you. Hope we'll meet again."

Chapter 18

London

The London Eye opened in 2000 to honor the Millennium. It was a modern take on the traditional Ferris wheel, a cantilevered observation wheel. Wildly successful, it carried three million paying customers each year. Intended to be in operation for only five years, the mayor of London knew a good thing and kept it in continuous service.

Thirty-two egg-shaped glass pods were evenly suspended around the wheel. Each sealed, air-conditioned pod held twenty-five passengers.

The young man reading the guidebook looked like any twenty-year-old wearing a white tee and scruffy blue jeans. Only his bright-red hair and green eyes made him stand out. He chatted up the ticket taker, a woman close to his age.

"Morning," he said. "Great ride, I hear. Go up on it a lot?"

"No." She smiled at this handsome boy.

"No? Now how could that be?"

"Too busy taking tickets."

"Well, I must take you up sometime. Wouldn't that be lovely?"

The girl forced a smile and said, "Maybe. But you need to move along. Your carriage awaits."

The boy stepped into the pod that had just emptied its passengers, ready for the next round. Since crowds were light, the pod carried half its capacity. The young man stood near the glass, looking out toward the Thames. Inside the pod was a little girl, nine-years-old according to her mother, who was talking to another couple. The precocious little thing was a chatterbox, talking freely to several people. Mom and Dad took a seat near him in the center of the pod.

The redhead winked at the little girl, and asked, "And how are you this fine day?"

The little girl pouted and leaned into her mother, who was surprised at her daughter's reaction. "Say hello." The little girl said nothing and looked away from him.

The mother shrugged and told the redhead, "I'm sorry. She's always so open with everyone. I don't know what's up."

He was unfazed. "No worries. You just never know, do you?"

The passengers snapped pictures and pointed out the sights below as the pod rose ever higher over London. The redhead was more interested in the pod and the wheel itself. He examined the steel cables holding the wheel in place. He tapped on the glass. He looked at the floor and around the bench in the center. He even held his hand over the air-conditioning vents.

The others were too caught up with the excitement of the ride and the view of London to notice. All but the little girl. She continued to peek at the young man with suspicion as her mother and father turned toward the glass.

It took a half-hour to return to the ground. The passengers disembarked, the redhead bringing up the rear. The little girl's mother held her hand as the girl kept turning to glance over her shoulder at the man.

"Come along," said the mother as she sheepishly mouthed, "I'm sorry" toward the redhead.

The redhead sauntered away from the crowd toward his red BMW S1000 bike. He unlocked it, put on his helmet emblazoned with an image of flames flowing from front to rear, and sped off into the streets of London.

Chapter 19

London

The brilliance of a firebomb would be more dramatic against the darkened sky.

The green-eyed redhead returned to the London Eye a half-hour before closing. His timing had to be perfect. The security check was brief. He had no backpack; he didn't need one. Everything he required, he wore. His instructions were to cause maximum physical damage with minimum collateral damage. Same as the church job. It didn't matter either way to him; although no one died in the church gig, he eliminated a witness after the fact.

Minimum collateral damage.

He calculated that the pod carrying him would end up high in the sky when the last passenger left the wheel below approximately 180 degrees behind him.

Perfect.

He entered the pod and took a seat in the center. Most of the other passengers pressed themselves against the windows to get the best view of Big Ben at twilight. No one noticed when he bent down and unzipped the back of his pant legs; it's not unusual to relax the cuffs when wearing boots. A girl about sixteen-years old glanced at him, but when he winked at her, she blushed and turned back to the window. Nobody saw him slide a package from each leg and stick both beneath the seat.

The redhead pulled out a cell phone and dialed it, feigning a conversation. No one was on the other end. He was testing the dialing. Another, unseen phone vibrated in his leather jacket.

Ready.

He finished his 'conversation' and returned the phone to his jacket pocket. He then took the other phone out as though it was the same one. He flipped through preloaded text messages. Satisfied he had not drawn any attention to himself, he reached under the seat and pressed the phone into the sticky package he'd just planted.

Now, job done and ready to imitate a tourist, he stood and walked to the glass to enjoy the view. Next to him was the girl he had winked at.

"Beautiful view, isn't it?" he asked the girl.

She glanced at her mother, who stood beside her before answering. "Yes. It is."

He turned to the mother and said, "This your little sister?"

The mother took the bait, enjoying the flattery. "No," the mother said. "She's my daughter."

"She looks just like you," he replied.

The young man knew that being social, however boring, was way smarter than keeping to himself. When suspicions fly, no one ever casts a thought toward the nice guy. He put the social into sociopath. He kept up the banter until they returned to the ground.

The mother and daughter said goodbye and the redhead relaxed on a park bench and waited. The attraction had not taken on any more riders; the man watched the sky as his empty pod slowly made its way back up to the top.

Perhaps the redhead could mask his ill intent to most people with friendly chatter. But one person on duty that night became suspicious, the attendant who had boarded the distinctive redhead a few days earlier. He remembered him being alone then as well, and he recalled how his girlfriend Tracy, a ticket collector, had complained when they returned to their flat that night about the sleazy redheaded guy coming on to her. Now the redhead had returned, alone once more, and was lingering on a bench looking at the wheel.

What's that bloke up to?

The attendant took a guard aside and shared his concern. "I'll keep an eye on that one," he assured the attendant. The guard walked toward the bench, stopped some distance away, and observed, pausing to tie his shoelace.

The redhead recognized the imaginary loose shoelace action.

Pathetic! Playing copper, is he? Just need a few seconds more.

The redhead saw his pod, now empty, reach the top as the last passengers departed below.

Now's the time!

The redheaded young man stood, took out his cell phone, and began to dial. The call took three seconds to connect, the phone planted in the top pod vibrated, the sensor in the explosives picked up the vibrations and performed as designed.

The pod at the very top of the London Eye burst into flames, issuing its own thunder across the city as shattered panes of glass rained down. The wheel rocked but did not fall as the pod burned like a bonfire in the sky.

As the redhead was returning his cellphone to his pocket, he looked up to see the guard now running toward him.

"Hey," he said. "Could I see some identification?"

"Sure," said the redhead, his hand still in his jacket.

The Beretta Alleycat was his favorite pistol. Small, but because it was detectable by security, he had attached it to the bottom of the park bench before taking the ride. Saying no more, the redhead pulled the pistol from his jacket and pumped two bullets into the guard. The crowd in the park didn't react to the fallen man; they were mesmerized by the explosion. However, within a few seconds, everyone scattered when they noticed the bloody guard on the ground. Other guards came running from the wheel.

It's time to go.

The redhead had parked his motorcycle among a line of bicycles. He would have been able to walk to his destination in a few minutes under normal circumstances. The wailing sirens in the distance announced these weren't normal circumstances. Still, he casually walked to the bike, so as not to draw attention.

Ignoring the men now chasing after him on foot, the redhead started his bike and roared down Chicheley Street, making a quick left on York Road. Suddenly, three police cars raced behind the motorcycle. He leaned the bike into a hard left and outpaced the police around the Park Plaza Hotel roundabout. A young couple leaving the Illy Caffé began to jaywalk across the street when the bike raced within a few feet, making them drop their espressos.

Heading along the covered tube of Waterloo Station, he cut another sharp left into the tunnel beneath the rail tracks. Darting between cars, he slid out of the tunnel to the left and zoomed up Approach Road past queuing taxis and headed for the station's entrance.

He pulled up in front of the station and onto a traffic island. Putting his helmet on the seat of the bike, he walked to the station. He hadn't gone more than twenty paces before the bike exploded into flames. But when it did, the redhead was gone, lost in the crowd of shocked passengers.

The young man took a deep breath, rolled his shoulders, and smiled. Fire had a calming effect on him, one that he sought. A benefit in his line of work. He walked among the confused crowd. Some commuters were talking, others were shouting. 'Did you see the motorbike explode outside the entrance?' 'Did you hear someone just bombed the London Eye?' The people around him were caught in psychological amber, unsure whether to go outside, run for their train, or duck and hide. The redhead knew what to do. He had a train to catch. He strode in that direction.

He took an escalator down to the lower level. As he reached the bottom, he heard a commotion behind him. Looking up, he saw a team of heavily armed black uniforms. The redhead was surprised they'd arrived so quickly. The team leader did not have time to yell halt before the redhead reached into his jacket and lobbed a small canister toward the men. The canister exploded like a Molotov cocktail, consuming the man and his fellow officers in fire.

As bystanders attempted to beat out the flames, the redhead once again disappeared into the crowd. But as he reached his train, he spotted two police officers approaching. He turned on his heels to retreat, only to fall into the arms of another two armed officers. As the officers closed in, he dropped to his knees and put his hands behind his head.

Chapter 20

London

The police officer charged with photographing suspects had witnessed his share of unsavory felons in his twenty-one years on the force, but this one was particularly unsettling. His bright red hair and green eyes were practically supernatural. His demeanor exuded superiority. Then his tattoo. Many fiends had tattoos, but this one was intricate, a series of shapes like a jigsaw puzzle, as though the man could be taken apart and put back together. Here and there were geometric shapes, triangles, octagons, and the like.

Weird.

The camera captured it all.

After the photos and the booking, they returned the suspect to a holding cell. The photographer overheard several people, some he knew and some he didn't, squabble over jurisdiction for the suspect. Scotland Yard had possession of him, but MI5 saw this as a case of terrorism. There were rumors that MI6 wanted questions answered. MI6 won, and the suspect was to be taken to their headquarters.

Paul was summoned to Vauxhall Cross. His boss, C, was waiting in a conference room with two other agents. The Bond movies popularized the boss as M, but the real MI6 honored the first leader of the Secret Service, Captain Sir Mansfield Smith-Cumming, RN, who signed all his notes with a green C.

Paul didn't recognize the other two agents. Both were wearing gray suits, one with a burgundy tie and the other with a blue one.

"Ah, Paul," said C. "Have a seat. We were just discussing this." C pointed to a small canister on the table that resembled a huge flashlight battery. "Have you ever seen anything like this?"

Paul took a long look at it and asked, "Have they emptied it?"

"Yes," said C. "Then you do know what it is."

"It appears to be a mini-Molotov. They say some crazy inventor created it and tried to sell it to military forces both east and west. A few terrorists have tried them, but their usefulness is limited. A hand grenade causes more damage in the same amount of space."

"It is an odd little beast," said C. "It contains a fuel no one can yet identify and a twist button to arm a small spark mechanism. The case is porcelain. When armed and thrown, it performs very much like a Molotov cocktail."

Paul jumped ahead. "This isn't what was used to bomb the London Eye. That device wouldn't have that much impact."

"No," said C. "It was likely plastic explosives. The lab is still analyzing it. The suspect used this 'mini-Molotov,' as you call it, in Waterloo Station. He set his motorcycle on fire with one as a diversion, and he threw another one at an armed response team. When we arrested the bastard, his jacket was lined with the little devils."

The most obvious question had not yet been asked. "Who is our suspect?"

C glanced at the open file before him. "The name's Aiden Hayes. Irish, living in Paris. He works at a bakery."

"A bakery?" asked Paul.

Agent burgundy-tie spoke up. "We talked to the owner of the bakery. It was Hayes and another man whose job it was to fire up the oven in the early hours each morning. Really old fashioned. They use a brick, wood-fired oven."

"Do we know his coworker's name?"

It was agent blue-tie's turn. "His name is Karl Lenoir. We're tracking him down. The owner says that Hayes and Lenoir switch off duties. Only one of them works each shift."

"That's a convenient arrangement for someone who needs to skip town for a day," remarked Paul.

C passed a file to Paul. "Here are photos of Hayes and Lenoir."

Paul glanced at the photos. There were several of Hayes, but only one of Lenoir. The ones of Hayes were from the Scotland Yard photographer. They included ones without a shirt which displayed his tattoos from different angles. The one of Lenoir appeared to be from a personal snapshot. He was with Hayes on a beach with two women. Lenoir was dark-haired and unsmiling.

Two officers loaded the suspect into a police van for his fifteen-minute journey to Vauxhall Cross. The van would have no other escort in order not to draw attention.

A sullen biker waited on the west side of the Vauxhall Bridge, his motorcycle engine idling. As the police van turned onto the bridge, the biker fell in behind. Midway across the bridge, the biker sped up beside the van. When the biker reached the front of the van, he threw a small canister onto the hood. It burst into flames, covering the hood and windshield with burning fuel. The driver couldn't see and panicked. He swerved to the right and cut off a car which crashed into the van's wheel well. The connected van and car screeched several feet to a stop.

The biker was now in front of the van, the flaming vehicle blocking all traffic behind them. With his door crushed in against the van and the airbags deployed, the driver wedged into the van had nowhere to go. The biker stopped his bike, put down the kickstand and calmly walked over to the van. He now commanded the situation.

The biker tossed another canister under the van. It exploded into flames. He walked to the back door and knocked as though he had come for a visit. Inside the van, the interior was already hot. The police officer inside was trained not to open the door when attacked, but training had not covered being boiled alive.

From inside the burning van, the motorcyclist heard the police officer shout to Hayes, "Get back!" Firearm in his right hand, he pushed the rear door open. Before he could discharge his weapon, the biker tossed another canister at the feet of the police officer. Flames engulfed him as he fell out of the vehicle. Hayes jumped out of the van and raced with the biker toward his parked bike. They ran by the driver of the van, now outside with a fire extinguisher in hand. The driver had a split-second decision to make, either drop the extinguisher and fire upon the escaped suspect or save his partner. Too late.

The biker jumped onto the motorcycle with Hayes behind still handcuffed. Hayes threw his hands over the biker and the two disappeared.

Paul waited with C and the two other agents. They expected Hayes to be delivered soon and anticipated a call upon his arrival. The call was not what they expected. "He's escaped," C announced to the assembled agents. "Come with me."

C led the way out of the meeting room with Paul and the two other agents behind. They rushed to a riverside window where they saw a flaming police van. The gas tanks caught, and a fireball rose from the wreckage. C turned to Paul.

"This man has to be stopped."

Ray's cell phone buzzed in his jacket. He pulled it out and looked at the caller information.

"What's up?" Ray asked upon answering the phone.

The voice said, "You know about the London Eye?"

"Yes," said Ray. "Who doesn't?"

"The bomber was our man."

"What? Which one?"

"The one who did the church."

"Did we authorize the Eye?"

"No, we did not."

Ray paused. He knew what this meant. "He was working freelance for someone else. What are we going to do?"

"This is just a call to keep you in the loop. We're taking care of it. The man escaped the police. He's headed back to Paris. We'll see to it that he can't talk to the authorities. You stay focused on California."

"I will. Thanks for the heads up."

Chapter 21

Rome

"Alessandro! It's been too long," Nick said, giving the old curator a hearty handshake.

"Nicholas, it is good to see you," returned Alessandro.

Nick and Tom greeted Alessandro at a small café where they had agreed to meet. Alessandro De Luca was the curator of The Golden Palace. The café was a stone's throw from the Colosseum, but more importantly, close to the Golden Palace.

Nick made the introductions. "Alessandro, I would like you to meet Tom Littleton. Tom, Alessandro De Luca." Tom and Alessandro shook hands. Alessandro's smile emanated warmth. His brown eyes constantly evaluating, but never betraying what he was thinking.

"Please, have a seat," Alessandro said.

A waiter came to the table and, since it was early morning, each man ordered a cappuccino. Nick knew the Italian custom. Espresso, you drink at a bar, standing up. Cappuccino is more of a leisurely table drink, and only consumed in the morning.

"So, my friend," Alessandro said. "You have been in the news, have you not?"

"You mean the cave?" Nick asked.

"Yes, and the tablet."

"Well," began Nick. "All of that was Tom's discovery."

"Ah yes, the famous cave explorer."

Tom grinned at the recognition. "Famous may be an overstatement. There are more accomplished cavers than me."

"But," responded Alessandro, "none of them discovered a ten-thousand year-old tablet, I will guess."

Alessandro, turned to Nick and asked, "You said on the phone you wanted to see the Domus Aurea, and I am happy to show it to you, but I did not quite understand your interest. Something about fire?"

Nick exchanged a glance with Tom, both men unsure how much of their wild speculation they should share.

"I've been doing some research on Pliny," Nick started.

"The Elder?" asked the curator.

"Yes. And I've been working with an expert on the writings of Josephus."

"Ah. Two men who lived at the time of Nero."

"Right. They wrote about Nero and the fire he started."

Alessandro laughed. "That is all centuries-old hearsay. Nicholas, you should know this. Yes, Nero took advantage of the fire and built his palace on land cleared by it. And yes, he blamed the Christians for starting it, but no, there is little evidence he did the deed. He was at his villa far out of the city."

"We believe someone working for him started it."

"That would be interesting," admitted Alessandro. "But what does that have to do with the Domus?"

"The information we have indicates Nero included a private room in the palace for this man," said Nick. "His name, according to a scholar of such things, may have been Filius Egnatius. Does that name mean anything to you?"

Alessandro spent more time than Nick on the history of the Golden Palace and responded, "No. I have not heard that name before. Could it be a myth?"

"Perhaps, but if we can find that private room, it would bolster the story."

"But we are sure no one actually lived there," protested Alessandro.

"This man, Egnatius, may not have lived in that room. It was more of a guild office," added Tom.

Alessandro's confusion was evident. "Guild? What kind of guild?"

Nick had gone most of the way through this far-fetched story. He pushed on. "A guild of fire starters."

Alessandro raised an eyebrow. "So, Nero built a room for these, what do you call, arsonists, to do their work?"

"Yes."

Alessandro turned to Tom. "And you believe this, too?"

"Yes," said Tom. "I have independent verification of it."

"Oh, well," said Alessandro mockingly. "If you have 'independent verification,' it must be so. Nicholas, you have been a good friend. I trust you. If all you have told me came from someone else, I would thank them for the cappuccino and be on my way. Coming from you, there may be something to this story."

The curator leaned back in his chair and addressed both men. "So which room is the one you seek?"

"We are not sure,"

"But, dear gentlemen, the Domus Aureus has three-hundred rooms, and none of them announce *Fire Guild this Way*."

Tom picked up the conversation. "We do, however, have details regarding the size and shape of the room and possible wall art. They described it as near the grand banquet room."

Alessandro sparked up. "That narrows it down greatly."

"So?" asked Nick.

Alessandro said, "Let's go for a tour."

Nick and Tom walked with Alessandro past the iconic Colosseum, already busy with buses disgorging tourists, to the lush park at the edge of the Colosseum area. The only hint of the Golden Palace was the name of the narrow, paved path to the site, Via della Domus Aurea.

Tom remarked on the name, "How long has this path used the name Domus Aurea? It is a recent find, isn't it?"

"Not a recent find," said Alessandro. "A young boy rediscovered it during the early Renaissance. I am sure that you know the story. But not until this century have we done extensive excavation. And it continues."

After walking a few minutes through the park, Alessandro led them to the left of the path and to a series of brick archways, each closed behind iron gates. One was open and men in hard hats were coming and going through it.

"These are Trajan's baths. The emperor built these baths on top of the Domus some years after Nero's death and after the Caesars had buried the palace."

A worker brought over three hard hats and handed one to each of the men. "Please put on this hat. There are no tourists today. They come only on weekends by appointment when no one is excavating. You are my personal guests. We've turned some exhibits off since you are on a particular mission and would not waste time with them."

Alessandro led Nick and Tom through the iron gates. They were soon overwhelmed by impenetrable darkness, but Nick knew that this was Tom's element — cool, dark, subterranean spaces.

Eventually, Alessandro switched on the lights. The lights provided only minimum illumination at the edges of the walkway. Although the walls were smooth, the floor was uneven from rough excavation.

"When we take people on tours," said Alessandro, "we project images on the wall and play an introductory narrative. People reserve a tour conducted in the language of their choice. That presentation is not available today, but I think you have done your homework and would not benefit from it. Let's go on."

They continued down the hallway to the original ground level of the palace. Another hallway greeted them, constructed of brick walls and an arched concrete ceiling.

"These walls were originally covered with marble before the palace was condemned and the marble stripped away," said Alessandro. "The Caesars following Nero's reign may have hated the excesses of the Domus, but they weren't crazy. Much of the art, the marble, and the gold ended up in their own houses."

Although the walls were stripped of adornments, many items remained. They soon came to the room in which the boy had accidentally discovered the Domus. It was now empty of the soil that had filled it, but the ceiling art that inspired the masters remained.

Alessandro gazed above and remarked, "We know that Michelangelo lowered himself into this room, such as it was during the Renaissance. Some say this style of ceiling painting inspired his work in the Sistine Chapel."

A room further on contained a well-preserved mosaic floor with black and white squares interlaced in repeating hexagons.

After walking through countless rooms, they arrived at the Domus centerpiece, the banquet hall. Five separate corridors converged on a large, round room with a domed roof. At the apex of the roof was a glass window, covered by earth for two-thousand years, but now open to the twenty-first century.

"This is the room you were asking about. Histories of the period tell us that Nero had a large device engineered into the ceiling that sprinkled rose petals over the guests. It was a magnificent dining experience."

Nick turned to Tom. "OK," Nick said. "Which one of these hallways leads to the fire starter's room?"

Tom smiled. "What Omni told me from her research makes sense now."

"Omni?" asked Alessandro.

"I'll explain later," replied Nick before turning to Tom. "You mean…"

"Where the first rays of the winter sun shine," said Tom.

"Alessandro," asked Nick, "Which way is east?"

Alessandro knew the excavation well. He stood in the center of the room and pointed. "That way."

Nick and Tom turned in the opposite direction.

"Adjusting for the first day of winter," said Tom, "Which way would the sun shine?"

"There!" said Nick conclusively as he pointed to a hallway on the left.

Tom was puzzled at Nick's quick response, "How do you know?"

Nick grinned. He knew that complex conclusions often come from simple experiences. "New York is at the same latitude as Rome. My townhouse faces east. The light through my front window on the first day of winter, hits the left side of my desk. If I stood by the window, it would be in that direction."

Tom asked, "How do you remember that?"

"I used to have a solar radiometer on the desk on the left side, and just before Christmas, it would start turning in the sunlight."

"A solar what?" asked Alessandro.

"One of those gizmos in a tube that has fins around an axis. Opposite sides are painted black or silver. When sunlight hits it, it starts to spin."

Alessandro laughed. "My friend, have you ever moved your desk or this gizmo?"

"Not in years. Let's go," said Nick as he took the lead down the hallway. His enthusiasm vanished as he looked down the hall. "But which room?" he asked.

"There are four rooms off this hall," said Alessandro.

"Then, let's look in each," added Tom, undaunted.

The men went room to room, looking for scraps of art or mosaics that might give them a clue. But all they found were blank, brick walls. However, in the fourth room, Nick stopped. "This is it!" he exclaimed.

"How do you know?" asked Tom.

Nick walked over to a wall where the faint remnants of a fresco remained. "What do you see?" he asked Tom.

Tom leaned in to get a closer look. "It seems to be a man with a hammer and anvil."

"Exactly," said Nick. "It's Vulcan, the god of—"

"Fire," said Alessandro, completing Nick's sentence.

Nick looked to the left of the sculpture. "What's this hole in the wall? Looks fresh."

Alessandro said, "We found a lead chest behind the wall."

"A lead chest?" asked Nick. "Where is it?"

"It is in storage," answered Alessandro. "We put it aside to examine more closely later. Would you like to see it?"

Nick and Tom both answered enthusiastically, "Yes!"

Alessandro led the men to a room outside of the tourist area, one cleared of debris but filled with relics. The dimly lit room was lined on four sides with rows of metal shelves all filled with pieces of bowls, statues, and glass.

"We store things in here from recent discoveries. Forgive the condition of the room. I have yet to catalog these items," Alessandro said with some embarrassment. "I remember the chest. I put it here myself."

Alessandro suddenly looked like a man who lost his keys but thought he knew where they were, just to be confused when they weren't there.

"What's wrong?" asked Nick.

"The chest. It is not here."

Chapter 22

Rome

Nick and Tom approached a Swiss Guard clad in colorful stripes. "We have an appointment with Monsignor Alonso Alberti," Nick said. The guard stepped into a booth and picked up a phone.

"I hope we have better luck here than we did at the Domus Aurea," Tom told Nick.

"I think we had extraordinary luck. We found the room in which Filius Egnatius held all of his meetings."

"You have no proof of that."

"The drawing on the wall is telling," Nick responded. "I know it has to be the place where Egnatius gathered his followers."

"But what was in the chest? Why is it missing?"

"Alessandro probably misplaced it," answered Nick. "He'll find it."

"I don't think so," replied Tom.

Nick smiled at his friend. "My Doubting Thomas. You're so aptly named."

"On the contrary, I believe the chest holds something key to the whole Filius Egnatius mystery. If so, wouldn't someone want to keep it out of our hands?"

The guard returned. "He will be with you soon."

"Thank you," said Nick, but they didn't have to wait long. Walking toward them was a tall young man, dressed in black pants, shirt, and jacket, with a white clerical collar at his neck. He could have easily been the local country priest, one with a smile that seemed perpetual.

"Mr. Foxe?" the man asked as he neared.

"Yes," responded Nick. "Monsignor Alberti?"

"That would be me," said Alberti as he shook Nick's hand.

"I would like to introduce my friend Tom Littleton."

"So good to meet you," Alberti said to Tom as they exchanged a handshake.

Turning back to Nick, Alberti asked, "How is Mr. Tanner doing?"

"You remember Tanner?"

"How could I forget? He seemed so determined to find answers to questions that bothered him. I showed him a book written by the first Spanish governor of Santa Fe, Juan de Ornate. He found the drawings in the book very interesting."

Alberti paused. "Tell me, did he find the answers he sought?"

Nick and Tom exchanged glances before Nick answered, "Yes. Yes, he did."

Alberti seemed pleased. "Ah. That is good, and now, Mr. Tanner's friends are seeking more answers."

Nick said, "I know it was a long shot when I called you, but I thought if anyone's records on Rome would stretch back to the time of Nero, it would be yours."

Alberti grinned mischievously, "So, you think we would have records on Filius Egnatius?"

Nick asked, "And do you?"

"Walk this way. We can talk."

Nick thought Alberti was pleased with himself. A simple 'no' could have been given, but it wasn't.

Nick and Tom followed Alberti, who sauntered along, nodding to fellow priests, and stopping from time to time to talk to someone confirming an appointment. They eventually found themselves in a vast hallway with a black and white checkerboard floor. Paintings adorned each panel of the marble wall and above in every cornice of the ceiling. Although the space could easily hold a crowd of more than a hundred, they walked alone.

"When we talked on the phone," Alberti said to Nick, "you mentioned having a meeting with Rabbi Isaac Genack."

"And when I mentioned him, I detected a pause. Did the name give you concern?" asked Nick.

"Rabbi Genack is a fine scholar," said Alberti in the way one politely does before revealing what they really think.

Alberti paused, allowing Nick to prompt with a "But?"

Alberti rotated his hand in a maybe-yes/maybe-no gesture as he said, "Sometimes he is given to what we now call conspiracy theories."

A wave of disappointment flowed over Nick, and he could see an irksome expression from Tom who asked, "So, we're on a wild goose chase?"

Alberti seemed to realize he had misled these gentlemen. "Oh, no, no. That is not at all what I meant. This time, the good Rabbi seemed to be on to something, but not in the way he thought. I'll show you what I mean."

Alberti led Nick and Tom to a smaller, but equally embellished room. A few rows of reading tables were installed, but only one other person was in the room. He was dressed in priest garb much like Alberti and stood by a huge old volume laying on the desk. When Alberti approached, the priest informed him, "This is the book you requested."

Alberti thanked the man, who then left the room. Alberti pointed to the book bound like an ancient altar bible and he told Nick and Tom, "This book points to what Rabbi Genack was talking about."

"Points?" asked Nick. "What do you mean?"

Alberti displayed a smug expression. Nick recognized it. It was the look his archeology colleagues used when they were going to tell about a discovery that everyone had overlooked.

"While I found nothing about a Filius Egnatius in Josephus' writings, I was aware of a mention of the man in this tome."

"What is it?" asked Tom, now obviously intrigued.

"This is a history of a family, written in 1512 AD. You might be interested in the family name."

"Egnatius?" ventured Nick.

"Close," responded Alberti. "It was Egnati."

"Egnati?" questioned Tom. "Well, that's interesting, but not quite the same."

"Ah," added Alberti, "but in this history, the family's roots are traced back to Filius Egnatius. Apparently, some liberty had been taken with the family name over time."

Nick glanced at his doubting Tom and saw him nodding his head, accepting the connection.

"There is more," said Alberti. "Do you know what the family business was?"

"Um, something to do with fire?" Tom responded hopefully.

"Greek fire," responded Alberti. "They were arms merchants."

"Greek fire?" asked Tom.

Nick explained. "Greek fire was a chemical first used by the Byzantine Empire. They built something in their navy like today's flame throwers to set enemy ships on fire using it. The formula remains a matter of speculation."

Turning to Alberti, Nick added, "But, it wasn't in use until the seventh century."

"True, but fire was used as a weapon by the Romans since the beginning of the empire. On the battlefield, a substance was lit and launched toward the enemy by catapult. Apparently, the Egnati family had a thriving business in supplying such things."

Nick wanted to know more. "You said the book was from 1512 AD."

"Yes," said Alberti. "Apparently, the family was doing well enough to have their history written. The author is unknown, and the truth of the document? Who knows? Much of it may be family lore."

"And what happened to the family? Where are they now?" asked Tom.

Alberti shrugged. "Who knows? Even families like the Medici fade into obscurity over time."

"This is very helpful," said Nick, "but I have to ask, how is it that you knew this book contained some mention of Filius Ignatius?"

"Well, that was where we were in luck," responded Alberti. "You may know that we have an effort underway to digitize the contents of our entire collection. The man who brought us this book today is responsible for the digitizing. When I asked him to search for Filius Ignatius, he found the reference in this book."

Tom looked peeved. Nick thought he knew why. Nick's suspicion was validated when Tom questioned Alberti, "When was this book digitized?"

Alberti appeared shocked at Tom's forceful manner in asking such an insignificant question and stammered, "Well, it was sometime this week. I'm not sure when."

Nick attempted to cool the situation by telling Alberti, "This is very helpful. It really is. Now that it is digitized, I assume we can examine the document further without having to bother you?"

Alberti, keeping a questioning eye on Tom Littleton who was clearly upset, responded, "Certainly, of course." Then, turning to Nick, he said, "But feel free to contact me. I would be glad to help in any way I can. Is there anything else I can do for you now?"

"No," responded Nick. "I think we've taken up enough of your time."

"Then, let me walk you out."

Nick and Alberti walked out the way in which they came, with Tom following silently a few steps behind. Alberti asked about Tanner and Nick brought him up to date talking in generalities. He told about his relationship with Lizzy which seemed to please Alberti on hearing there was a woman in Tanner's life.

They returned to the Swiss Guard where they had started, and Alberti shook hands with both men. Once again, Alberti told them he was available for any follow-up they might need.

As they walked out beyond the gate, Nick turned to Tom. "I know why you're upset."

"It's obvious, isn't it?" Tom pointed to a quiet spot just beyond the guard's station. "Let's go over there and talk to Omni."

Tom pulled out his cell phone and to any passerby it would appear Tom was calling a friend. Although Tom did not put the call on speaker, the connection was loud enough for Nick to listen in.

"Omni," said Tom. "I'm very disappointed in you."

"Why would you be disappointed in me?" asked Omni.

"We asked you to find references to Filius Egnatius and you found none."

"That is true."

"We are standing outside of the Vatican Library, and we just found out that a book had been digitized mentioning Egnatius. Why did you not see it?"

"Well," responded Omni in her unflappable tone, "you asked me about Filius Egnatius fifty-two hours ago and the Vatican released its digitized reference thirty-seven hours ago."

Nick couldn't help but grin at Tom's facial contortions, not unlike those of a teacher frustrated by a smart aleck student.

"Omni," said Tom after regaining some patience, "you've got to be more proactive."

"I shall," responded Omni. "In the spirit of being proactive, I have further information for you."

Nick mouthed to Tom 'in the spirit of?' noting such an unusually human construct for a computer. Tom ignored Nick and asked Omni, "And what would that be?"

"The document that mentions Filius Egnatius is in a history of the Egnati family," replied Omni.

Tom rolled his eyes. "Yes, we know that."

"Do you know that a villa was recently discovered near where you are now that belonged to the Egnati family?"

Nick and Tom exchanged an astonished expression.

"No," said Tom. "Tell me more."

"I will send you a recent news article that tells more. It does not provide the coordinates but reports that it is located on Aventine Hill close to the Circus Maximus."

"I will contact Alessandro," said Nick. "He probably knows all about it."

Omni overheard Nick and responded, "Do you mean Alessandro De Luca, the man you met with recently?"

Nick was puzzled at how Omni knew that information.

Does she have access to my calendar?

"Yes," Nick answered.

"Alessandro De Luca was mentioned in the article. He was asked for comment and reported that he looked forward to exploring the find."

"Well," said Nick, "He's going to have that chance. Thanks, Omni."

A man, hidden amongst the swirl of tourists some distance away, saw Nick and Tom talking on the phone. He reasoned they would not recognize him from any other worker at the Domus Aurea, but he remained in the shadows just to be sure. He had worked tirelessly to excavate the chest of Egnatius and now had it in his possession. He would make sure the men he kept under surveillance would never have it.

Chapter 23

Rome

Alessandro knew the man responsible for the recently discovered villa and that colleague welcomed him to accompany Mr. Foxe and Mr. Littleton on a visit.

A modern-day apartment building sat beside the villa. It was not until a janitor explored a seldom used part of that building's subbasement that the villa was discovered. He was investigating a water leak when he tripped over a mop handle and fell against the wall which cracked open. He alerted the authorities, and the excavation soon began.

For the first year of the discovery, workers entered through the apartment building and through the opening the janitor had accidentally created. They soon installed an exterior metal staircase adjoining the apartment building. It was there that Alessandro met Nick and Tom. He was as excited to see what lay ahead as Nick and Tom were. His colleague trusted Alessandro and told him that a workman would let him in. It would be a self-guided tour of sorts, but the workman would be available for questions.

Alessandro greeted Nick and Tom. "Welcome. We meet again so soon."

"So it appears," said Nick. "Thank you for setting this up."

"No problem. It is a treat for me as well," responded Alessandro. "But tell me, why do you believe this villa may have belonged to the Egnati family?"

"The book I told you about when I called stated the family had a villa around this location," said Nick.

Alessandro shrugged. "But there are many villas. Most have not yet been discovered. Probably most have been totally destroyed."

"Well, we know what we are looking for."

"You mean more paintings of Vulcan?" Alexandro asked, referring to the discovery in the Domus Aurea.

"Something like that," said Nick.

Alessandro had his doubts and turned to Tom for further verification of Nick's theory. "Do you hope to find something like that as well?"

"We won't know until we look," responded Tom.

"Then why don't we look?" asked Alessandro as he led the men down the staircase.

The room they entered was in far better condition than those of the Domus Aurea. Workers had erected bright tripod lights which made the floor look as though it had been laid yesterday, not nearly two-thousand years ago. The walls fared less well. The white and gold patterns were faded and cracked, still remarkable for their age.

A workman dressed in overalls walked up to the men with a portfolio under his arm. "*Signor* De Luca?"

"*Si*," responded Alessandro.

The man handed Alessandro the portfolio and said a few words in Italian. Alessandro translated for Nick and Tom. "He said that my colleague, his boss, asked him to give this to me. An artist has made drawings showing how he imagined the rooms to have been when the family lived here."

Alessandro set the portfolio on a small worktable and opened it. The first drawing was of the room in which they were standing. The drawing depicted the floor with the intricate gray and white pattern just as it appeared now, but the artist had enhanced the faded frescos on the walls to their original gold luster. The second showed a chamber in which the artist had adorned the walls with a rich red color popular in Rome during the empire. "This would have been a bed chamber," said Alessandro.

Another drawing was of a room that Alessandro identified as the

134

dining room. Two more drawings of rooms with unclear purpose completed the collection.

Alessandro turned to Nick and Tom. "None have the insignias you are looking for, no?"

"Why not look around?" asked Nick.

Alessandro asked the workman if they could guide themselves. The workman said yes, but he had things to do and would remain there.

The men wandered through the villa, seeing the rooms from the drawings in their faded condition. Alessandro noticed how carefully Tom examined the walls. Nick explained why. "You see," said Nick, "Tom is a cave explorer with an unusual gift. He has a keen peripheral sense."

"Peripheral sense?" asked Alessandro.

"You know how it is when you believe someone behind you is looking at you? You do not see them, but you feel the stare. Many people sense they are near a sudden drop-off, even though it may be pitch dark. That's peripheral sense. Tom's gift of that sense allowed him to discover a passage behind a cave wall no one else knew was there."

As Nick explained the phenomenon to Alessandro, Tom continued to be focused on the walls. He was at the end of a hallway between openings to rooms, and he was running his finger around the indentation of three separate panels at the end of the hall. Most of the panels in the villa were faux creations by an ancient artist. These were exceptional in that they were carved into the plaster wall.

"What's behind this wall?" asked Tom.

"I believe it's nothing but earth," offered Alessandro. "I'll ask."

With that, Alessandro walked back to the workman and brought him to Nick and Tom. The workman confirmed that the hallway ended there with nothing behind the wall. As Nick asked the workman what techniques were used to ensure that nothing was there, Alessandro noticed out of the corner of his eye that Tom had taken out a pocketknife and was probing around the indentation. As a man accustomed to carefully probing digs with brushes, Alessandro was alarmed. He thought Tom was treating this wall like a rocky cave rather than an ancient treasure. Before Alessandro could say anything, the workman showed his alarm by approaching Tom spouting a host of Italian invectives Alessandro understood but was sure Tom did not.

Tom calmed the workman as best he could with hand gestures. Then he asked the workman, "Put your cheek up close, like this," and Tom put his cheek close to the wall where he was probing. The workman followed suit and jerked away surprised. Tom explained why. "Cool air is escaping from the other side of the wall through the opening I made. There's a room there."

Tom stepped by and examined the center panel. "I believe this whole panel opens, perhaps on a hinge, if it hasn't rusted away."

Alessandro walked with the workman back to the hall's opening, explaining what Tom had said. Nick joined in the discussion. The three men talked excitedly over each other. The workman said he must talk to his boss. Nick wanted to open the panel right away. Alessandro reminded Nick about the steps one must follow, as he expected Nick would understand as a fellow archeologist.

None of the men noticed Tom until they heard a dull thump when he pushed his body hard against the panel. All three stood mouths agape. When Tom backed up a few feet, they could not believe what he was about to do. Alessandro and the workman yelled, "No!" in unison as Tom ran full force putting his shoulder into the panel. The panel fell into the newly discovered room in a cloud of dust.

Tom stood smiling and offered a simple, "Whoops."

Alessandro was shocked. The workman went ballistic and directed his ire at Alessandro telling him that he was headed above ground to use his cell phone to call his boss.

136

Alessandro could not believe Nick was grinning. Tom's theatrics were outside the boundaries of archaeological conduct and Nick seemed to acknowledge that fact when he wiped the smile off his face and told Alessandro, "Well, what's done is done. Nothing's left but to take a look."

Alessandro could not help but be as curious as Nick and reluctantly walked with him to where Tom awaited at the opening to the mystery room. Tom moved one of the tripod lights into the room and was outlined by shadow and a diminishing cloud of dust.

They stepped into a room unlike any of the artist concepts of a rich Roman's villa and more like the imagining of a star chamber. The floor was mosaic tile and was as well preserved as the one they first encountered in the villa. This one was bordered by a series of triangles with a large circle in the middle depicting flames as though they were rising from a campfire.

Nick pointed to the border of triangles. "The triangle is the Greek symbol for fire, one of the four basic elements." Nick looked at Alessandro. "With that, and the fire featured in the middle, can there be any doubt this was the villa of Egnati? I can see him working deals in this very room."

Alessandro considered Nick's assumptions but was distracted by Tom's close examination of another one of the walls.

He's not going to attack another wall, is he?

"There is something written on this wall," noted Tom. "It's faded but is definitely there. Can either of you make it out?"

The wall was covered by pale frescos. Unlike the pleasant pictures in the other rooms, these were pictures of demons resembling gargoyles atop a cathedral. The letters were large and spanned most of the wall. Alessandro stepped back to garner a better view of the words.

"It is Latin," Alessandro read the letters as he made them out. "I, c, en, d, m, a, t, s."

Nick put it together. "*Incendium Artis,*" he said. "Fire Arts."

Tom's peripheral sense refocused. "There's someone out there," he said, nodding toward the opening.

"Perhaps it is the workman returning."

Everyone heard a slight click and then the hallway erupted in flames. The opening to the room became the door to a furnace. Everyone backed away from the heat.

"What is this?" asked Alessandro. "There was nothing that could burn in the villa."

"This is a firebomb. It has its own fuel," said Nick.

"It's sucking the oxygen out of the room," warned Tom. "We have to get out of here!"

"How?" asked Alessandro.

"Help me pick this up," said Tom as he bent down to grab the edge of the stone panel he dislodged, now laying on the floor. "We'll toss this out and separate the flames so we can escape."

Nick grabbed the other side of the panel and Alessandro held the end.

Tom told Nick, "Lift your side up a little more so we can be sure to clear the opening. On my count of three, we'll run to the opening and toss it. One!"

With that, Tom led a rhythmic rocking of the heavy panel toward the opening. "Two!"

The flames were well fueled and began licking into the opening.

"Three!"

The men rushed toward the opening and threw the panel across the flames. It landed with a loud thud and provided a path through the fire, almost. The flames still rose at the end of the panel creating a wall of fire two feet deep.

"We can make it," yelled Tom. "But we have to be quick."

Alessandro wondered if he would be fast enough to save himself, but as he paused, he saw shadows of two men on the other side of the fire. Then a cloud of gas billowed through the flames.

138

"*Da questa parte!*" yelled the man behind the gas cloud, now smothering a path through the fire. "*Freta! Freta!*"

Nick and Tom motioned Alessandro to go first and the two men each followed closely behind. They encountered two men dressed in yellow and blue jackets and pants, paramedics, one who continued to use a fire extinguisher against the blaze and the other asking in Italian if the men were all right.

"*Si, si,*" responded Alessandro, attempting to catch his breath.

"How did you know we were here?" asked Nick.

"The *polizia* received a call that men might be in trouble here and that medical attention might be required," said the paramedic. "When we arrived, we found an unconscious man near the entrance. When he came to, he said he worked here and that someone attacked him. Then we saw the flames. Do you think the person who attacked him set this fire?"

"Undoubtedly," answered Nick. "But who placed the call to the police?"

The paramedic shrugged. "This, I do not know." Turning to Alessandro, he asked, "Do you think you are able to climb the stairs out of here?"

"Yes. I will be OK," answered Alessandro.

"The fire is almost under control," replied the paramedic and turning to Nick he said, "I will assist you all. We have a vehicle at the entrance, and I want to check each of you further."

Alessandro had regained his balance and had no trouble climbing the stairs to the entrance with the others. When they arrived aboveground, they saw a paramedic tending to the workman, now sitting by the open doors of an ambulance. A policewoman had a pad out taking notes from an interview with the victim. When she saw the men emerge, she walked over to them.

"Which of you is the American who created a hole in the wall?" she asked.

"That would be me," said Tom. "Was that the first thing the gentleman was concerned about?"

The policewoman was all business and offered only a slight smile as she said, "No. He was more concerned about who knocked him unconscious. He did not see him and said he must have sneaked up from behind while he was on the phone."

"Is he OK?" asked Nick.

"The medical technician said he would be OK. He wanted to be sure someone would keep him awake for the rest of the day and he said his wife would have no problem doing that."

Alessandro asked, "Who would have done this? Do you have a witness?"

"None that we have identified yet," she replied. Pointing to a surveillance camera mounted on the corner of the apartment building she said, "We hope that camera will reveal the culprit."

Turning to Alessandro, the policewoman asked, "Can you tell me more about what happened?"

As Alessandro and Nick filled in the policewoman about the events of the day, Tom walked to a corner where he could make a private call. He pulled out his cell phone and touched an icon. "Omni?" asked Tom.

"Yes, Tom."

"Did you make a phone call to the local police?"

"Yes, Tom. I did."

"How did you know we were in trouble?"

"The surveillance camera focused on the entrance. I saw you enter, then I saw someone come out and that man was attacked by another man."

"Did you get a good look at the man who attacked?"

"Yes. His face was quite clear."

"The police would like to have that image."

"They already do," said Omni. "Although I will make sure they know where to look."

"Good work," said Tom.

"I was just following your instructions."

"My instructions?" asked Tom.

"You said that I had to be more proactive."

Tom smiled. The essence of Omni was a storehouse of enormous knowledge. That was a great gift. Tom believed he had fathered the artificial intelligence enhancements, and he was proud of his creation.

"Tom," said Omni, "I took the liberty of searching police records using the perpetrator's face. He has a record. Would you care to know what his previous conviction was for?"

"Yes," replied Tom.

"Arson."

Chapter 24

Rome

Mateo Guerra was a determined man. The nuns at the orphanage where the bastard child grew up recognized it. Though they beat him for playing with fire, he never cried. They tried to keep matches away from him, but he always found a way to get them, even at an early age. When he turned sixteen and left the orphanage for good, he took pride in his last act of setting fire to the place. He relished the flames reaching the sky over the horrid building. Mateo may have been determined, but he was careless. The police had no trouble pinning the act on him. The judge told him he was lucky no one was killed, before giving him a reduced sentence as a juvenile.

Mateo saw prison as a rite of passage. He became a man there, but most importantly he learned what direction his life would take. His cellmate bore an odd tattoo. This man told others a fabricated story as to its meaning, but for Mateo, he told the truth. Perhaps it was their shared love of fire that loosened the cellmate's tongue. Perhaps it was because the story was too farfetched for anyone to believe, but Mateo believed it.

The cellmate told of an ancient organization to which he belonged, one that traced its roots back to the time of Nero. This organization used fire for retribution and there was money to be made. Over time, the cellmate told tales passed down in the organization from one fire starter to another, but there was one that fascinated Mateo the most. The cellmate told the legend of the founder, the man who worked for Nero, the man who set fire to Rome. He was important to Nero, so much so that when Nero built the Domus Aurea, he built a room especially for him to hold private meetings. The founder recruited a league of disciples who fanned out across the Roman

Empire taking direction from the shadow government he created. The cellmate proudly claimed he was a soldier of that organization.

Mateo begged him to join the group. The cellmate would just smile and promise that when they were released, he would tell Mateo how to join. Unfortunately for Mateo, his cellmate didn't leave jail alive. An encounter with a crudely made knife from an unidentified assailant put an end to him.

When Mateo was released from prison, he plied his pyromania trade as best he could working for shadowy mafia figures on small jobs in and around Rome. He learned how to be more careful in escaping detection. At the same time, he worked in his small apartment on more sophisticated firebombs, hoping to find a way into the mysterious organization to which his cellmate had belonged.

When Mateo heard that the people at the Domus Aurea dig were looking for laborers, he answered the call. He hoped he would find clues to the organization. He felt lucky when a room was uncovered with a picture of Vulcan in it. Even though Mateo was a man of limited education, when it came to fire, he knew everything. Of course, he knew Vulcan was the god of fire. When an iron chest was removed from this very room, Mateo knew he must have it and stole it from the storeroom. It was sealed shut, but he could hear something rattling around inside. He tried to open it but was careful not to pry it loose, damaging whatever was inside. He believed it was the key to the organization.

Before he could pursue the contents of the chest further, men named Foxe and Littleton appeared in the Domus Aurea. From what he overheard, he knew these men were on the same trail as he, but it was unlikely they were interested in joining up. Mateo was a pyromaniac, but he was also paranoid. He could have followed Foxe and Littleton to see if they uncovered clues to the mysterious organization. However, no one had ever done anything to help Mateo. He saw plots against him around every corner. He overheard Alessandro tell these men he had the chest of

Egnatius. That was his chest now. No one was going to take it away from him. After following them, waiting for them to emerge from the Vatican, he was certain they had to be stopped.

Mateo planted his latest bomb creation in the villa Foxe and Littleton found. It was portable but produced a self-sustaining inferno. He set a short timer on it to allow him to escape before ignition. It was only when he reached ground level and passed the workman he had rendered unconscious, that he spotted the camera high on the corner of the apartment building. He cursed himself for being so stupid not to have noticed.

The next day in his apartment, Mateo's paranoia was at full tilt.

What if someone identified him?

His hand shook as he adjusted the firebomb on which he was working. He sat back and took a deep breath to calm his nerves. He looked at the iron chest from the Domus Aurea and smiled. The fire organization would prize the return of their icon, whatever it might be, and surely they would honor Mateo for protecting it from Foxe and Littleton.

The loud pounding on the apartment door snapped Mateo back to reality. *"Polizia!"* shouted the man demanding him to open the door. Mateo stood up, knocking over his chair. He did not notice that he had tripped the timer on the firebomb. Mateo backed up against the opposite wall as the pounding continued. He spotted the ticking counter too late. The impact of the explosion crushed Mateo against the wall as flames embraced him. Mateo stumbled forward, engulfed in fire. Before he passed out from the unbearable pain, his last sight was the iron chest, still withholding its secret.

Chapter 25

Rome

Nick received the call from Alessandro. The curator told him that the police had attempted to apprehend the man who tried to kill them in the villa, but he apparently blew himself up. However, they recovered the iron chest. Unbeknownst to Alessandro, the villa assailant worked as a laborer at the Domus Aurea and had apparently stolen the chest.

"Have you opened it?" asked Nick.

"No. Not yet. As you might imagine, it did not just flip open. We have a man trained in such things. I haven't gotten it to him yet. Would you and Mr. Littleton like to be present?"

"Of course!"

Nick and Tom were soon on site at the Domus Aurea aboveground in a building used by workers examining recovered relics. The chest sat on a table near the entrance.

"The chest is quite heavy," Alessandro said as he pulled out a pair of latex gloves and offered them to the men. "Who would like to carry it for me?"

"I'll do it," Tom said as he took the gloves and put them on. He picked up the chest and found it to be unexpectedly heavy, a real strongbox. "Lead the way," he told Alessandro.

Alessandro led Tom and Nick to a young man in a lab coat who was studying a small coin through a magnifying glass.

"Alonzo," said Alessandro. "I have something for you to look at."

Alonzo was a thin man in his early thirties with a trim goatee and an athletic build. He didn't speak in response to Alessandro, and one would suspect he said little to anyone. Alessandro motioned Tom to place the chest on the lab table. As Tom set the chest before Alonzo, the young man studied the artifact as intently as he'd been studying the coin.

"We would like to open the chest which the centuries have sealed shut."

The chest was constructed of thin lead with thicker lead bands around the rim and corroded hinges at the rear. Alonzo gently rubbed his latex-covered fingers around the lid, looking closely at where the top sat upon the bottom. Specialized tools were scattered around the workbench, no doubt for use by only a well-trained individual. All eyes were on Alonzo.

Which tool will he use to work his magic?

Alonzo sat down on his stool and rested his hand against his chin. Then he reached into a backpack beside him and brought out a can of Teflon bike lubricant. Alonzo pointed the long red straw from the nozzle and sprayed the hinges and then the edges of the lead closure. He then picked up a tiny ball-peen hammer and tapped the edge. The chest popped open as if it was brand new.

Alessandro shared Nick and Tom's surprise at this man's simple solution. But they lost little time in their surprise as they peered in to see the chest's contents.

"Alonzo, please remove the item," requested Alessandro.

Alonzo pulled out an iron triangle with two letters welded to its base.

"What is it?" asked Tom.

Alonzo pulled something from a tray on the table, almost as rare as these artifacts, a piece of carbon paper. He laid a piece of white paper on the desk and placed the carbon paper on top of it. Alonzo took the item from the chest and tapped it onto the carbon paper. He removed the carbon to show a perfect image.

"It's a branding iron," surmised Nick.

They looked at the image on the paper. If one were branded, it would appear like what they saw on the paper. It was a simple triangle with the letter I on the left side of the base and the letter A on the other.

Nick said, "The letters stand for the words we saw in the Egnati villa. *Incendium Artis.*"

Chapter 26

Paris

Paul's temporary apartment was directly across the street from the Châtelet–Les Halles train station, more of a modern shopping mall than a train station in Paul's way of thinking. The apartment was listed on Airbnb, but the listing was a ruse. Agents and embassy personnel always booked it in the service of Her Majesty. Once the residence of a successful television producer who moved out when he started a family, it remained a well-equipped one-bedroom apartment.

But the over-riding consideration for using this apartment was its location near the bakery where Aiden Hayes and his buddy Karl Lenoir were employed. Surveillance cameras showed the two men had not yet returned to work there. However, it was a start.

Paul was about to visit the bakery where the arsonist worked when a call from Nick stopped him.

"Hello, Nick. How's Rome?"

"Paul, do you have a minute? There's information I want to share with you."

"Sure," said Paul as he closed the door to his apartment, walked to a couch in the living room and settled in for a chat.

Nick said, "Tom and I found something of interest. I'm sending you a photo."

"A photo? Of what?"

"It's a very simple design, a triangle with the letters I and A below it. Look, I'll send it to you now."

In a few seconds, Paul was looking at a photo of the carbon-paper print Alonzo made in Rome.

"I and A? What do they stand for?"

"Incendium Artis."

"Fire arts," interpreted Paul.

"Yes," confirmed Nick, "But there are Latin words for different types of fire. *Ignus* means fire or light. *Flamma* means blaze, love. *Incendium* means burning, arson."

"So, we have arson arts."

"Exactly," said Nick. "But there's more, Omni found that this image appears throughout history. The Museum of London has pottery from the great fire of 1666. It bears this symbol. In 1871, the Chicago police took a photograph of a man in their custody who was accused of setting fire to a business. He had a sound alibi, so the police released him. That fall, a great fire destroyed three-square-miles of the city. The suspect they released had a tattoo with the very same symbol."

"So, it wasn't Mrs. O'Leary's cow?" Paul joked. Nick was clearly enthusiastic about this conspiracy theory, Paul thought. Yet, there was something familiar about this symbol.

"Nick," Paul said, "I would like to talk more about your discovery, but I'm busy with something else."

"I see," said Nick, pausing for a moment. "I don't know why I thought I should tell you about all this. Maybe I was caught up in the moment. Omni can process a lot of connections in the blink of an eye, but she lacks a gut feeling. However, my gut is telling me there's some connection between all of this and what you may be pursuing right now."

Paul didn't see a connection, but he was gracious about his doubts.

"Nick," he said. "I have to ring off."

"Ok, keep me posted. I mean, as much as you can."

"You bet." And with that, Paul hung up, dropped his phone in his pocket, and went to leave. He started to open the door when a nagging doubt made him close it. Paul went back to the couch and pulled out the Hayes file from his briefcase and laid it on the coffee table. He flipped through to the photos Scotland Yard had taken. He picked out the one of the arsonist showing his tattoos, the one that had a continuous maze of shapes over his body. Then he saw it. Something no one would have paid attention to amongst the noise of the rest of his heavily illustrated body unless they were looking for it.

He picked up the phone and called Nick back.

"Hello?" answered Nick.

"Nick, the fire starter guild is alive and well."

Chapter 27

Paris

The bread was fantastic. Paul enjoyed all the breads produced by the French. Not necessarily just 'French bread,' which in England was a term for baguettes. But the *pain de campagne*, a rustic favorite in round loaves; *de mie*, what American loaf bread should be; *aux noix*, full of nuts; *perdu*, what others would call French toast, but much, much better.

Paul was enjoying a slice of *pain perdu* at the Boulangerie Marceau as he watched customers select breads and pastries from behind the glass cases. In particular, he watched the proprietor, Louis Marceau, a large, round man in his sixties with a handlebar mustache and meaty hands created for kneading dough.

Paul knew the authorities had interviewed Marceau regarding the whereabouts of his employees Hayes and Lenoir. He told them he had no knowledge of their location and was angry he had to come in early to fire up the oven himself. What Paul found surprising was one item everyone seemed to have missed. Hayes was married to Marceau's niece.

Paul enjoyed his sweet bread and coffee as he studied Marceau. He saw a friendly man with a gruff exterior. Marceau would tease a new customer who requested some standard fare, telling them they lacked imagination. Then he would produce something else for the customer, adding a compliment, telling them he knew they had fine taste just by looking at them. He knew they would enjoy whatever selection he suggested. It was classic up-selling.

Most of the customers appeared to be regulars, as Marceau knew each by name. He would ask someone who looked grim, what the matter might be. If someone was happy, he would ask if it was a special day.

As the store cleared of the morning crowd, Paul walked over to the counter. *"Bonjour,"* he greeted Marceau.

"Bonjour," returned Marceau.

"Votre pain est excellent."

"Merci. Vous êtes anglais, non?"

"Oui." Although it was clear he was English, Paul's French was good, and he continued the conversation with Marceau in his native tongue. "I have heard about your establishment, but this is my first time here."

"What a shame. I hope it is not your last. Do you live in Paris?"

"No, but I visit often. I have a daughter here." Paul followed this fabrication with a sad grimace which he trusted Marceau would notice. The baker did not disappoint.

"My friend, that should be joyous, but you seem to hold some problem."

Paul paused and assessed Marceau as though judging whether to go further. He said, "She is married to a man who's no good. He's been in trouble with the law."

Paul could see Marceau couldn't wait to commiserate.

"I know how you feel," said Marceau.

"You do? How?"

"I have a niece who is married to a very bad man. I did not know it until lately. He was a good worker."

"He worked here?"

"Yes. He and his friend lit the fire in the oven very early each morning. One or the other boy was here every day."

"What happened?" Paul asked.

"Well, they accused him of a terrible crime, although I cannot believe he did it."

"How is the niece taking it?"

152

"She is holding up as well as one can expect. Her husband is in hiding, but I see her every day. She helps close up the shop in the evening."

Paul had the lead he needed.

Time to go.

Paul reached over the counter and offered Marceau his hand. Shaking it, he said, "I hope all will be well."

"You too, my friend."

"But before I leave, I would like a few slices of your *pain aux noix*."

The authorities had not made the connection to the niece since she had not taken her husband's name, Hayes. Paul had discovered her name was Marie Marceau. He had her name but was uncertain where she lived. He would find that out that evening.

Later in the day, Paul enjoyed his dinner at a sidewalk café across from the bakery and waited for Marie to come and help her uncle close up. As the end of the business day neared, a young woman entered the bakery as the last customer exited. Paul knew it had to be her. Petite and pretty, Paul imagined her role in life being played by a young Audrey Hepburn. Unfortunately, Marie had chosen a tattooed felon over a Cary Grant.

Once Marie locked up and exited, Paul left money on the table and followed her through the busy streets to her apartment. He verified her name on the entrance call box and now he knew where she lived. He would return the next day.

Paul wandered the streets and walked along the Seine, checking out the tourist art for sale and watching young lovers enjoy a beautiful day. The movies show a secret agent's life as a non-stop adventure, from the evil deed being done to an exciting finish. The truth is there is a lot of waiting.

Paul reviewed what he now knew. Nick had added quite a twist, a society of arsonists. Paul knew Hayes didn't operate alone. Someone had hired him. Some pyro-mafia was at work here, and like the mafia, it was carried out for profit. Hayes' background was hardly one of a terrorist sympathizer, although he could have been working for such a group, one with sufficient funding. However, no terrorist organization had thus far claimed credit for the London Eye bombing.

Crazy people have money as well. Someone who just hated the London Eye could have hired Hayes. It was controversial when built. Hayes seemed to take care that no one was hurt, setting off the explosion once everyone had gotten off.

One thing Paul was certain of: only one person could answer 'why?'

I must get to Hayes.

The next day near closing time, Paul was outside Marie's apartment building when she left. Marie exited and walked in the direction of Marceau's bakery. Once out of sight, Paul walked to the door. He had done his research on this building and knew that three of the units were on Airbnb. That meant the occupants would be accustomed to seeing strangers come and go. He waited.

But he did not wait for long. A couple walked out, busily chatting with each other, out for an evening on the town. Paul grabbed the door as they left and walked in. Now he had only the apartment door. He knew that it was on the first level, and he found it was at the end of the hall. The lock was simple, and his pick set made quick work of it.

The apartment was a one-room studio. He could see the entire place with a quick scan. Marie was neat. The magazines were lined up, the pillows on the couch fluffed. No clutter anywhere. Paul took care not to disturb anything. Marie was evidently compulsive and would notice.

Paul heard a noise at the door. As soon as he entered the apartment, he had identified a planned escape route out a window on the backside of the apartment should it prove necessary. Luckily, the noise was from a couple across the hall. Paul didn't have to execute his plan.

Paul found a notepad on a table beside the couch. Marie had scratched down an address and time. 14 Rue Saint-Denis 1400.

He recognized that street. There was a music street festival going on near Paul's apartment, and Rue Saint-Denis was one of the streets where it was being held. He was banking on Marie meeting Hayes at that address tomorrow at two pm.

I will be there.

Chapter 28

Paris

The next day at 1:00 pm, amid a swirl of festival goers on Rue Saint-Denis enjoying music of alternating styles filling the air, two young men sat at a table outside a coffee shop. They chose the location for their meeting to blend into a crowd. The two were the same age but were different in many ways. One was a redhead with a ruddy complexion. The other, dark with jet black hair. Unseen under their long sleeves were matching tattoos. The redhead was more casual in his manner, which seemed to infuriate the other man.

"You don't get it," said the dark-haired man, Karl Lenoir.

"Get what?" asked the laid-back Aiden Hayes.

"You don't mess around with The Company."

"The Fire Company," sneered Hayes. "What a joke."

"That joke," as you call them, "paid us well for the church."

Hayes became less cavalier when Karl mentioned the church. "Us? What did you do? I did all the work. I was on site at Notre Dame mingling with the workers. I even took care of the only witness."

Karl's anger grew as he glanced around at the crowd. "Don't use that name. It's the 'church.' You're going to give us away. *This* is the city where it happened, you fool!"

After he cooled a bit, Karl continued. "It was me The Company called. I arranged everything. You just had to set the fire and get out, and without being seen. That was a loose end we didn't need."

"And I took care of it," insisted Hayes.

Karl escalated the argument. "I got your ass out of London when you got caught. And for what? A job The Company didn't hire us to do."

Hayes yelled, "You! You always think you're my agent. My business manager. Well, I have connections, too! Our client hated the London Eye. Sure, he was nuts, but he had money. Lots of money. You don't seem to be bothered by the half I gave you."

Karl made a counterpoint. "*After* the job was done. Had I known about it ahead of time, I would have stopped you. The Fire Company does not mess around. With what you know about them, you're a risk. Not only to you but to me, too."

The previous day, just after figuring Hayes would be at this location at this time, Paul had contacted French authorities experienced in dealing with terrorist operations. He was no longer a lone wolf. The *Groupe d'intervention de la Gendarmerie Nationale* or GIGN had men stationed around the square. Lieutenant Yves Dupont, the commander, was with Paul in a building across the street from the two arsonists.

"Looks like we have a bonus capture today," said Dupont.

"Yes. That's Karl Lenoir, the man who helped Hayes escape," Paul remarked.

"We need not wait for the wife, do you agree?"

"No," said Paul, "but I still want to talk to Hayes first."

"As you wish, but it appears that Lenoir is leaving," said Dupont as he took his walkie-talkie and gave commands to his team to follow Lenoir and arrest him.

Paul was not the only one who broke into the niece's apartment and saw the note about the meeting today. The other intruder was a master of his trade, much like Paul, but very much at counter-purposes. The man wore a black bicycle outfit. He blended into the crowd that was populated by many men who were biking that day. He wore a small biker's backpack, but with a very different load inside.

The man in black noticed the GIGN operatives about, although only someone trained like him would spot them. He entered the building next to the one from which Paul and Dupont observed Hayes and Lenoir. He made his way to the roof after easily picking the lock to the top staircase. He positioned himself on the roof and waited. His job, like Paul's, involved a good deal of waiting.

Hayes remained at the table, presumably waiting for his wife. Paul walked up and took a seat with a friendly, "Hello, Aiden."

Hayes started to bolt, but Paul stopped him. "That wouldn't be smart," Paul said as he nodded toward the men on opposite street corners watching them.

"Who are you?" asked Hayes.

"Let's say I'm a researcher."

Hayes looked Paul up and down. Then his eyes darted around as if still contemplating an escape. "What type of research?"

Paul realized that Hayes was buying time, but he pushed on with his questions.

"I'm very interested in *Incendium Artis.*"

"The Fire Company," added Hayes, using the modern name for the organization.

Paul was taken aback by his openness but also pleasantly surprised. "The work in London. Who authorized it?" Paul was playing the odds. If Hayes thought Paul was with The Fire Company, he might believe The Company was so vast that Paul would not be in the know. The other possibility was Hayes might think Paul was testing him, knowing The Fire Company hadn't authorized the job.

158

The last bet was the one.

"Look, I did well at the church. Historically well, in fact. I know you coordinated it with Karl, but I did the deed." Hayes was fluffing up his value. "I'm good, and what if I took on a side job?"

Paul was now sure Hayes assumed he was from The Fire Company.

"Who did you work for?"

Hayes ignored the question. "Look, Karl told me all about the next job. It is far bigger than the Eye. Let me do that one. You'll see."

Paul was making better progress than he had imagined. But it's the little things that get in the way of crossing the finish line. Such it was when the walkie-talkie on one cop blasted a question from another cop. It was barely discernible, but it spooked Hayes. He leapt to his feet.

Spies are not the only professionals with patience. Assassins have it as well. The man in the black biking outfit was a professional, and steely patience was all part of the job. He enjoyed the hunt, but the kill, the gentle pull of the trigger, the power of launching hot lead into someone's heart, that was the ultimate thrill. He made good money, but nothing compared to the thrill.

The assassin had followed his target, getting to know his habits, his moves. He soon found another man was doing the same. That man had secret service written all over him. A cop was hindered by warrants and pretty-please may-I's. A man like that, one in the cloak-and-dagger business, made for the best prey. A challenge. He would like to take him out as well. But he was a professional, and his job was only one target.

But what if this agent got in the way?

The man in black kept Hayes in his sight, waiting for a clear shot. When Hayes stood, he had his opportunity. His client told the assassin Hayes carried mini-Molotovs in his leather jacket. Hayes was wearing his leather jacket. The man smiled.

This will be something different.

Hayes stood and Paul rose to block his exit. Hayes halted and looked down at a small hole in his jacket. Someone had just shot Hayes. The next bullet found its target; the mini-Molotov was fuel for a hot lead slug. It burst into flames, consuming Hayes from the waist up. Another final slug struck Hayes in the chest, knocking him to the pavement.

Paul ripped the tablecloth from the table and rolled Hayes in it. The tablecloth caught fire and Paul pulled one from another table and rolled the burning man in it. A server came out with a fire extinguisher. Paul snatched it and sprayed its foam over Hayes.

Hayes was bleeding out. Moans emanated from the foamy mess. Paul took out a sharp pocketknife and cut the tablecloth from head to toe like one would open a dish baked in parchment paper. He carefully pulled the cloth away from Hayes' body, easily exposing his legs, but the young man's flesh had already stuck to the cloth above his waist.

With the amount of blood pouring from Hayes' wounds, Paul knew he had little time.

"Aiden, for God's sake, tell me, what's the next job, the one far bigger than the Eye?"

Hayes managed a weak smile. He was near death, but still playing games, offering a clue with his last words.

"We're going to destroy the planets."

Chapter 29

London

"One fire starter is dead, but another is on the loose," Paul told Nick in a phone call. He briefed Nick on what happened in Paris.

"Are you headed back to London?" asked Nick.

"Already there. I'm calling you from my place."

"I'm leaving Rome. I'll meet you there."

Nick arrived at Paul's flat the next morning. Nick scanned the place with an appraising eye. "Your flat looks like modern retro. I thought it would be more Sherlock Holmes. You know, tapestries, worn embroidered chairs, and you in an old robe and fez hat."

Paul laughed. "We could use a Sherlock Holmes right now. This case has me stumped. Too many moving parts."

"Let's sit and talk. You wouldn't have any coffee, would you?"

Paul grinned. "I keep some on hand for my Yank friends." He pointed toward a couple of chairs separated by a side table. "Have a seat. I'll get it."

After Paul brought a coffee for Nick and a tea for himself, Nick continued. "You told me only enough about what happened in Paris to pique my interest. You said one fire starter was on the loose. Didn't the police capture Karl Lenoir?"

"No."

"Why?"

Paul grimaced. "He escaped. Vanished in broad daylight."

"And what did you say Hayes told you, just before he died?"

"We will destroy the planets."

Nick laughed. "A rather lofty goal, don't you think?"

"I rather think so," said Paul before changing the subject. "By the way, I have a neighbor you may know."

"Who might that be?"

"Ray Woodward."

"Ray?" Nick exclaimed. "You've got to be kidding."

"So, I take that to mean you do know him."

"Sure. The kid grew up in my neighborhood. He got into a scrape with the law when he was a teen. That's when I first met him. I ran into him again in a coffee shop before he was headed off to college. I asked him to keep in touch and I get an email from him from time to time. He sent me a note some time ago and told me he had moved to London. But to a place next door to you? What are the odds? I guess he's doing well."

Paul snickered. "I would say so. I can barely afford a flat in this area. He owns a house."

"So, what else do you know about Ray, other than where he grew up?"

"There was one thing that I couldn't find out," Paul continued. "I know, from old records, that the NYPD called you in for something to do with Ray, but I couldn't find what it was."

"That makes sense," responded Nick. "He was a juvenile. Protected records. Ray was setting fires in the neighborhood. I saw him set one, and the police asked me to identify him."

Paul looked surprised. "What is it?" Nick asked.

"I think Ray still likes fire," said Paul.

Paul related his story. "I met him when I was waiting for delivery of the right key to my flat. He invited me in out of the rain. His place is very nice. Very expensive."

"I believe he works for an investment firm," Nick added. "Guess that's working out well for him, but why do you say he still likes fire?"

"He has a butler, but he insisted on lighting the fire in the fireplace himself. I saw the enjoyment he got from it."

"Well, enjoyment is understandable," noted Nick.

"It wasn't enjoyment as much as it was a sense of release; it worked like a sedative."

"Paul," Nick said. "That makes sense. I learned some things about pyromaniacs when the police booked Ray. They build up a tension that only setting a fire releases. Ray underwent counseling. Perhaps his lighting of the evening fire is a controlled, socially acceptable means of release."

"Psychiatric counseling? Who was the doctor?" Paul asked.

"I can't remember. Not sure I ever knew." Nick waited a moment, but then asked, "What?"

"I think I need to learn more about Mr. Woodward."

"You do that," said Nick. "In the meantime, why don't I contact Ray? It's time we meet again."

To: Raymond Woodward

From: Nicholas Foxe

Subject: I'm in London

Ray,

As luck would have it, I'm in London. Want to get together?

Nick

From: Raymond Woodward

To: Nicholas Foxe

Re: I'm in London

Nick,

Sure thing. How about tomorrow afternoon? Not sure where you're staying, but how about something central to the city around where I work. I favor the Peacock Lounge on the corner of Haydon and Minories. It's on top of the Montcalm Royal hotel. Say around five pm?

Ray

From: Nicholas Foxe

To: Raymond Woodward

Re: I'm in London

Sure. See you then.

Nick

Chapter 30

London

The Peacock Lounge was located on top of the Montcalm Royal London House hotel across from Finsbury Square. This was London's business district, surrounded by new office towers of fanciful geometrics. When the City of London built the glass egg on the Thames for their municipal offices, it sparked a competition for more imaginatively shaped buildings. Busy during the day, the streets among these modern structures were empty after hours, except for the pubs that marked every corner seemingly plucked from a hundred years ago. Young professionals flowed onto the streets, drinks in hand.

Nick walked up the chrome and glass steps from the penthouse level of the hotel to the rooftop lounge. After passing a stuffed peacock at the top of the stairs, he discovered this place to be a meet-and-greet for young professionals. The rooftop bar, just beyond a small dining area, overlooked the square. It bustled with young London singles dressed to mingle. The men wore an array of white open shirts and black pants; women, in tight skirts and heels, definitely having changed from their office outfits.

As Nick admired the scene, Ray walked up with his hand out. "Nick, it's been a long time!"

Nick shook Ray's hand. "I can see why you like this place."

Ray followed Nick's gaze to the crowd. "It's a fine place to meet a lovely lady." He turned to Nick with a smile. "For a short-term relationship."

Ray pointed to a table in the corner, away from the crowd. "I have a table over there. Let's sit and catch up."

Few tables had diners at this early hour and the service was prompt. Following Ray's lead, Nick ordered a twenty-year-old scotch. Ray eagerly started the conversation. "You were all over the news some time ago. What was that all about? A tablet in a cave?"

"Yeah. It was quite the mystery. It was ten-thousand years old, but it looked like titanium. Had a code on it we finally solved."

"What did it say?" asked Ray.

"It said a lot about the people who left it, but it also proved to be a treasure map of sorts. It eventually led us to a device left by these ancients."

"The Omni Scientia?"

Nick smiled at his young friend. "So, you've been keeping up with things. The press got tired of the story and the Omni wasn't the big news the initial discovery was."

"Yet, it was the story I noted. If it had Nick Foxe in it, I paid attention."

Nick knew what the press reported. He didn't want to get into murders in Venice associated with him and knew that would be next on Ray's list. So, he changed the subject.

"I want to know about you. How's the world of high finance?"

"It's been good to me. I bought a house in Kensington. I'm comfortable." Ray paused. "So, you want to know how I'm dealing with my little problem, don't you?"

"I wasn't going to bring it up…"

Ray raised his palm to stop Nick. "No, of course. But I want to talk about it."

"OK," responded Nick.

Ray continued. "I take drugs. Small doses. Probably will for the rest of my life. I find outlets. I have a butler…"

"A butler?"

Ray smiled. "Yes. I told you I'm living comfortably. Anyhow, I have my butler place kindling and logs in the fireplace waiting for me when I come home. He does everything but light the fire. I do that. You might have a cocktail after a hard day. I light a fire."

Nick knew the odds were long that Ray would have anything to do with the modern fire starters, but after talking with Paul, he had to probe.

"I've been doing a little research into people who start fires," Nick said as the drinks arrived at the table.

"Oh?" Ray said as he clicked Nick's glass in a small toast.

"Yes. Have you heard of the Domus Aurea in Rome?"

"The Golden Palace? Nero, right?" Ray asked and then realized something which amused him. "They recently started excavating the place. Why doesn't it surprise me you got involved? It must be an archeological treasure chest."

"Well, I was working on the histories of Pliny and that led me there."

As he told his tale, Nick searched Ray's face for a reaction.

How much of this story does he already know?

"I don't believe Nero started the great fire of Rome. There was a man who worked for him who did it at Nero's direction. His name was Filius Egnatius. I was in a room in the Golden Palace where Egnatius met with his disciples."

So far, Ray showed nothing but rapt attention. He seemed to be hearing all this for the first time.

Nick continued. "We found something. An artifact from Egnatius' meeting room."

"What?" asked Ray.

"It was the head of a branding iron. We believe Egnatius required his disciples to bear that mark."

Nick noticed that Ray, previously rapt in his telling of the story, now showed some discomfort at the mention of a mark. Ray asked his next question as one who didn't want to hear a particular answer. "What was the mark?"

"The mark was a triangle, the symbol for fire, with an I and an A at the bottom."

"What could those letters stand for?" asked Ray.

"*Incendium Artis*. It's the name of the guild."

Ray said nothing.

"You know of the London Eye bombing?"

"Of, course," Ray responded. "A horrible event. I hope they get the terrorist who..."

Nick cut him off. "The man who did it wore the guild symbol tattoo."

Ray looked like Nick had just slapped him across the face.

Ray tried to recover. "Did they catch the man who did it?"

"He's dead," Nick said flatly.

This time, Nick saw only a confused look from Ray.

He didn't know.

Now it was Nick who was puzzled. If Ray had anything to do with the fire starters, he wasn't fully vested in its operation.

"Dead?" asked Ray. "How?"

"Agents were closing in on him, but someone took him out first. Guess they didn't want him talking."

"Nick, I haven't seen any news about this. How did you know?"

It was Nick's turn to hedge. "Friend of a friend," he responded.

Nick could see Ray wasn't buying it. He quickly changed the subject. "Well, enough of that. All these lovely ladies out there made me think. How's your love life? Anyone special?"

If Nick intended to distract Ray from further questions, he succeeded. Nick could see a dark cloud form over Ray.

"Well," responded Ray. "There was someone. Another American that I worked with. Her name was Jean."

"Was?" Nick asked.

Ray paused. "I haven't told anyone this, but a woman who meant a lot

168

to me ... I was responsible for her death."

Without waiting for any response from Nick, Ray forged on. "We were coming home from a bar. We took a turn down a side street. It was a nice section of town, one with old houses being renovated. All empty. No one was on the street, except this one guy. He was running from one of the houses. A moment later the house burst into flames."

Nick could see Ray becoming distraught in the retelling of these events. Ray took a long draw of his scotch and continued. "Nick, I went to the flames. I thought they were beautiful. So strong, so powerful. I stretched out my arms to absorb their warmth. It freaked Jean out. As well it should have. Any normal person would have been. She tried to get me to leave the place. She feared for me.

"Then, there was an explosion from the upper levels. A brick from the house hit Jean squarely on the temple. She was unconscious when they took her to the hospital. She came to, and I thought everything was going to be okay. But ... she died later that night from a blood clot."

Nick said, "I am so sorry."

Ray downed the rest of his scotch. He looked at his watch and said, "Nick, there's somewhere I've got to be. How about walking with me down to the street?"

Nick walked with Ray down the steps and to the lifts. On the way down, Ray turned to Nick. "You know, we've only been in touch off and on, but I always thought of you as the big brother I never had."

Nick laughed. "Thanks for not saying I was like the father you never had. I feel old enough already."

They reached the street, and a cab pulled up. Ray opened the door and turned to Nick. "Can I drop you off somewhere?"

"No," replied Nick. "I think I'll walk around for a while."

Ray shook Nick's hand, "Let's stay in touch," Ray said.

"Sure thing."

With that, Ray's cab drove away.

Nick walked the streets. He thought about Ray and hoped for the best but feared the worst concerning Ray's possible involvement with criminals. Nick was eager to compare notes with Paul.

Chapter 31

The Cotswolds

Ray enjoyed his drive to the Cotswolds. It was the England he had always imagined. Villages that kept their thatched-roof charm, some that didn't post street names, let alone house numbers. Roland Fiedler's home was one such place. The GPS was useless. Ray followed specific turn-by-turn directions to get there.

Ray knew Roland Fiedler only as Roland up until the call he received two days ago. As managing partner of The Fire Company, Roland had always been just a voice on the phone. Ray figured he was old by his slow, crackling voice, like that of a wizened grandfather. Despite his presumed age, Roland's take on the business was always spot on. He understood the risks and had cultivated connections that reaped rewards. The upcoming California job was an exception; there was no outside client. Ray was bringing his finance expertise to bear in this venture. Perhaps that was the reason for the summons.

After miles of narrow, hard-surfaced roads with nothing but the flat fields at the base of the Cotswolds Hills around him, he arrived in a village with only five houses. At its center was an old church, long since abandoned by a congregation. The house was as Roland described it, an old home behind an older wall with a patchwork of extensions that had been attached over the years.

Ray parked in the driveway, walked to the front door, and rang the bell. The chimes rang an unidentifiable tune. Roland answered the door. Before him, Ray saw the man he had imagined behind the voice, with two exceptions. Whereas Ray imagined a rotund Englishman, Roland was slim.

He was also taller, perhaps a little less than six feet tall. But when Roland smiled, the wrinkled face mottled with liver spots was exactly what he expected.

"Raymond?" asked the man. "Come in, come in."

Ray followed Roland as he shuffled into a room filled with curios. A grandfather clock, worn from a century of use, ticked in one corner. A taxidermy black bear, on his haunches with his teeth exposed in a menacing growl and his paws poised for attack, occupied another corner. Next to the bear stood a bookcase filled with aged leather-bound editions, and beside that a stuffed chair and footstool for a reader to enjoy the books.

"Coffee?" asked Roland.

"That would be fine. I hope I'm not putting you out. You probably prefer tea."

Roland turned to Ray and provided a comic scowl. "Don't let the English accent fool you. I may have been born here, but my family was German. We always had coffee. In fact, I planned to make a *cafe latté*. Would you like one?"

"Sure."

Roland walked over to an espresso machine sitting on a wet bar. He expertly steamed small pitchers of cream and poured them into two large mugs, followed by espresso from cups under the machine.

"German, you say?" Ray asked.

Roland smiled as he worked the machine. "Well, Grandmother was Italian. I suppose that is the source for my appreciation of a good espresso."

Roland handed Ray one cup and held the other for himself. He watched Ray as he sipped, awaiting his approval.

"Very good," said Ray.

"Let's sit in the conservatory," Roland said as he turned to walk through a kitchen bare of counter accessories and much too neat for regular use. The conservatory was on the far side of the kitchen. Two chairs with a

172

table between them faced a picture window looking out upon a lush flower garden. The morning sun lit the blooms and warmed the room.

"Have a seat," said Roland, waving toward the chair on the right of the table. Roland took the other chair and collapsed with a sigh.

"You like my garden?" he asked.

"It's beautiful. Who cares for it?"

"That would be me. I live here alone, and I didn't hire a gardener. I rather enjoy it. Do you know what my secret is to having such healthy plants?"

Ray shook his head.

"Ash," Roland shared conspiratorially.

"Ash? What type? I mean, what wood does it come from?"

Roland smiled. "Not from wood. I have a friend who runs a crematorium. Many poor souls have no one to claim the ashes."

Ray was taken aback. "You use human ashes?"

Roland remained nonchalant. "My dear boy, ashes to ashes, dust to dust, and all that. We all return to the soil. The circle of life, you know."

Roland came to the matter at hand. "You may wonder why I asked you here."

"Well, yes. But I welcomed it. I wanted to know the man behind the voice."

"And now you have," said Roland. "Do you know anything about me?"

"Until today, I didn't even know your last name."

"That's fair. Let me tell you about my family."

Roland related a saga starting with his grandfather, Richard Fiedler, who invented the flame thrower for the German army. Ray detected a sense of pride in Roland as he related this dubious achievement. He could think only of the black and white World War II movies showing US Army soldiers spraying caves on some Pacific island and Japanese men racing out on fire.

173

Ray had an indelible attraction to fire, but those scenes troubled him.

Roland seemed to relish the story. He told Ray he had a working flame thrower in the shed, and he would be glad to show it to him.

Roland continued his story. His family suffered in Germany after the Great War. The unbridled inflation and worldwide depression crushed his grandfather's business, of which his father was a part. The family immigrated to England, where his father was offered a job as an engineer for a coal mining company in Newcastle. Roland was born during that time as an English citizen.

When Germany declared war on England, Roland's father was called by the war department to a new assignment. His engineering genius was invaluable, and his command of the German language was particularly useful. As the war progressed, Roland's father proved his worth and rose in the ranks of civilian war planners. He helped to plan the firebombing of Dresden.

With this detail, Roland paused and said with a wink, "I guess fire is in our blood."

Ray protested. "But Dresden was horrible. 25,000 people died."

Roland scoffed. "You Yanks sent over three-hundred bombers to Tokyo and dropped more napalm than you ever did in Vietnam. Japanese deaths were four times the number in Dresden."

Roland continued, his agitation rising. "Canals boiled, metal melted, human beings burst spontaneously into flames. Then you invented the atom bomb. Fewer people died, but those hit were vaporized and those who survived were shunned as untouchables. All things considered, the firebombing seemed humane."

"None of it," said Ray, "is something to be proud of."

Roland replied calmly as a teacher of a student who didn't understand. "I agree about the atom bomb. It's a beastly creature. It is a genie I wish we could put back into a bottle. But fire, it's purifying, don't you see? I don't mean in the way the witch hunters thought that it would release demons. I mean in rising again, the phoenix effect. Look at Tokyo today, a modern powerhouse. A beautiful city. And Dresden has reclaimed its glory as well."

Roland then moved the discussion to the present. "And for us, when we performed the church job, it brought people together to consider what was important. We were a modern-day Victor Hugo."

"I don't understand."

Roland, again the teacher, said, "There was a time that the people of Paris thought Notre Dame should be torn down. It was decrepit. Then Victor Hugo wrote *The Hunchback of Notre Dame* which romanticized the icon. The book was wildly popular, and the cathedral was saved."

Ray interjected. "I thought we were doing it to appease a well-paying client who was brutalized as a child in that place."

Roland shrugged. "And Victor Hugo made money on his book. What's your point?"

Ray struggled with what was bothering him. Perhaps he had not dealt with it yet himself. But he unloaded his burden on the old man. "I recently lost someone in a fire. Someone very close to me."

Roland put his hand on Ray's arm and sympathetically said, "You mean your girlfriend?"

"You knew?"

"We know about our people. But I understand that she died of a concussion."

"She wouldn't have if I wasn't so enamored with fire. She was trying to get me to step away."

Roland patted Ray's arm. "My boy, we are not trying to harm anyone. No one died in the church fire. Your California operation should not touch a single soul. We are working on another contract. Again, just property damage."

Ray smiled a weak smile. "I'm sorry. Guess I'm a little more sensitive about it than I thought."

"No problem. Time heals all things," Roland said, then changed the subject. "May I ask you something?"

"Sure."

"Why do you not yet have the tattoo?"

"How do you know I don't?"

The old man smiled and replied simply, "I'd know."

Although Roland had it covered with a shirt and a warm twill sweater, Ray knew he meant the *Incendium Artis* tattoo.

"I don't like tattoos."

"How unlike others of your generation," said Roland. "My grandfather had the tattoo. As a kid, I didn't know what it was. But my father told me, and I was hell-bent on getting into the organization.

"You know, Ray, it is ancient. Goes all the way back to Nero's time. Our founder orchestrated the great fire of Rome. He also engineered Nero's suicide. So, the order has always had political clout as well, albeit behind the scenes.

"You, Ray, represent a new direction for the order. One in which modern finance, not external patrons, controls our destiny. That's why I wanted to meet you face-to-face. I wanted to take stock of the man who may represent our future."

Ray shrugged off the faint praise. "On another matter," he said, "How about our renegade who did the London Eye?"

Roland smiled like a Cheshire cat. "We have taken care of it. As I told you earlier, focus on California."

"I will," Ray said as he rose from his seat. "I guess I'd better be going."

Roland stood. "I'll see you out."

They retraced their steps and Ray paused by the door to eye the bear one more time.

Roland noticed. "It's a reminder to me that danger lurks always."

Ray reacted unsure how to take that remark, but he said only, "Thank you for the *lattè*."

"You are welcome." Then a gleam came into Roland's eye. "I told you about the flamethrower I have. I want to show it to you."

Ray wasn't so sure he wanted to see it. Starting a fire was one thing. Tossing flames broadly seemed to be dangerous to the operator.

Roland led him to a small tool shed at the end of the driveway. The throw latch was secured with a simple twist combination lock suitable for a gym locker. There was barely room for one person inside, so Roland told Ray, "Wait here. I'll get it."

What Roland brought out surprised Ray. Ray expected some World War vintage relic, but instead, Roland brought out a fresh and shiny chrome canister resembling a diver's air tank mounted on a backpack.

"This is the modern version of Grandfather's creation. A company in Ohio makes them. You may have trouble getting a firearm, but no trouble at all in getting one of these beauties. Let me help you slip it on."

Not waiting for Ray to protest, Roland held the backpack up behind Ray and he slipped it on.

"Now let me get the rest of it," Roland said as he re-entered the shed and came out with a thick hose with a long silver wand attached. "Hold the wand and I'll connect the hose."

Ray held the wand in both hands, and it felt good to him, for reasons he could not say. Roland screwed the hose into the rear of the unit at the bottom of the backpack.

"There," he said. "Let's give it a go. Follow me."

Ray followed Roland through a thicket of trees and into an open field. The field had been freshly plowed. Amid the turned soil were two large bales of hay.

"All right. Let me turn this on," said Roland as he turned some unseen valve on the backpack. "OK. Ready. Light it up."

Ray, uncertain, asked, "Uh, how?"

"Just aim at one bale and pull the trigger right here," Roland said as he pointed to the trigger and then stepped behind Ray.

Ray pulled the trigger and a fifty-foot stream of fire propelled out of the nozzle to the left of the hay bales. He stopped. He fired again. Ray held the trigger and moved the flaming stream to the first hay bale. A feeling of power came over him. His desire to set fires was now weaponized. He pulled the trigger once more and held it. Moving the flame to the other bale and then back to the first, the burning accelerated until scarcely anything was left.

The remains of the bales slowly burned. Ray breathed as though he had completed a sprint around the village. Roland smiled. "You liked it?" he asked.

"Yes," was Ray's simple reply.

Roland put the flamethrower away and Ray thanked him for the thrill, said his goodbyes, got into his car and left for London.

As Ray drove down the M40 back to the city, he reflected on his morning.

Did Roland really expect me to be the leader of the next generation of The Fire Company, the one who would steer them in a modern direction?

Ray then considered the California project. It promised to be the organization's most lucrative operation yet. It would be his moment to shine.

Chapter 32

Wyoming

"So, what do you know about horses?" asked Tanner, who knew next to nothing.

"Mom took us to rodeos," replied Lizzy.

"I thought she took you to Grateful Dead concerts."

Lizzy smiled playfully. "She wanted me to be well-rounded."

In Jackson, picking up supplies, Lizzy pointed out a poster advertising a horse auction coming up in a couple of days. Tanner saw how much it captured Lizzy's attention. He could hear the wheels in her head spinning. Lizzy said she wanted to go.

"Well, this is an auction, not a rodeo," said Tanner. "I doubt there'll be roping acts."

Lizzy shrugged. "I know that. It's the horses themselves I like. So much animal power under your control." She winked at Tanner. "Reminds me of you."

"Not sure if I like that comparison."

Lizzy hugged Tanner and leaned back, arms still around him. "Come on, my stallion, it'll be fun."

Tanner looked more closely at the poster. "Hey, this is in Cody. That's four hours away."

"Is Yellowstone between here and there?"

"About halfway."

Lizzy lit up. "Perfect. We can spend the night there. You know I love Yellowstone. Then, we'll head out the next day."

Tanner provided the best horse whinny he could muster and said,

"OK."

They spent the night in a cabin on Yellowstone Lake. Maybe it was the cabin, maybe the evening mist settling over the quiet lake, but Tanner considered their lovemaking that night was special. They were wrapped in each other's arms as the sun rose over the lake and into Tanner's eyes.

"Hey," he whispered. "We got to go."

"No…" she said between snuggles.

"Lizzy. Horse auction."

Lizzy snapped to attention and sat up. "OK."

After leaving Yellowstone and traveling through bucolic countryside, they arrived in the small town of Cody, Wyoming.

Tanner had been to Cody, but Lizzy hadn't. As they entered the city limits, Lizzy saw convenience stores and small businesses like in any other small town. She was disappointed. "Where's the saloon, the sheriff's office?"

"Uh, Lizzy," said Tanner. "You're thinking of the old town they keep for the tourists. Cody's as modern as any other. Don't worry. I'm taking you somewhere you can get a taste of the old west."

"Where's that?"

"Buffalo Bill's Irma Hotel. We're getting breakfast there."

"Yahoo!" whooped Lizzy.

When they arrived at the hotel, a police officer was directing traffic to a parking area.

"Must be a mob here," said Tanner, not too pleased at the prospect.

After they parked, Tanner and Lizzy walked to the Irma Hotel, which wasn't too hard to find since everyone was walking in that direction. After a few blocks, they arrived at the simple two-story brick building with its name high above it on a bright red sign.

They barely noticed the hotel, as directly in front of it, a corral had been erected over the asphalt street, and a mob of men and women in cowboy hats milled around it.

Tanner pushed through the crowd with Lizzy following until they reached the front of the hotel which had a line out the door. Tanner approached a woman in a cowboy hat and asked, "Is this the line for the dining room?"

"Yep," she said.

Tanner and Lizzy grudgingly joined in behind her.

The woman's age was difficult to define. She was tan with a face full of creases, earned by years of working outdoors. Ramrod straight, you could envision this woman tall in the saddle, proud and no-nonsense. She wore jeans that were accustomed to riding, the blue faded around the knees and cuffs. A red bandana tied around her neck looked as if it had been through a dust storm or two.

She made banter easy. "You folks come for the auction?" Tanner sensed she knew they were tinhorns.

"Yes," he answered.

"I want to see the horses," Lizzy said with the excitement of a child. All that was missing was saying 'horsies' rather than horses.

The woman was either genuinely friendly or charmed by Lizzy's enthusiasm. "That's good. You'll see plenty. Hi, I'm Joanie," she said, sticking her hand out and giving each of her new friends a firm handshake.

"Tanner."

"I'm Lizzy."

"Tanner. Lizzy. Good to meet you."

"How long do you think we're going to wait?"

"Well, that depends. Would you like to join me at a table? The wait will be shorter."

Tanner wasn't sure why it would be shorter. Perhaps it was in her taking a full table versus a table for one. The decision was made by Lizzy, who said, "Sure."

Tanner guessed wrong. A young woman with a clipboard walked along the line of people and when she reached them, she said, "Miss Fitzwell, your table is ready."

"Come along," Joanie said. "You're with me."

The hostess led them through a large open dining room with red plastic tablecloths, and vintage woodwork on the columns and along the wall. Tin tiles adorned the ceiling and sketches of Buffalo Bill and his associates lined the walls. She showed them to a booth in the corner under a ten-point stag trophy.

"Your server will be with you shortly," said the hostess.

Tanner looked around at all the full tables. "They seem to like you here."

Joanie laughed. "When you've been coming here as much as I have, people get to know you. So, do you folks live around here?"

"I have a place near Jackson," replied Tanner.

"God's country, for sure," said Joanie.

"Well," confessed Tanner. "My uncle left it to me. I can't really say I live there, although it is my mailing address. I came here to see about selling it."

Joanie looked shocked. "Now, why on earth would you do that? Your uncle left you a special gift."

Lizzy piped up. "See, I told you not to sell."

Tanner put his hands up to push the arguments away.

"OK, OK. I'm *thinking* about selling."

Joanie looked to Lizzy. "And you, sweetie, how do you busy yourself?"

"I keep this guy in line."

Joanie considered Tanner's bulk and replied to Lizzy, "You sure you don't break horses for a living?"

The server came and took orders. Steak and eggs for Tanner. Two eggs over easy for Lizzy. Joanie cautioned Lizzy, "Better get some bacon and toast with that." Joanie ordered the steak and eggs, too, which made Tanner wonder how the woman stayed so slim.

"Are you buying today" asked Tanner, "or selling?"

"Well, sometimes I'm a consignor," said Joanie, stopping to answer their questioning looks by adding, "Seller. But this time, I'm just looking. A friend told me he was bringing a chromed-out sorrel mare to the auction. She's about fifteen hands high and I figure her for a good riding horse."

The order came quickly. Tanner dug into the steak, but Joanie first slathered hers with ketchup. Lizzy looked taken aback by the pile of smoked and greasy bacon on her plate.

Joanie gave her a wink. "See, aren't you glad you got some meat on your plate?"

Between bites, they each shared their life stories. Joanie was a person who, in her style of friendly, direct questioning, got to know everything about someone she shared a meal with. Tanner related his career as an Army Ranger and his meeting Lizzy in New Mexico. Lizzy shared her trailer park upbringing by a single mom. Both Tanner and Lizzy skipped the parts they played in discovering a ten-thousand-year-old tablet. They skipped the part about Lizzy setting herself free from a castle in the Adriatic and rescuing Tanner. Little details like that. They didn't mention Nicholas Foxe either. That name was newsworthy.

When they finished, Joanie looked at her wristwatch. "Well, it looks like it's time for the auction. Let's mosey on out."

Lizzy looked at Tanner with a chuckle.

"Yes, Lizzy. We say 'mosey' in these parts."

The crowd was thick around the corral. There were benches up close to the action, and Joanie found them seats. The corral had an auctioneer and announcer behind a rough-hewn table with a windscreen in front of them. Their voices boomed out of loudspeakers.

"Welcome to the Cody Country Horse Sale!" said the announcer as the crowd whooped and cheered in return.

They wasted no time. A handler led the first horse into the corral. The announcer read out the details. He described the five-year-old gypsy draft, named Little Joe, as a gentle horse anybody could ride. The gelding was brown with a shaggy white mane.

"Looks like a horse for kids to ride," Lizzy said.

The auctioneer started into his rapid-fire selling approach with a "I hear two-thousand, who will give me two-thousand five." Little Joe sold for $3,500.

"That's affordable," offered Lizzy.

Joanie smiled. "The prices are all over the place," she said. "Depends mainly on age and who their mommy and daddy were. They're mixing things up. Next up is a star."

The next horse was a mixed gray and beige stallion with a shaggy mane named Iron Man.

"Not a cute horse, is it?" asked Lizzy.

Joanie said simply, "Just watch."

Lizzy's open mouth grew wider and wider as the bidding started at ten-thousand dollars and topped off at thirty-two thousand.

"Wow!" she exclaimed. "Who was his mommy and daddy?"

Joanie laughed. "Good breeds. Iron Man is a stud horse. Considering they will get two-thousand a shot for stud service, it's not a poor investment."

Lizzy looked up at Tanner with a suggestive expression.

"What?" he said.

"Nothing."

Joanie leaned into Lizzy and whispered, "And he doesn't even have to be there. They ship the sperm in an ice pack."

"What fun is that?" Lizzy exclaimed.

The auction continued with a mixture of horses fetching a variety of prices. The proceedings were winding down when they brought the horse Joanie had come for into the corral.

"Here we have Fancy Pants," the announcer declared. "Fancy Pants is a three-year-old chromed-out sorrel mare complete with a blaze face and four white socks. She stands a perfect fifteen hands and weighs in at 1,150 pounds. Fancy Pants has been used in every aspect of ranch work and performs like a pro, despite her young age. Fancy Pants has sorted cows, both in competition and on the ranch, has pulled calves to the branding fire, and moved cows in a feedlot. She has a big stop, nice turnaround, and effortlessly switches leads. She is very athletic and has a huge motor when asked for it; she can go all day, no problem!"

Tanner had no idea what half of the announcer's terms meant, but he could see that for Lizzy, Fancy Pants was love at first sight. He noticed that Joanie saw it, too. He had no idea what the horse was worth, but he thought Joanie may have paid too much.

The auction over, Joanie led Lizzy and Tanner to check out her new purchase. Along the way, they bumped into another horse lover Joanie knew.

"Denise!" said Joanie. "Good to see you."

Denise Anderson was a well-scrubbed blonde who seemed to reside at the well-bred end of horse country. She looked as if she would ride steeplechase, not herd cattle. Joanie was all western saddle, and Denise was definitely English saddle.

"Did you buy anything today?" Joanie asked.

"Not today, but I like to look."

"Denise, this is Lizzy and Tanner. This here is Denise Anderson. She has a fancy ranch down in Santa Fe."

Denise shook hands with both Lizzy and Tanner and told them, "Don't let Joanie sell you a line of hooey. I've seen her place. It's a fine ranch."

Denise looked at Joanie. "You used to have a ranch here, didn't you?"

"That's right," replied Joanie. "I don't anymore. I know it's crazy to come all this way for a horse."

"They tell me you can buy them on the internet now," added Denise.

Joanie laughed. "Well, that wouldn't be me. I like to get up here and see old friends. Years ago, when my daughter asked me to come to her place in California, my husband and I sold everything and moved down there."

Joanie paused. "Then she died."

Denise put her hand on Joanie's arm. "I'm sorry. I didn't mean to open old wounds."

Joanie offered a weak smile. "That's OK."

"Well, I've got to go," said Denise. "Good to meet you, Lizzy, Tanner." Then to Joanie, "If you ever need anything…"

"I know," replied Joanie.

As Denise walked away, Lizzy turned to Tanner and muttered, "I've heard her name before. I'm sure she's friends with Nick."

They walked over to the man holding the reins for Fancy Pants. The cowboy told Joanie, "Well, here she is. The boss will be pleased with the price she fetched."

Joanie rolled her eyes and said, "I'm sure he will be."

But Tanner watched Lizzy; she was oblivious to the conversation. She was already stroking Fancy Pants and whispering into her ear. Tanner was surprised to see how comfortable Lizzy was around the horse.

"I'm loading up Fancy Pants tomorrow to take her back first thing in the morning," said Joanie.

"Where's your ranch?"

"California, outside Sacramento."

Lizzy was crestfallen. "I guess I assumed your ranch was somewhere nearby. I'd like to get to know Fancy Pants better, maybe ride her."

Tanner was incredulous. "Have you ever ridden a horse before?"

"No, but how hard could it be?"

"You want to go with me? I mean, it's a long trip. It will take three days. But if you two have the time, you're both welcome. I've got a crew cab, so there's plenty of space."

Lizzy practically jumped up and down on the spot. She turned to Tanner. "Let's go!"

"I can't. I got people lined up to appraise the place in Jackson, real estate agent, lawyer…"

Lizzy's face fell. "Tell you what," he said. "Why don't you go, and I'll catch up with you later?"

"Sure?" asked Lizzy.

"Sure. Go on. Have a good time. I expect to see you riding when I get there."

"Deal," said Lizzy, hugging Tanner.

Chapter 33

California

"You're a natural," Joanie told Lizzy as she trotted Fancy Pants around the paddock. Lizzy beamed with pride.

Their trip from Wyoming, towing Fancy Pants in a horse trailer, was a long one. Joanie appeared grateful for the company. In the three days on the road, they had plenty of time to get to know each other. Lizzy shared with Joanie that she never knew her father. Mom followed The Grateful Dead and Dad was a roadie. The Hispanic name came from Dad, the red hair from Mom.

Lizzy told Joanie that her mom was smart. "Home schooled," Lizzy said, "even if 'home' moved around a lot." Her mother purchased a set of second-hand encyclopedias, easy to come by in the days of Wikipedia. Mom insisted Lizzy study each new place they visited and write a report. When they headed out on the road, Mom had Lizzy look at the gas consumption mpg reported by the truck and do the math on how far they could go before filling up.

Thankfully, they stayed in one place through most of Lizzy's high school years. She was constantly underrated by the other girls, until she put one girl in her place. The girl was on the debate team, smug and dismissive until Lizzy successfully debated her right in the hall on a history topic. One of Lizzy's teachers took notice and encouraged Lizzy to go to college, but Lizzy never thought college could teach her what she could learn on her own.

Lizzy knew all about Italy and the history of the Roman empire but had never set foot in the country until Nick's team traveled there. Once she

188

connected with Tanner, they traveled all over Europe.

Lizzy learned Joanie's story. She and her husband realized their dream when they moved to the ranch in California and fixed it up. They boarded horses and sold rides to anyone who wanted one. Her husband died, much too young, followed by her daughter two years later, and for the last ten years, Joanie had been running the place on her own with the help of a few hands she employed.

They broke up the trip by stopping in two places. The campsites were located in deep woods with spectacular views. Joanie would bring out a propane camp stove and Lizzy would help cook the soup, the beans, and hot dogs. She loved it.

When Lizzy looked at the moon, she said she would like to go there one day, just to see the earth from that vantage point. The photos astronauts took from outer space made the earth appear like a blue and white pearl to Lizzy. She told Joanie she read that if you took the earth and shrunk it to the size of a cue ball, the cue ball would be rougher. "Imagine, the highest mountains and the deepest oceans, all of them so challenging to us, in the bigger scheme, are so small."

Looking at the night sky, she wondered out loud, "Where are those people from ten-thousand years ago now?"

"What people?"

Lizzy wasn't sure how much she should reveal about Nick's discoveries, and she made up some feeble story to mask her question.

Now, Lizzy was riding Fancy Pants. She rode the horse around in circles in the paddock until Joanie said it was time to take to a trail. Joanie took her favorite saddle-bred mare from her stall, put a western saddle on, mounted her, and led Lizzy and Fancy Pants out of the paddock.

The trail began in low-lying sage but quickly entered a forest of oaks and ponderosa pines. Lizzy followed Joanie's lead, who took a steady pace she said she used for day-riders with little experience. But when they reached an open meadow, Joanie gave her mare a kick, and she started a trot. Lizzy was right behind.

In a minute, Lizzy pulled up alongside Joanie. "This, I like," Lizzy said.

Joanie pulled on the reins and slowed her horse. Lizzy mimicked Joanie's rein-work and slowed Fancy Pants. They rode side-by-side.

"You know, I think you've graduated," announced Joanie.

"What do you mean?"

"This afternoon, we have some school kids coming to ride. Want to help out?"

"Sure. I like kids."

"OK, then."

That afternoon, a school bus rolled in with a dozen middle-school girls. Lizzy sized them up as private school kids. They were dressed too well, all in fresh jeans and boots.

"Have these girls ridden before?" Lizzy asked Joanie.

"Some have. Most haven't."

"Well, their moms have decked them out pretty well."

Lizzy noted how the girls grouped in the expected best-friend cliques, leaving one girl by herself. The girl was taller than the others, skinny with long hair emphasizing her thin frame. Lizzy identified with the loner and, as the girls went to the paddock where a couple of ranch hands were bringing out horses, she approached the girl.

"Been riding before?" Lizzy asked.

Lizzy startled the thin girl who wasn't expecting to be singled out. "Yes, once," she said.

"Did you like it?"

"I'm back, aren't I?" the girl quipped.

Lizzy smiled. "Oh, a smart ass, huh?"

190

The girl squirmed.

Lizzy winked and said, "I think I like that."

The ranch hands helped the girls onto the saddled horses. Lizzy led her new sassy friend to a small chestnut mare and helped her mount.

"I'm keeping an eye on you," Lizzy jested.

The girl returned a weak smile.

Joanie welcomed everyone, laid out the ground rules for the ride, and then left the paddock with herself in the lead.

The thin girl was the last girl in line with Lizzy behind her.

The ride was much like the one Joanie and Lizzy had taken earlier, sans galloping in the meadow. Although it was a rear view, Lizzy saw the thin girl sit high in the saddle. When they returned to the stables, the girl was beaming.

That evening, Joanie's cook prepared a spread for the ranch hands and for Joanie and Lizzy. The ribs and mashed potatoes were the best Lizzy had ever tasted.

After dinner, Joanie and Lizzy took to the rocking chairs on the porch. It was a fine summer evening with dry, cool air wafting aromatic scents from the pines.

"Get enough to eat?" Joanie asked Lizzy.

"Too much! I'm a pig. Didn't think I could eat so much."

"You know, you were real good with those kids today."

"Thanks."

Joanie paused, studying Lizzy. "Could I ask you something?"

"Sure."

"What do you think about staying on here? I could use another hand."

Lizzy's gut said yes, but her head interfered.

"Joanie, there was a time I would jump at the chance. I was free and easy, used to moving around. But now…"

Joanie smiled. "Now, there's someone else to consider."

"Yes. There is."

"Tanner has something that would keep him from coming here? Some job?"

"No, Tanner lives on a pension from the Army. I inherited money from my mom, a surprising amount. Didn't think she had that much. We live modestly. So, we don't have obligations."

"You know," Joanie responded, "they have some fine places here to live."

Lizzy didn't respond. Joannie interrupted the silence. "Just think about it."

"I will. Tanner is headed this way. Should be here in a couple of days. We'll talk."

With that, Lizzy and Joanie continued to rock and silently enjoy the evening.

A few miles away from Joanie's ranch, high in the mountains, Grumman inspected the electrical infrastructure. It was in even worse shape than Wyoming. The high-tension wire supports were installed in the middle of the last century and were rusted and weak. Trees had grown tall that should have been removed years ago. A few explosive charges would easily topple one onto the wires, and a little accelerant would finish the job.

Grumman smiled.

This will be easy.

He set to work.

Chapter 34

California

Lizzy saw the smoke first. It was far away, on the horizon. The news said the fire was on the edge of a regional park. She was frightened, but Joanie, a long-time Californian accustomed to natural disasters from mud slides to earthquakes and occasional forest fires, seemed calm.

Joanie provided Lizzy with the latest reports. "They say the fire is moving east, away from us. As long as we keep our eyes and ears open, we should be OK."

"Shouldn't we take the horses somewhere safe?"

"There are few places where we can move sixteen horses. Most ranches are looking at the same fire."

Lizzy wrinkled her forehead and pursed her lips. Joanie squeezed her shoulder and said, "It'll be all right, sweetie."

Tanner sipped his morning coffee as the news about the California wildfire flashed across the TV screen. Realizing it was near Joanie's ranch, he loaded the truck and headed out. If he had to, he would drive all night.

Road-weary but still alert after popping energy drinks, Tanner had another six or seven hours to go as he drove past Elko, Nevada. Then he saw him. He recognized the bright green motorcycle waiting to merge onto the highway. He could not miss the matching green helmet. Although he was driving in the opposite direction separated by a median strip, Tanner knew this was the man he'd talked to at the gas station in Jackson, the guy with the odd tattoo flicking a Bic lighter. Something bothered Tanner about the guy. He had to see what he was up to.

Tanner did an illegal U-turn across the median, stirring up desert dust. He floored the truck to catch up. The flat, sandy plains of Nevada offered unobstructed views. The motorcycle was in his sights when the rider took an exit. Tanner was right behind him. The motorcycle cut through several side streets, but Tanner kept pace. The rider turned into the Elko Regional Airport. Although the motorcycle slowed, a car taking its time pulled in between and blocked Tanner. The rider didn't enter the small terminal; rather, he headed to the general aviation area. Tanner parked and rushed out just in time to see the rider enter the side door to a hangar.

Tanner followed and cautiously opened the door the man had entered. He crept into a small, enclosed room attached to the hangar. It was a storage area with metal shelves holding aviation tools and spare parts. Tanner crept amongst the aisles. Suddenly, the lights in the room went off, and he was plunged into the dark. Tanner didn't see what hit him.

Tanner was disoriented when he came to.

Did I dream this?

His throbbing head told Tanner it was no dream. It was still dark in the room, but as Tanner rubbed the goose egg on his skull, the lights came on. Tanner shielded his eyes from the glare.

"Hey, you OK?" asked a young man in grease-smeared overalls.

Tanner stumbled to his feet, and the young man froze in the shadow Tanner made towering over him.

"Did you see the man who rode here on a motorcycle?"

"Yeah, uh, he drove here about an hour ago and took a private plane out."

"Where was he going?"

"I don't know, but you could ask at the desk."

"Where's that?"

The young man, more relaxed now that Tanner appeared to be no harm to him, said, "I'll show you."

He led Tanner out and into the small passenger area where a blonde woman with a ready smile sat behind a counter. Tanner thanked the young mechanic and walked up to the counter.

"May I help you?" asked the smiling blonde behind the counter.

"A young guy rode here on a motorcycle and came into this building. He was maybe in his twenties, about your height, shaggy brown hair. Did you see or speak to him?"

The blonde was flirtatious. "How do you know my height? I'm sitting down."

"Five-five?"

Not responding told Tanner he was right on the mark.

"Are you police?"

"Not exactly, it's just that I've met him before and I was curious who he was and where he was going."

"Well ... I shouldn't do this," she began as Tanner gave her a wink and she looked at a log before her. "His name is Francis Grumman, and he's headed to Baltimore."

"Anything odd you noticed about him?"

"Only that he was the solo passenger on a private jet. He didn't look like money. Maybe he's a rock star?"

"Thanks. I'll get you his autograph."

Tanner knew someone who could help. He pulled out his cell phone and dialed.

"Nick," he said.

"Tanner. How's it going? Are you in Wyoming?" asked Nick.

"No. Long story. Is Tom still with you?"

"No. He's back in Basel."

"I need to get a make on a guy. I suspect he has a record. You think Omni has the info?"

"You have a photo?" Nick asked.

"No, but he has a distinguishing mark. He's got a tattoo of a triangle on his upper left arm."

"What?" exclaimed Nick.

Tanner, taken aback, continued. "Yeah, and it has two letters below it."

"Are the letters I and A?"

Now Tanner was astonished. "How did you know that?"

"Tanner, we believe there is a group of fire starters at work. They nabbed one in England. He had the same tattoo. When Tom and I were in Rome, we found this group's origins go back a long way, but they still seem to be active. Let me ask you, have there been any fires in Wyoming lately?"

"Yes. When Lizzy and I first arrived, they were just putting one out, a forest fire. Look, I have his name, it's Francis Grumman."

Nick said, "That name sounds familiar, but I can't place it."

Tanner continued. "He just boarded a private jet headed to Baltimore."

"A jet from Wyoming?"

"No, from Nevada. That's where I am now."

"What? Why?"

Tanner realized Nick wouldn't know all that had happened recently: The horse auction in Cody, Lizzy heading to a new friend's ranch in California. He brought him up to date.

"And so, Lizzy is with this woman on her ranch near Sacramento?" Nick asked. "There's a forest fire in that area. Is it near them?"

"It is," answered Tanner. "That's why I'm passing through Nevada. I'm headed there now."

"Tanner, I don't want to alarm you, but I'm checking out the latest weather status in that area as we speak. The wind is shifting. Overnight,

196

they are expecting strong winds from the east. That doesn't bode well."

"Then, I've got to get there. Now."

Chapter 35

New York City

Nick wasted no time in calling Tom, who he knew had returned to the Basel lab. "Tom," Nick said without saying hello, "we have a fire starter in the States."

"What? You mean a member of the same group?"

"Same group. Same tattoo."

"How do you know?"

"Tanner called me. He saw a guy with the tattoo in Wyoming, and it was right after a forest fire there. Then he saw him in Nevada, most likely heading away from the forest fire currently raging in California."

"What's Tanner doing in California?"

"Lizzy's there. She's at a horse ranch near Sacramento, close to the current fire. Long story. But I need information on the fire starter."

"Have a name?"

"Francis Grumman."

"Let me ask Omni. Omni, can you find anything on a man currently living named Francis Grumman?"

Omni was quick in her response. "There are eight men named Francis Grumman."

Nick, now on speakerphone, spoke directly to Omni. "He would be between twenty and thirty years old."

"I have two such men named Francis Grumman."

"He may have a police record."

"I have one such man."

Nick knew he was getting somewhere now. "Read us what you have."

"Francis Albert Grumman was born twenty-eight years ago in New York City."

Nick thought the name was familiar. Grumman was born in his city, but it's a large place.

"Since you asked about a police record, shall I skip other details and go there first?"

"Yes," Tom and Nick replied at the same time.

"The police arrested Grumman as a youth. The record is sealed since he was a juvenile. Shall I unseal it?"

"Yes," replied Nick.

"The arrest was for arson. They gave him a suspended sentence and remanded him to the care of the psychiatrist Milton Perry."

Nick now remembered the connection. "Milton Perry?" he exclaimed. "That was the doctor who treated Ray Woodward."

"Who's Ray Woodward?" asked Tom.

Omni interrupted. "Ray Woodward was another patient of Milton Perry."

"Yes, Omni," said Nick. "What you may not know is that I identified Ray for the police as the kid I saw light a waste can on fire."

"I see that, Mr. Foxe," said Omni.

Nick loved the way Tom had worked with Omni to make her interactive, but sometimes it was irksome. Now was one such time. "OK, Omni," he said. "What you are unlikely to know is that I met Ray again just before he entered college. He was accepted at an Ivy League and just recently moved to London.

"Tom, when I visited Paul Allerton on the way back from Rome, he told me that Ray was now his neighbor. Ray was in finance and doing well. Well enough to buy a pricey place in Kensington. Paul was suspicious of Ray. So, I had drinks with Ray on the pretext of catching up. I told him about what I learned in Rome about the fire starters. When I mentioned the tattoo, he

199

reacted. He knows something."

"Omni," Nick asked, "do you see any connection between Grumman and a man named Ray Woodward?"

"No. The only record is that of the treatment of both by Milton Perry."

Tom had another thought. "Omni, do you see any connection between Grumman and England?"

"Yes. Last year, Francis Grumman traveled from JFK Airport in New York City to London Heathrow Airport on a British Airways flight. He rented a car from Hertz and two days later checked it in at Birmingham Airport for a trip to Paris."

Nick thought about this for a moment and asked, "How many miles did he drive? The retail receipt probably reports that."

"It does," replied Omni. "He drove 125 miles."

"How many miles are between the two airports, driving the quickest route?"

"105 Miles."

"Thanks, Omni. Tom, what's between London and Birmingham?" Nick asked.

"Did he meet Ray Woodward?" asked Tom.

"Perhaps, but if he drove into London to meet him, it would be twenty miles one way. Then why leave from Birmingham?"

Tom asked, "What's next?"

"I am going to call Paul and tell him what we know about Grumman — as well as his neighbor Ray."

Nick had another thought and asked, "Omni, is Milton Perry still practicing in New York?"

Omni replied, "Milton Perry was killed in a firebombing of his car twelve years ago."

Nick told Tom, "I'm calling Paul!"

Chapter 36

California

"Wake up, Lizzy. We got to get moving."

Joanie's pleading with the somnolent Lizzy didn't make sense.

It's still dark. What's that smell? Why is it so warm?

"We've got to get the horses out of here. The fire's coming," said Joanie.

Lizzy threw on a pair of jeans, her shirt from yesterday, and slipped into her boots. When she went outside, she first felt the wind, then saw what blotted out the rising sun: Smoke, thick smoke, stoked by yellow flames below. A large plane came across the view dumping a pink powder. She had fallen asleep to a peaceful evening breeze. She awoke to a fiery maelstrom.

Two ranch hands were leading horses out of the stables with Joanie coordinating. Lizzy had only one thought.

Fancy Pants!

She didn't see her favorite horse among those now out of the barn and in the paddock and ran up to Joanie. "What happened?" she asked.

"A freak shift in the wind happened last night," replied Joanie. "They had a fire block carved between us and the fire. I don't know why that didn't hold, but it didn't."

"Where's Fancy Pants?"

"She's a little scared. Won't leave her stall. I'll help with these other horses and then tend to her."

Saying nothing more, Lizzy ran toward the barn. Lizzy could see that the fire was now both east and north of them. She turned and saw the hills on fire to the south.

It's circling us. We got to get Fancy Pants out of here!

When she arrived at Fancy Pants' stall, the mare was stomping and backing away from sensed danger.

"Hey, girl," Lizzy said as she approached her horse. "It's me. Let's get you out of here."

Lizzy had learned how to put a bridle on her horse, but when she approached Fancy Pants with the tack in hand and began to put it over the horse's head, the horse reared up on her hind legs, her front legs knocking Lizzy on her ass.

Lizzy was barely grazed and remained calm. "OK, you. That was not called for. We have to get this on you."

Joanie came in and sized up the situation. "Let me help."

"How about the other horses?"

"Fortunately, we had two eight-horse slant trailers here. The men got the others loaded. I told them to take off. We'll meet up with them later when we get out of the fire zone."

"I'll ride her out of here," said Lizzy.

"No, you won't. Don't you see how spooked she is now? If she sees the flames, no telling what she'd do. I have the trailer we brought her in. It's got to be hitched up to the truck, but that's what we'll use. Now, let me help you with this bridle."

Joanie and Lizzy were able to keep Fancy Pants quiet enough to put on the bridle.

Lizzy held the leather reins and was about to walk Fancy Pants out when Joanie stopped her. "We've got to put this on her," Joanie said as she took a long piece of cloth she brought with her and tied it around the horse's head, covering her eyes. "We don't want her more spooked than she is already."

Lizzy followed Joanie out of the barn, a blindfolded Fancy Pants trailing behind. Lizzy was stunned by how far the fire had advanced. The tops of the pines on the property's edge blazed like enormous tiki lamps.

"We better hurry," Joanie said.

They walked to the single-horse trailer parked beside a shed. The trailer was unhitched, the tongue setting on cement blocks. "We can't hitch the trailer with her in it. Hold on to her reins good and tight while I fetch the truck."

The fire, now a short hundred yards away, toasted her body; it was like standing before a hearth, but this was not the cozy warmth of a living-room fire. This was angry heat.

Lizzy stood next to the horse while Joanie ran to the truck by the ranch house. The nearby trees were now ablaze from top to bottom. She jumped into the truck as a flaming tree collapsed onto the ranch house, crushing the roof with a thunderous report.

Lizzy shouted, "Joanie!" frightening Fancy Pants, who backed away, but Lizzy held on tight. She turned back toward the truck. The burning house lit the interior like a klieg light, creating a clear silhouette of Joanie in the driver's seat. Joanie started the truck and raced over to the trailer.

She positioned the vehicle in front of the trailer and leaned out the window. "Tell me when to stop."

"Stop!" Lizzy yelled when the ball hitch neared the trailer's socket.

Joanie rushed out of the truck toward the hitch.

"Let me help," said Lizzy.

"Just hold on to Fancy Pants," replied Joanie as she picked up the trailer hitch.

An explosion rocked the air as a superheated propane tank at the ranch house exploded. It blasted a fireball into the air and shot debris toward Lizzy and Joanie. A foot-long piece of wood struck Joanie in the side and made her drop the tongue of the trailer. It scraped her right shin, landed on her foot, and bounced off. Joanie fell to the ground.

Lizzy kneeled next to Joanie and asked, "Can you stand?"

Joanie moaned, but despite her obvious pain, she stood and hopped on her left leg, avoiding the right foot which appeared to have a broken bone or two.

"Here," Lizzy said, handing the reins to Fancy Pants over to Joanie. "Hold her and I'll hitch us up."

Having lived in a trailer in her youth had its advantages; Lizzy was accustomed to hitching one up to a truck. Lizzy hefted the tongue in place and clipped it down securely. Joanie leaned against the trailer while Lizzy took Fancy Pants from Joanie, who was braving a weak smile. Lizzy led the horse into the trailer and shut the door.

She came back to Joanie and announced, "I'm driving. Let's get you into the truck." Lizzy gave Joanie a shoulder to lean on and was able to lift her into the passenger's seat. Then Lizzy hopped in the driver's seat. The truck had a keyless ignition and Lizzy assumed Joanie still had the key fob in her pocket. She pressed 'Start' and the engine came to life.

Lizzy spun the tires on the dirt before she remembered she was towing a trailer and eased off the accelerator. Hard to do when tall flames were licking the sides of the gate she had to drive through. The opening, never very wide, was now made narrower by the encroaching flames. Lizzy closed the windows and picked up as much speed as she could.

She held her breath as she aimed the truck toward the fiery opening.

Tanner was livid. "You got to let me through!"

Tanner was an imposing man, but he was well-matched against the deputy that operated the roadblock. The man in a smokey hat stared Tanner down as he told him, "No one in. We allow only those who are coming out."

Tanner had driven straight through from Nevada once he heard that the wind had shifted, and his girlfriend was in danger. He had tried Lizzy's cell phone several times, to no avail.

Her phone must be off.

Tanner refused to consider other options. He could see up the rise where the road to the ranch *should* be, but he saw nothing but flames. As he tried Lizzy on the cell for the umpteenth time, the cops moved the roadblock barriers to let a truck with a long horse trailer rush through it, passing Tanner. A second rig, much the same, followed a few seconds later. Both pulled off further down the road, and the police and firefighters walked over to talk to the drivers. Tanner joined them.

A cop put his hand up to stop Tanner, but Tanner was already close enough to yell out to the man. "Where did you come from? Was it Joanie Fitzwell's ranch?"

"Yes, it was."

"Is Joanie with you?"

"No. She and one of her guests had trouble with the last horse. They told us to go on ahead and they would catch up."

Tanner remembered Joanie had called him on his cell phone once back in Cody.

Why hadn't I thought of that before?

He pulled out his cell phone and scrolled through received calls until he found the likely number. He called it. Joanie answered. "Hello?"

"Hello, is this Joanie?"

Joanie recognized the voice. "Tanner?"

"Yes. Is Lizzy with you?"

"Yes, she is. She's driving. I'm putting you on speaker."

"Hey, sweetie," Lizzy said in the calmest voice she could muster.

"Where are you?"

"We're on the road traveling away from the ranch," said Joanie. "Where are you?"

"I'm sure I'm on the same road, but the police have set up a roadblock and won't let me through."

"We'll be there soon."

Joanie clicked off before Tanner could say more.

"You did a good job of sounding calm," said Lizzy.

"Thanks. You, too."

Had Tanner been in the truck's cab with the two women, Lizzy knew he would have deemed their phone performances Oscar-worthy. The truck and trailer were driving through an amber sea, its waves crashing against them from both sides of the road.

They sped past by a stand of pines, blazing like a furnace. As they passed, tops of trees began shedding flaming branches. One landed directly in front of the truck on the road. Lizzy didn't hesitate to run over it. As she cleared that one, another fiery branch dropped onto the hood with a loud thud. Lizzy swerved to the left, and the branch fell off. Lizzy heard Fancy Pants' loud whinny.

"Sorry, Fancy Pants," shouted Lizzy.

Fancy Pants had more jolts ahead of her when a large pine fell across the road and Lizzy slammed on the brakes. Fire engulfed them on the right side, a flaming tree blocked the road ahead, and the blaze was closing in quickly on the left.

Lizzy sized up their only option. On the left was a narrow shoulder with a ten-foot drop to the field below. Fire was licking at the stone that created the small cliff. Lizzy looked at Joanie. She knew they were thinking the same thing. They had to try going around the tree on the narrow shoulder, but if they slid off the shoulder they would roll into a conflagration.

"Hold on," said Lizzy.

Tanner paced, carving a trench in the ground. The fire had advanced toward the roadblock.

A cop came to Tanner and said, "We've got to move back down the road."

"No," said Tanner stubbornly.

The cop stared at Tanner and said, "You don't understand. Where we're standing will be on fire in a few minutes. We've got to go!"

The cop took Tanner by the shoulder to shift him, but Tanner swatted the arm away and growled. It was a stand-off. Tanner was moments away from slugging the man when the cops near the roadblock yelled, "Look out!"

Tanner turned to see a truck with a horse trailer crash through the barricade. Two ornamental flags atop the trailer burned brightly, as though part of a planned display.

The truck's horn blared in celebration, and Tanner saw Lizzy smiling behind the wheel. She pulled off to where the cops directed her and hopped out. Tanner was already there to lift her off her feet and hug her like he had never done before.

"Easy, guy," Lizzy said. "I can't breathe."

An EMT stood nearby at an ambulance. Lizzy yelled to him. "Hey, there's someone in the truck who has a smashed-up foot. You better take care of her."

Tanner smirked. "Still bossing people around." But as the EMT helped Joanie from the cab, he released Lizzy and walked over to Joanie. "You OK?" he asked with genuine concern.

Joanie winced. "Just dropped the fool trailer on my foot."

Lizzy added, "And got hit by a flying two-by-four."

Joanie worked out a smile. "I'll be OK. Lizzy had to drive. She's a real champ."

Tanner agreed. "Yes, she is." He then looked where Lizzy had been standing, but she was gone. Noticing the back doors of the trailer open, he walked over to see Lizzy removing the cloth from the horse's eyes and stroking her crest."

"She OK?" asked Tanner.

"Sure, she is, now."

An officer approached them, "We have to move. Just drive behind me. I'll lead you out of here."

"Ready?" asked Tanner.

"You bet. Follow me."

"You sure you're OK to drive? You've been through a lot."

"Hey. I can drive this rig. Guess you could say I got my trial by fire."

Chapter 37

California

Joanie answered on the second ring and put the call on speakerphone.

"Joanie! It's Denise, Denise Anderson."

"Denise, good seeing you in Cody. What's up?"

"I wanted to call you after all the news about the fire out there. Did it touch your ranch?"

"Tell her the truth, Joanie," Lizzy whispered.

"Well," responded Joanie, "it wiped me out. The horses are OK. We have them at a friend's ranch. That's where I'm now. But it leveled all the buildings."

"On, Joanie, that's awful. Were you hurt?"

"I dropped a trailer hitch on my foot and have a beauty of a cast on it, but that's all. Lizzy has helped me get around. You remember Lizzy? You met her in Cody."

Denise had plenty of practice, as a senator's wife, in remembering people she met. "Of course, I remember. Did she come out to California with you?"

"Yes, she took a shine to a horse I bought there and has become quite the cowgirl."

"May I speak to her?"

"Sure thing. She's right here with me now."

"Hello?"

"Lizzy, it was a pleasure meeting you in Cody. How's Tanner?"

Lizzy was impressed that this woman would remember her and her boyfriend after only a brief introduction. "He's fine. He came down to help."

"Well, I just want to thank you both for helping Joanie out and I'm glad you're safe."

After a few more minutes with Joanie, Denise ended the call.

"Well," said Lizzy, "I'm impressed that she remembered me and Tanner."

"She has a knack for that," said Joanie.

Chapter 38

London

The misfortune of others can make another person rich. Within a few days of the fire in California, PG&E was found at fault. Powerlines sparked the conflagration. At his desk at Barstone Capital, Ray delighted in watching the rapid decline of PG&E's stock value. He created a short sale on the stock and its decline racked up millions with each point the stock dropped. However, this was not a sale for Barstone Capital, but rather a side deal he had made for The Fire Company.

Later that evening, Ray continued to monitor the decline of the utility from his home office when Roland rang him up. "Well, my boy. Where do we stand?"

"So far," Ray responded, "we are up eight million dollars."

Ray sensed an expression through the line, one of shock. Roland originally had a hard time convincing the other partners to lend him the necessary ten million dollars, but when Ray added two million of his own funds to show he had skin in the game, they relented. The Fire Company had made an eighty percent return in the two months it took to plan and execute the project. It only took one man and a match.

"Ray, dear boy, you are leading The Fire Company into a new age." *Yes*, Ray thought, *I'm not just working for rich clients with a need for arson. Now, they can direct their own destiny.*

Roland took the conversation in another direction. "I believe you know the man who did this job in California, Francis Grumman."

Ray was puzzled. "Francis? He's been just a voice on the phone."

"So, you don't know him?"

"Roland," said Ray, somewhat annoyed at the senior fire starter's little game, "what do you know that I don't?"

"You both come from New York City and the same psychiatrist treated you both."

"Dr. Perry?" Ray didn't relish bringing up his treatment by a psychiatrist. It embarrassed him, and he would rather forget it. It particularly annoyed him that Roland knew, although he felt Roland and most of The Fire Company agents could make good use of thorough head shrinking. Ray dismissed the connection. "I don't remember him."

"Well," Roland said, "he is younger than you. That may explain it. But get to know him better. He's going to work the planet job in the US."

"Oh?" said Ray neutrally. Roland was handling the planet job, and Ray had just a passing knowledge of it. Now, more than ever, Ray was glad not to be too involved. He was averse to harming people, but he could see that Roland took glee in such prospects. Although Roland reassured Ray that the project would be completed when no one was around, this job could hurt thousands if something went amiss.

Yet, Ray couldn't help himself; he was still interested in the job. "Who is doing the London part of the job? We had Aiden Hayes slotted to do it until he betrayed us by going rogue with the London Eye."

"Ah, yes. Lucky for us, his partner, Karl Lenoir, has stepped up for us."

Ray sneered. "Well, wasn't that noble of him."

"Ray, I detect some cynicism. We checked him out. He's capable. Plus, he's seen firsthand the price that comes from disloyalty."

Ray said nothing. Roland was considering his next request carefully before breaking the silence.

"Ray, you know that the London piece will occur quite near you. I would like to get you involved."

"Doing what?"

"Meet with Lenoir. I want to make you the point of contact in this. Will you do it?"

Ray wasn't keen, but Roland made a good point. It was going to happen in his neighborhood. For that reason alone, he should monitor it.

"Sure. I'll help."

"Great! I'll send you Lenoir's contact information straightaway."

Roland ended the call and Ray began to think more about his personal connection to Francis Grumman than he did Lenoir. He tried to remember Grumman and wished he had a photo of him as a kid. He remembered that someone killed Dr. Perry by firebombing his car. At the time, Ray suspected that the good doctor must have owed money to the mob.

But what if a patient did it?

Paul had his suspicions about his new neighbor Ray, and Nick's call cranked them up higher. Nick told Paul about the arson in the US, Francis Grumman, and the fact that he had made a trip to England. He'd met someone somewhere between London and Birmingham. That was the only thing that made sense. It was unlikely that it would have been Ray, since he lived in London, but it was troubling that the same psychiatrist treated them in New York.

Did they know each other?

Paul didn't have enough evidence to get an order to monitor Ray's phone calls, but he didn't need one. Although skirting the law, he had the skills to do it himself.

Paul was in his flat, listening to Ray's conversation with someone in the Cotswolds about the success of a job in California. From the conversation and the fact that Ray was an investment guru, Paul took only a few more pieces of evidence to piece together what had happened. He had read reports about the collapse of PG&E stock after the company was blamed for the California wildfire. Ray must have entered a short contract on PG&E.

Hence the millions of dollars he made for the organization to which Ray and his caller belonged. Someone had set up PG&E to take the fall, but someone in Ray's organization had started the fire.

Now Paul had a name for the man who did the deed, Francis Grumman. What the 'planet job' could be would be anybody's guess, but part of it was going to take place in the United States. Paul would alert his contact at the FBI.

But it was the next portion of the conversation that especially caught Paul's attention. 'The London part of the job.' A job assigned to Karl Lenoir.

Lenoir. He's showing up again like a bad penny.

Ray was going to meet with Lenoir.

I'm going to be a part of that conversation.

After Ray and his unknown friend ended their call, Paul stood and paced. He thought about his last visit with Nick. He had been skeptical of his Omni thingamabob. Too sci-fi for Paul's taste. But the Omni knew a lot about this so-called fire guild organization.

I need Tom and his magic machine here.

Chapter 39

New York City

Nick wondered what had transpired since the last phone call with Tanner. Last time they'd spoken, Tanner knew about the fire and was headed to find Lizzy. Nick worried for their safety and hoped one of them would phone soon. While waiting for their call, he focused on the fire starter spotted by Tanner and pondered the man's destination.

Baltimore? thought Nick. Nick immediately thought of BWI, Baltimore Washington International. A little research told him the only other airport where a private jet could land would be Martin State Airport. That was unlikely since it was a joint-use airport between military and civilian. But BWI meant Grumman could be headed to anywhere in central Maryland or DC. Nick thought he should involve the police, but he knew the flimsy evidence he had wouldn't gain their attention.

After several tries, Nick got Tanner on the phone. By the time he got hold of him, Lizzy was safely by his side. Tanner recounted his dash to California and Lizzy's narrow escape. The big man needed little encouragement to come east to track down the guy who could have killed Lizzy. Nick told Tanner he would send his jet to pick them up in Sacramento and bring them to DC, where he was booking rooms at one of the hotels he favored.

Nick shared with Tanner the call he'd received from Paul about Grumman, Ray's involvement, and Lenoir.

"I'm relieved to hear that you are both safe and well, and I'm looking forward to seeing you again soon." And with that, Nick hung up the phone

When Nick last spoke with Paul, his British spy friend let him know he had contacted the FBI and that they would be in touch with Nick. Nick put aside his reservation about the authorities' disinterest now that MI6 and the FBI were involved.

It was the last thing Paul requested that surprised Nick. He asked if Tom would join him in London. Paul explained he needed his help, particularly from the Omni. Paul had dismissed Omni and hadn't accepted her as another being. He called her the 'Omni thing.' However, when Nick contacted Tom, he volunteered to leave right away to join Paul. Nick requested that Tom provide him with full access to Omni as well. Her help was demanded on his side of the Atlantic, too.

Nick was confident that Lizzy would insist on accompanying Tanner. That left one remaining member of the team.

Rachael.

Chapter 40
Washington, DC

"Angie! How good to see you," said Rachael as she left the Uber in front of her friend's apartment house on 14th Street, NW. Angie Fullerton was waiting at the Starbucks beside the building, sipping a *latté* at curbside seating as she anticipated her friend's arrival.

Rachael had described Angie as having cheerleader looks and Einstein's brain. When Rachael said that in front of Angie, her friend would snort. "Look who's talking." People told Rachael she was pretty, but Angie was another level. She was magazine-cover beautiful with natural blonde hair and well-defined cheekbones. Rachael accused her of 'dolling' herself up. Whereas Rachael forgot where she kept her lipstick, Angie always wore fresh red color on her lips and a touch of mascara and liner on her eyes. When Rachael chided Angie on her makeup, Angie would fire back the logic of having pale lips and hair needing those touch-ups to have any facial definition at all.

Both were mathematics and physics wizards; the two were best friends in college and study pals. After college, Rachael went to MIT and Angie to Princeton. They stayed in touch throughout graduate school. Then careers got in the way. Rachael remained at MIT to teach, and Angie got a government job with the Nuclear Regulatory Commission in Washington. They seldom connected. Rachael had taken care of that oversight.

"Would you like a cup of coffee?" Angie asked.

"How about something a little more relaxing?" replied the travel-weary Rachael.

Angie smiled. "I got just the thing. Let's go to my apartment."

Rachael rolled her suitcase behind her and followed Angie as she walked next door to a new high-rise glass-walled apartment building; the type where the tenant had to spend a mint on curtains to gain some privacy. Angie punched in a code and the door to the lobby opened. She held the door for Rachael to roll in.

While they waited for an elevator, Rachael took in the lean, modern, and expensively furnished lobby. "Nice building you have here. I just have a walkup in Cambridge."

"It's my little splurge. Several professionals my age moved into the area. A friend of mine at work lives here and got me interested in the place."

"A male friend?" asked Rachael.

The elevator arrived. As they stepped in, Angie answered, "Yes, a man."

"So, what's going on with that?" Rachael asked with a sly smile.

"I think he wants more than being just friends, but I don't see that happening. He seems to be OK with that. But, enough about me. From what you said on the phone, you seemed to be here to escape a man."

They reached their floor, and the door opened.

"That's not exactly the case, but we can talk after ... maybe some wine?" Rachael said as she looked hopefully at her friend.

"You bet. My place is to the right."

Even though the lobby was an indicator of what to expect in each apartment, Rachael was astonished by Angie's place. The floor-to-ceiling glass wall in the living room presented an excellent view of the city. Over the rooftops of clustered century-old rowhouses, you could spot the Capitol dome. Next to the living room was an open kitchen behind a counter with four bar stools. The furnishings were soft, warm tones. It looked like a designer had just staged the place for sale.

"What do you do at the NRC?"

Angie laughed. "Don't get used to it. I'm house sitting."

"Come again?"

"A director at the NRC and his wife are living in Los Alamos on a one-year assignment. They leased me the place for an affordable amount."

"How did you get such a deal?" asked Rachael.

"You know the guy I mentioned, the one who got me interested in this building?"

"Yeah."

"He's their son."

Rachael laughed.

"Come on," said Angie. "I'll show you your room and you can freshen up while I get some wine. Red or white?"

"White would be good."

Rachael's room equaled the style of the living room. Fortunately, these glass walls had curtains, so she could avoid exhibitionism.

Rachael soon joined her friend with two glasses of sauvignon blanc and the bottle in a marble wine chiller. Rachael settled onto the couch with Angie at the other end. Angie handed Rachael her glass, they clicked a silent toast, and each took a sip. Rachael closed her eyes and let the wine work its magic. She quickly relaxed.

"First," said Angie, "it's great to see you. It's been too long."

"True. It has."

"Second, what's up with you in the romance department. I thought you and the famous Nicholas Foxe were an item."

Rachael knew her friend hadn't changed, and they were back in college again. "You always were direct."

"No really, what's up? The man spent time with you in your apartment in Cambridge. You ran off to see him in Venice. I mean, Venice, one of the most romantic places on earth. And now, you need time to yourself? What's up with that?"

Rachael felt like a secret agent under interrogation.

"It's complicated."

"Oh, don't hand me that tripe. That's like a tired old line from a movie. 'It's complicated.' Look, we have all night. I'm your best friend. Spill it."

Rachael thought she needed to adjust her simple description of her friend.

Cheerleader looks with Perry Mason tenacity.

"You may have seen Nick in the news some time ago."

"Sure. Back when you guys discovered that tablet in a cave. Tall and handsome, what's not to like?"

"And cocky and full of himself," Rachael added.

"So, you weren't attracted to him? Remember: One long sleep over at your place and then Venice. Oh yes, no attraction."

Rachael snickered at the obvious and gazed into her glass as she spoke, as though her answer would rise from the wine. "I love my work, but I didn't realize how boring living inside my head all the time could be until I got swept up in the Nick Foxe hurricane. We found secret passages under a castle in Italy, a treasure in a grotto. At first, I felt like I was living inside an Indiana Jones movie."

Angie looked incredulous, but Rachael forged on, lifting her eyes to meet Angie's. "We even had a sword fight in the Doge Palace."

"I knew you were quite the fencer in college, but I didn't know they had competitions in the Doge Palace," Angie responded.

"Angie, it was in the attic with a man who was trying to kill us."

Angie's jaw dropped. "You have to be putting me on."

"No. I'm not."

"Wow, now that has to be a rush."

Rachael smiled weakly. "Yes, I admit it was…"

"But?" said Angie.

"Angie, it *was* exciting, but more than anything, I was terrified. There was an assassin after Nick in Venice, and I was with him when he attacked.

The man knocked me out cold. When I came to, the room was soaked with blood, the assassin's blood. Nick was unharmed, and he held me close for a long time. But something snapped."

Rachael, near tears, continued. "I asked myself. What am I doing here? This is not me. This is not my life. I love Nick, but I can't do this." She looked into Angie's eyes as though her friend could offer absolution. "I just can't do it."

Angie put her glass down, scooted down the couch, and hugged her friend. Rachael burst into tears, releasing for the first time all the emotion she'd been hiding.

Chapter 41

Severna Park

Grumman arrived at the BWI private terminal aboard a jet provided by Anthony Egnati. When Grumman stepped off the plane, a limo and driver were waiting for him. Grumman's ride from BWI was a short one but silent. The driver, a beefy no-nonsense man in a black suit and sunglasses, hardly spoke a word on the trip. Grumman liked to chat but his attempts to do so with this man failed. He welcomed the arrival at his destination.

Egnati's home was at the end of a private road, deep in the forests lining the banks of the Severn River. The house was more like a mountain lodge than a lake house. It featured a dark brown roof and cedar siding above stone walls. Large picture windows on the first floor looked out over a stone patio and Adirondack chairs. Under the right side of this large house, three garage doors spoke of at least a moderate degree of wealth.

The driver pulled up the crushed-stone drive and stopped in front of the double entrance doors. He silently opened the car door for Grumman, who said, "Thanks," eliciting no acknowledgment in return. Grumman walked to the front door as the driver stood by the car, now looking around as though on guard.

As Grumman approached the house, a man a couple of inches under six feet tall greeted him. He was a trim man with black hair streaked with silver. A nose slightly bent from a punch in a fight long ago was the only blemish on an otherwise handsome face. He wore casual clothes, a polo shirt and khakis, but ones that came from a store in a better part of town than where Grumman bought his gear.

The man thrust his hand out. "Francis Grumman?" he asked.

"Yes," was Grumman's simple reply as the man shook his hand in a firm grip.

"Tony Egnati," said the man. "It's good to meet you. Come on in."

Grumman followed Egnati into a large foyer which opened into a larger living room with a stone fireplace in one corner. Picture windows offered a view of the river peeking through the forest beyond a stone patio. A tall, blonde, middle-aged woman in a tennis outfit who Francis suspected had a facial Botox shot or two, walked in. She turned to meet the recently arrived guest.

"Honey," said Egnati, "this is Francis Grumman. Francis, this is my wife, Monica."

Monica extended her hand to Grumman in a delicate manner making him wonder if he should kiss it or shake it. He decided on a gentle shake.

"Will you be staying for dinner?" she asked.

"Well..." mumbled Grumman, unsure.

"We'll see," said Egnati. "We have business to discuss."

Monica reacted as a wife of a husband who frequently hosted people with whom he had business to discuss. She said, "Well, I have a tennis lesson to get to. It was a pleasure meeting you Francis," and she walked away.

"Let's have a seat and talk," said Egnati as Grumman followed him to a couple of chairs in the living room. Grumman was out of his element. He was accustomed to cheap hotels and back alleys. Now he was in a rich, laid-back gentrified environment.

Grumman's assignments with The Fire Company had been few, but he hoped for more in the future. He knew he was being tested. He had found his way into The Company by shadowing Ray Woodward's email trails, and it was Ray from whom he had taken his orders. The old man in the Cotswolds that Grumman visited had assured him that the organization was far greater than just an old man in rural England. Roland told him that a Company partner in the United States would be reaching out to him, that is, if the California job proved successful. That job proved to be just that, and before Grumman knew it, the man now seated across from him had sent his private jet to fetch him. The planet job would require more than the simple tools he used in California, and Egnati would provide them.

"So," began Egnati, "I hear good things about you."

"Thanks, Mr. Egnati."

"Please, call me Tony."

"Yes, sir ... Tony"

"Were you aware of the reason behind your starting the fire in California?"

"It was a financial deal, wasn't it? Ray Woodward cooked up a stock scheme that would make a lot of dough if the stock for PG&E took a dive."

"That's right."

"The Fire Company is moving into a new direction."

Egnati looked displeased. "The Fire Company? Please. I don't even know if I like the name, but if anyone would have a right to it, it would be me."

Egnati was about to continue but stopped when the driver came into the room. He walked over to Egnati, bent down, and whispered something in his ear.

"Good!" said Egnati and with a "thank you," from his boss, the driver exited.

Egnati paused to examine Grumman, taking stock of him.

"I want to show you something," Egnati said as he stood. "Follow me."

Egnati walked back to the foyer and toward the garage, but just before reaching the garage, he turned to a door on the left with a keypad lock. After punching in a short code, he opened the door and started down a flight of stairs with Grumman following. At the base of the stairs, they turned right into a hallway lined with stone similar to the mountain rock on the front of the house. Egnati stopped by a picture hanging on the left wall and turned to Grumman.

"See this picture? Know what it is?" asked Egnati.

Grumman examined the old photo of a destroyed city with only a few walls remaining here and there as though it had been bombed. He hadn't a clue and answered, "No."

"This is what the city of Baltimore looked like in the winter of 1904. Fire destroyed more than a thousand buildings. Twelve-hundred firefighters took two days to bring it under control."

Egnati stood for a moment appraising the photo as though it had layers of meaning. "You know why I'm showing you this?"

"No."

Egnati grinned a wicked smile. "My great-grandfather started this fire."

Grumman was both appreciative of the magnitude and mystified why someone had done this. Egnati could read Grumman's confusion.

"My great-grandfather didn't intend to torch the whole city. A landlord was going belly-up and hired him to set fire to one of his office buildings to collect the insurance money. He collected. A bunch of people collected." Then a look of remorse skimmed Egnati's face. "But a lot of people didn't."

Egnati looked at Grumman. "I'm telling you this to let you know this picture represents a turning point in our family and our family goes way back. My family came to this country early in the 1800s. The land of opportunity! Especially when everything was built of wood. We trace the family back to Milan and some say they can trace it back to Rome."

Egnati looked Grumman in the eye and said, "This is the point where we need to firm up our level of trust. You now know some things about me that are, for the most part, harmless. But before we go further, I need your assurance that what you learn from this point forward will never be repeated."

"You want me to sign a non-disclosure agreement?" asked Grumman.

He realized how lame he sounded as soon as he said it.

Egnati laughed. "No. You must just understand that if I believe you may tell someone who I don't think should know…" Egnati paused to brush unseen lint from Grumman's shoulder. "I will execute my own type of NDA. Understand?"

Grumman gulped and uttered, "OK."

Egnati turned his ear as though he didn't hear Francis well. "OK, what?"

"I understand."

Egnati smiled broadly and stuck his hand out. "Good! Let's shake on it."

Grumman shook the hand that seemed to envelope his more than it did upstairs when they first met. Grumman had not resorted to his Bic-flicking habit ever since he had left the airport. He ached for that relief now.

Egnati put his hand on Grumman's shoulder to lead him into a room the size of a comfortable study. Again, lined with stone as was the hallway, with one wall covered with oak paneling and featuring a large television. Stuffed leather chairs were positioned to enjoy TV watching.

Still capturing Grumman by the shoulder, Egnati said, "I like you, Francis. Now that we have our agreement in place, I want to show you something. Have a seat."

Grumman sat in one of the leather chairs as Egnati stood at the front of the room as if about to deliver a presentation.

"I told you that the Baltimore fire was a turning point for my family. One of the things that survived the fire was Shot Tower. You know Shot Tower?"

Grumman shook his head no.

"That's not surprising, but everyone from Baltimore knows what I mean. It's a tall brick tower that looks like a chimney. A man built it back in the days when rifles were loaded with gunpowder, fodder, and shot. That shot, a round ball of lead, was made by melting lead and pouring drops of it from inside the top of the tower. The lead retained its spherical shape as it cooled on its trip down the inside of the tower.

"Family legend has it that Great-Grandfather was walking around the ruins of the city when he came across Shot Tower. I think the tower, and the fact that the Spanish-American War had been all over the papers, gave him an idea. Why not change the business from fire to firepower? Some in the family said we dealt with arms way back when."

Egnati pushed buttons on a keypad beside him and unseen motors sprang to life. The oak paneling and TV moved back into the wall. Other motors took over and a display lifted from below, replacing the area where the TV had been. The display took Grumman's breath away.

Arrayed across the display was a variety of weaponry. Some, like the semiautomatic rifles now carried on the streets of America, he recognized. Others, far more lethal looking, he did not. There were handguns and rifles, some bearing rocket launchers.

Egnati smiled like a proud papa as he relished Grumman's astonishment. "You are sitting where many clients from around the world have sat, eager to buy the latest in arms."

"Do you make these things?"

"No. There are plenty of manufacturers. I'm a middleman who protects the identity of the customer."

As impressive as this display was, Grumman could think only of fire. He had to ask, "So, does this mean you're not in the fire business anymore?"

"Not at all. There are uses for fire other than to launch lead into someone's heart," Egnati responded. He turned and picked up a small canister which he tossed to Grumman. "Recognize this?"

Grumman caught the canister. "Sure. It's a mini-Molotov."

Egnati laughed. "A mini-Molotov? So, is that what Fire Company agents call it? I guess that's more appealing than compressed incendiary grenade. My father worked with some buddies of his when Dow Chemical laid them off and they came up with a special liquid. It would create a burst of fire bigger and better than anything developed up until that time, probably anything even now."

"So, it's not compressed gasoline?"

"Gasoline is already a liquid, Francis. It's already compressed. That's simple hydraulics. That item you hold contains a special formula." Then with a wink, Egnati joked, "Patent pending."

"So, what's next?" Grumman asked, eager to get to the reason he came.

Egnati knitted his brow. "Can I ask you something?"

"Sure."

"You've known Ray Woodward for a long time, haven't you?"

Grumman was uncertain how to answer. He thought it may be a loaded question, depending on what The Fire Company thought of Ray. He thought he would play it safe. "We knew each other when we were kids."

"I've talked it over with my partners. We thought it best, for various reasons, if Ray didn't lead the planets job. We believe that you know all you need to carry it out."

"But I need equipment."

Egnati smiled broadly. "Ah. That's where I come in."

Chapter 42

Severna Park

Grumman returned to the limo with the silent chauffeur and Egnati joined him. Grumman was pleased that Tony Egnati sat beside him this time, if for no other reason, to break the silence.

"I think you'll like what we're providing you," said Egnati as the car left the paved road and onto a gravel one, deeper into the forest. Although Grumman didn't know where he was, he figured it must be close to Egnati's house because they had been on the road for just a few minutes.

They arrived at a one-story house constructed from large timbers, a modern log cabin with a large garage attached. As they drove up, a man came out the front door to greet them. He was dressed in overalls and a flannel shirt. Grumman thought the young, dark-haired man looked like a mechanic. He was soon to find out the man was indeed a mechanic, one with an unusual specialty.

The driver stopped the car, opened the door for Egnati, and stood guard. Grumman opened his own door and walked around to join Egnati, but Egnati had already reached the porch. Egnati opened his arms as though he was going to hug the man, but the dour man was definitely not the type to hug.

When Grumman reached the porch, Tony made the introductions. "Francis, this is Virgil Wagner. Virgil, Francis Grumman." There were no handshakes exchanged, just a nod from Virgil. "Virgil is my main engineer. He does all our custom work and modifications."

Virgil maintained his unemotional demeanor although Egnati was effusive in explaining what Virgil did.

"So, is everything ready?" Egnati asked Virgil.

"Yes," was the simple response and the first thing out of the man's mouth.

"Let's see it," said Egnati.

Virgil walked over to the garage. The garage door was wide, but Virgil did not open it to enter. Instead, he opened a door just beside it. Egnati and Grumman joined Virgil in a small hallway and Virgil closed the door. He treated this small area like an air lock. One door had to be closed before the other was opened.

Virgil opened the second door and stepped into the garage. When Grumman walked in, he was blinded by the intense glare of high-powered LED lights against walls lined with stainless steel. The floor was a polished gray tile with not a speck of grease or dirt on it. The interior was an unexpected modern contrast to the woodsy exterior.

Red roll-around toolchests lined the back wall. Workbenches were to the left. Grumman noted that each tool was meticulously lined up on top of the workbench.

He doesn't look it, but Virgil is a type-A sort of guy.

In the middle of the garage was a single vehicle, a large, black SUV.

Egnati smiled as though the SUV was a Christmas present waiting to be opened. "Virgil, show us what you've got," he said.

Virgil walked to the rear door of the SUV. Egnati motioned Grumman to follow behind. When Virgil opened the back door, the quiet man suddenly transformed into a professor lecturing on his creation occupying the rear of the vehicle.

"These are stainless steel canisters. The windows are blacked out, but I painted the canisters black to prevent any stray sunlight from reflecting. On top is a package containing plastic explosives with a detonator. When the detonator sets off the explosives, a wave radiates outward at three miles per second through the canisters which contain a mixture of ammonium nitrate fertilizer and fuel. The energy of the detonation wave causes the ammonium nitrate in the fertilizer to vaporize—the solid fertilizer becomes a gas in an instant. Ammonium and nitrate molecules break down, and an enormous amount of oxygen gas is suddenly formed.

"The gas released from the decomposing fertilizer drives the explosion. A rapid release of oxygen, along with the energy from the detonation wave, ignites the fuel. When the liquid fuel ignites, it rapidly combusts, and it releases even more gas.

"Pressure waves traveling at the speed of sound emanate from the mixture, doing massive damage to any structure in its way."

Virgil issued the first smile of the day. It was a wicked smile. "And, in honor of Tony's family invention, we have included a large canister of the fuel used in his compressed incendiary grenade along with another canister of good-old napalm."

Virgil looked lovingly over his creation while he talked. Upon finishing his description of the special fuel and napalm cocktail, he looked toward Grumman and added, "It should make quite a bright, fiery explosion, something out of the ordinary. It will spread flames everywhere."

Grumman smiled at what was a pyromaniac's dream.

"Thank you, Virgil," said Egnati. "Excellent work, as usual. Any questions, Francis?"

"Just one," said Grumman. "Cell phone or timer?"

"Timer," answered Virgil. "Look here." Virgil flipped open the lid on a stainless-steel box on top of the assembly. "This is a read-out. You set the time of the explosion here with this adjustment, flip this cover up, and throw the toggle switch underneath."

Virgil turned to Grumman. "You know the time this beauty is to light up?"

"Sure, we could set it now," said Grumman

Virgil stared at Grumman. "No. We can't. You must save that for the last thing you do when you park the SUV, just before you leave. Once you set the time and throw this switch, you cannot undo it. If you rip this box off, it explodes. If you try to reset the clock, it explodes. When you throw this toggle, you've pulled the pin on a live grenade. A very big grenade. Got it?"

Grumman tried not to betray his growing fear for this rolling firebomb and answered, "Got it."

Grumman was the first to leave the garage as Egnati continued to speak with Virgil. Grumman pulled out his Bic lighter and began flicking it. He stopped for a moment and held the flame before him, admiring it. He was deep in a forest with dry leaves all around. He imagined torching the whole forest, just as he had done in California. The forest fire was such a grand achievement, so much power over so much land, and he had created it.

But he put that thought out of his head and focused on the task at hand. He had rigged firebombs before. He enjoyed torching the motel room in Wyoming with devices of his own creation, but now he had met the master. Virgil had created something magnificent. He could imagine the great conflagration of a notable building in the heart of the nation's capital. It would be beautiful, and he would have delivered it.

But why me?

Grumman wasn't stupid. If a monkey could drive, that primate could deliver a bomb and flip a switch. He liked to flatter himself as a rising star in The Fire Company, but that may not be the reason he was chosen for this job.

Maybe they think I'm expendable if something goes wrong.

Grumman decided he would prove he wasn't expendable. Washington, DC had the most places with the highest security in the land. He thought he would visit some public buildings to check out what security might be evident. Maybe he would get some ideas as to what to expect. Besides, there were a few museums he had been wanting to see.

Chapter 43
Washington, DC

Rachael would be the first to admit it; Angie was an excellent tour guide. A veritable tourist guidebook on all things Smithsonian. She explained they built the Air and Space Museum just in time for the celebration of the nation's bicentennial in 1976. It contained the most notable of the Smithsonian's aviation collection. Hanging from the ceiling were the Wright brothers' airplane, the plane to first break the sound barrier, and the Spirit of Saint Louis. A lunar landing module rested on the floor. The museum also contained one of the first IMAX theaters in the United States, where its premiere film *To Fly!* thrilled audiences. Angie wanted to save Air and Space as the highlight of the Smithsonian museums. Over the course of three days, Angie walked Rachael through half of them.

I can't believe you have never visited before," said Angie.

She knew Rachael loved mechanical things, so the huge steam locomotive they were currently standing in front of in the Museum of American History fascinated her.

"You know," Angie said, "they had to bring the train in first and then build the museum around it."

But in an out-of-the-way room on the top floor, there was a section that absorbed Rachael immediately. There she saw a curated collection of musical instruments.

"I forgot," said Angie, "you play the piano."

"And my mother was a professional violinist," said Rachael as she recalled another, special museum of instruments. "I visited a fantastic museum in Basel, Switzerland. It had several small rooms, each dedicated to variations on one type of musical instrument."

"What took you to Basel?"

Rachael hesitated to say it, the name having been the subject of way too many conversations. But at last, she did. "Nick."

"Nick? Why Basel?"

Rachael knew most of the exploits she shared with Nick were now common knowledge, but the ultimate resting place of the Omni was not one of them. It became known to a group of people who wished her friends harm, and she hoped its location would remain unknown. So, she told her close friend, "Just a business trip."

They left the museum and headed up the Mall toward the Air and Space Museum. It was a sunny day and a pleasant break from being indoors in dimly lit museum space. The Capitol's white dome gleamed in the distance.

They reached the museum and walked up the wide staircase toward the center lobby where the featured exhibits were housed. When they reached the glass doors, a short, shaggy-haired young man was exiting. He held the door for them, smiling broadly. Both women returned the smile, but Rachael turned for another look.

"What?" asked Angie.

"I don't know. Look at that guy. Is that a lighter in his hand?"

"Guess so."

"He's just flicking it on and off."

"Odd habit, I guess," remarked Angie.

Rachael continued to watch the man as he flicked the lighter, stopping only when he hailed a cab, dropped into the backseat and left.

Rachael loved the museum and ran Angie ragged right up to closing time. As they left, Rachael spotted a movie poster. "What's this? They have a theatre?"

"Sure. It's an IMAX theatre."

"I've never seen an IMAX movie," Rachael confessed.

"Girl, you've got to get out more. Look, it's too late tonight, but how about coming back tomorrow and seeing a movie?"

"That would be great. This one looks interesting."

Angie read the title of the movie. *The Planets.*

Grumman drove the bomb-ladened SUV into the center of DC and along Independence Avenue to his destination. The ramp to underground parking would be busy later in the day, but not now. He stopped and flashed his counterfeit pass to an attendant and the parking gate rose. Once inside, he took a ramp to the top level where access to the public was restricted. No one else was around when he backed the vehicle into a space. He had scouted out the spot previously and knew it was directly beneath the section of the building where the most damage to the most people would occur.

The Fire Company warned Grumman that his contact had a problem with 'collateral' damage. He was to play along, and pretend ignition would occur when that part of the building would be unoccupied.

Whatever.

Chapter 44
Washington, DC

James Lucas lived alone. Now, leaving the doctor's office, he realized he would die alone.

James' modest brick rowhouse on Capitol Hill seemed emptier than ever. Ava, his wife, passed away five years ago, one year after their daughter Julie graduated from college. Julie moved to Atlanta where she met and married a man from work. She kept in touch after her mother died, but now, as she settled into a new life of her own, James felt her slowly vanish from his.

He poured himself a scotch and leaned back on the couch, taking stock of the recent news. The doctor reported James had pancreatic cancer, late stage. He recommended chemotherapy but held little hope that it would extend his life. No way he was going through that. Ava tortured herself with chemo ten years ago for ovarian cancer, and for what? It got her anyway.

James reflected on their life together. They met in college. He was ROTC with an eye on becoming an officer in the Marines; she, pre-law, with her sights set on immigration law. Upon graduation, they married in the college chapel. James became a lieutenant in the Marines and entered flight school, learning to handle choppers. Ava studied law remotely, a daunting challenge. But when the Marines sent James to the Middle East, Ava stayed behind and entered law school full-time for two years. James returned for R&R but requested redeployment to allow Ava to finish law school unhindered.

James finished his tours as a captain assigned to Joint Base Andrews. Ava got a job with a law firm in nearby Washington. It wasn't immigration law, but corporate. Not her first pick, but the pay was good and the location great. Finally, James and Ava were together like a proper couple. James flew Marine One and, being the president's main ride locally, his assignment would likely keep him in the DC area for years. It was time to start a family.

Their daughter was born within their first year in DC, and the new parents decided they needed more space for their budding family. Ava had a salary that could cover a down payment on a Capitol Hill rowhouse fixer upper. James found he had a knack for carpentry. Ava loved painting the rooms, starting with a nursery for their baby daughter.

James got to know several security people while flying the president. Most were secret service, but several were FBI. It was a friend in the FBI who offered him a job as an FBI Tactical Aviation Pilot. He would fly choppers, but instead of taxi service for high-level dignitaries, he would support surveillance and SWAT teams. James was retirement eligible and was all-in.

James relished his work as a special agent and pilot. He flew teams into domestic hot spots that reminded him of his days flying into war zones. Much milder, but exciting enough. Meanwhile, Ava's career flourished, and their daughter was becoming a young lady. It was the best of days.

Then Ava got sick. Their grown daughter was already settling into her life in Atlanta. She took time off when mom was going through chemo. That treatment extended Ava's life a little. The next time their daughter came home was for her mother's funeral.

James continued with his work another four years flying choppers. He volunteered for additional assignments no matter where they were. He had to stay busy. Then came the annual physical he needed to pass to continue flying. He failed. His blood pressure was too high, so he started medication to lower it. In the meantime, his surveillance work would have to be done from the seat of a car.

He wanted to fly again and decided to go for a comprehensive physical. He did it with his private doctor, just to be sure the FBI didn't get the details if the results were bad. His blood pressure was fine, but something far more serious was diagnosed. That was what led to the fatal diagnosis. James asked the doctor to keep the results confidential. He wanted to work until he dropped.

Chapter 45
Washington, DC

Nick booked rooms for Tanner, Lizzy, and himself at the Willard off Pennsylvania Avenue. Nick never intended to be in the same city as Rachael. He wanted to honor her need for space and didn't want her to know he was there. Rachael was traumatized by Nick stabbing a man to death in their room. Until she came to terms with it, he didn't want her involved in something that might have a similar ending.

FBI Agent James Lucas contacted Nick soon after MI6 had alerted the FBI. He arranged for himself and his partner, Agent Ralph Newsom, to meet in Nick's hotel suite. But before the agents arrived, Nick asked Tanner and Lizzy to drop by. Now that Tom had extended direct access by cell phone, Nick took advantage of Omni to learn more about the agents.

James Lucas, age fifty-four, was a hockey player in college and a Marine officer after that. Nick saw a grin of appreciation from Tanner at the thought the agent was a vet like him. He was the father of an adult daughter and husband to a wife who passed away five years ago. What Omni discovered about Lucas was information the FBI would never make public. The agent had recently been diagnosed with stage four pancreatic cancer. His doctors noted his general robust health masked that he had a tough time ahead of him.

Omni reported Ralph Newsom, age thirty-three, had a more limited career. He was recruited right out of college and had served the FBI for ten years. He was definitely the apprentice to his partner. No wife. No children.

When the agents arrived, Nick saw a man in Lucas that hardly looked sick. He was a compact figure under six feet with a military posture and no-

nonsense bearing. Agent Newsom, although the same height, was lean and wiry.

Nick introduced the agents to Tanner and Lizzy. Tanner was his usual unexpressive self, but Nick suspected he wanted to compare notes with Lucas on overseas experiences. Nick recapped what they knew about the situation, most of it a repeat of their initial phone conversation.

When he finished, Lucas looked to Tanner. "I understand you've seen Grumman."

"Yes, more than once," responded Tanner.

"We want you to go with us to ID him. Is that OK?"

"You have a photo of him?" asked Nick.

Nick was pretty sure they didn't since he had asked Omni for a recent photo of the man, and she had only been able to access a photo of him as a teenager.

"No," responded Lucas. "Only as a young man. He's the ideal terrorist. No criminal record, not much of a record at all. MI6 reported that the suspect killed in Paris, the one responsible for the London Eye firebombing, said the attack here in the States had something to do with 'the planets.' We are working on what that might mean."

Nick wasn't surprised; he'd already asked Omni for a connection. Omni was a wealth of information, but she lacked analytical tools. Lateral thinking was not in her wired DNA.

Nick wanted to tell the FBI about Omni and how it could help, but that would only be a diversion they could not afford.

Tanner spent time with a sketch artist at FBI headquarters and was able to come up with a decent drawing of Grumman. Agents began sharing the drawing with security groups at public places in Maryland, DC, and Virginia. Later that day, with Tanner and Lizzy in the hotel, Nick shared it with Omni.

"Omni," Nick said, "gain access to security cameras within one-hundred miles of my location and tell me if you see a person who looks like the drawing I am showing you now."

"Right away," responded Omni.

Omni had a response within one minute, but it was a disappointing one.

"The drawing is too vague for accurate facial recognition," she reported. "I have a wide range of qualifying subjects. Please show me a photograph or the person himself."

"That's the best we have," replied Nick.

Omni took the initiative. "Then I will assemble possible suspects to narrow the search."

"Could we see the collection you now have?" Nick asked hopefully, thinking that human eyes could help.

"I have nine-million, four-hundred and thirty thousand, two-hundred and ten videos in the collection. How would you like them delivered?"

Lizzy rolled her eyes.

Nick, aghast at the quantity, sadly replied, "Never mind."

While Nick was conversing with Omni, Tanner took a call. Nick and Lizzy heard Tanner's end of the conversation.

"Ok, yes. That's right. That's what I told you. OK. Good news."

Tanner ended the call and told Nick and Lizzy what was going on.

"That was Agent Lucas. Looks like the human touch came through for us this time. A security guard at The Air and Space Museum saw a man matching the description. He followed him outside. He had an odd habit of flicking a Bic lighter."

"That's promising," said Nick.

"There's more. The museum is showing a movie in their IMAX theatre. Has a name we might be interested in."

Lizzy had a smug look as though she could guess, but asked, "What's it called?"

"The Planets."

Chapter 46
Washington, DC

The Four Seasons Hotel restaurant was bustling. A premiere establishment in Georgetown for the movers and shakers of Washington, DC; for Rachael, it was Angie's treat. Rachael guessed Angie wanted to lift her spirits; she realized she wasn't being an easy guest. Over cocktails, the women shared observations about men. Rachael mentioned her affair with a guitar player in Cambridge. Gorgeous guy, good lover, but dense like lead. Angie talked further about the guy in her apartment building. Nice guy, but she didn't want to get serious about someone down the hall.

They drank and enjoyed a calamari appetizer, but mainly, they drank. Rachael noticed a large man come in with a couple. The man stood out, not only for his hefty bearing, but his dress. He wore a suit with a bolo tie and a gray Stetson cowboy hat. The maître d' gushed over the party.

"Who is that?" she asked Angie.

Angie turned to look. She didn't know the complete slate of characters in Washington politics, but this man was known around the Energy Department. "That's Rex Richardson. He's big in the energy field."

"Who's that with him?"

With Richardson was a tall man with trim sandy hair and a ready, highly enameled smile and with him, a middle-aged blonde with well-scrubbed good looks. "They look like a senator and his wife," surmised Rachael.

"I don't know," replied Angie, "but you're probably right."

Rex Richardson, a Texan through and through, had worked his way up in an oil company to CEO, a job he held for years until Exxon bought the company. He took the rich rewards amassed from that buy-out to found a diversified company that retained interests in alternative sources of energy, plus a medical division that brought new drugs to market. Rex named his company Potestas and was seeking ways to build his brand. Hence, the purpose of tonight's meeting.

Senator Pete Morrison was a senator from New Mexico and his wife Denise Anderson, besides running a horse ranch near Santa Fe, sat on the board of The Kennedy Center. Denise was seeking corporate sponsorships for the Center. She was aware her husband had done some sort of business with Rex and begged him to arrange the meeting. Pete reluctantly agreed.

The maître d' showed the group to their table in a private dining room. Rex ordered a bourbon on the rocks. Pete had an old fashioned and Denise a glass of wine.

They took a quick look at their menus and set them aside. Pete started the conversation. "Rex, what have you been up to lately?"

"Well, we have folks looking for an energy source in the Adriatic. You know, lots of underwater work."

Pete assumed Rex meant oil exploration, but it was odd he used the phrase 'energy source.'

Did he mean geothermal or something of the sort?

Since Pete knew Rex played things fast and loose, he thought better of asking. 'Deniability' was his watch word.

Rex turned his attention to Denise. "But it is this lovely lady I want to talk to tonight."

Rex was widowed; Pete and Denise attended his wife's funeral six years ago. His company was bought out the next year and Rex went from being rich to being obscenely rich. Pete had heard that Rex had put everything into this new venture, and Pete suspected he was attempting to fill a hole in his life. Something else happened. Afterwards, Rex became a different man. Sure, he was still gregarious and larger than life. The cowboy persona was not all for show. Yet, Pete saw a new dark side to the man. Put simply, Rex had become mean.

But it was the cavalier cowboy with them tonight, fortunately.

Rex began with personal chit-chat. "Denise, I heard you went up to Cody to the auction. Get any new horses?"

"No, but I ran into an old friend, Joanie Fitzwell. Do you know her?"

"Can't say I do."

"She runs a ranch in California. There was a recent fire in her area."

"I hope she's all right."

"She is. I called her. She hurt her foot, but otherwise fine. She's tough."

Denise got down to business. "Rex," she said, "I want to talk more about what we discussed on the phone."

Rex smiled. "OK."

"As you know, I'm on the board of The Kennedy Center. The National Symphony Orchestra reached out to me. They are starting a new season and the director wants to raise awareness of the NSO. Do you remember Great Performances on PBS sponsored by Mobil?"

"Indeed, I do. My wife loved them."

"These performances lifted the status of Mobil, and the branding was so strong, people thought Mobil sponsored Great Performances long after the relationship ended. That's what I want to offer to Potestas."

Rex provided Denise with a thoughtful frown and said, "Tell me how that would work."

"We would start with Potestas announcing the company is underwriting the season," and in an aside to appeal to his business interest, "it would be a fraction of the cost of something like buying the naming rights to a stadium."

"How much?"

"I'll leave you with a proposal you and your people can review."

Rex grinned. "That much, huh?"

Denise laid her hand on Rex's arm. "Rex, it's affordable, and it's a good deal."

Rex looked toward Pete. "I pity the person doing horse deals with this woman."

"Rex," said Denise, "there is something else. The season starts soon. I would love for you to make the announcement on stage at The Kennedy Center just prior to the performance. It's a special event, and PBS is taping it for broadcast. I will make sure they include your remarks."

Rex showed his discomfort. He preferred to work one-on-one and, when needed, in the background. Rex had his share of standing in front of stockholders and others, reading prepared statements. He thought that's what we had politicians for, to be the front men for special interests.

"I don't know about that," he said.

"Please, Rex. You'll be great."

Pete knew Rex couldn't resist Denise's charm. "OK," he said. "Let my people take a look at the numbers. If they make sense, we're in."

Denise glowed. Pete had wrangled with the savage beast inside Rex, and he admired how his wife made him positively docile. He picked up his cocktail glass. "To great beginnings," he toasted.

Rex and Denise responded with their glasses held high.

Chapter 47

London

Ray arranged to meet Lenoir at a bar around the corner from his Kensington house. It was a place where he could sit with the latest addition to The Fire Company in relative privacy. The table near the window was set apart from the main barroom, and Ray tipped the bartender well to ensure he was left alone.

Karl Lenoir walked past the window where Ray was sitting. Ray had been given a rough description of the man, but in the flesh, unlike Roland who looked just as Ray expected, Lenoir's appearance disconcerted Ray. The name Lenoir, with its French origins, was fitting for a man with dark hair and dark eyes. Despite being a man in his twenties, Lenoir resembled a moody teenager.

When Lenoir walked into the bar, Ray caught his eye and waved him over to his table. Lenoir acted sullen, too — as though Ray was the stern father he resented.

"Do you want anything to drink?" Ray asked.

"No," responded Lenoir.

Ray had no drink of his own, so he began with, "The Fire Company thought you could do this job."

"I can," Lenoir said as if there was no question about it.

"Look, let's walk to the site. It's not far from here."

Ray knew better than to talk details on the street, so he tried to get a better idea of who this man was. "I understand you worked in a bakery with Aiden Hayes," he said.

"That's right."

Ray was uncomfortable with the next question, albeit a natural one for a member of The Fire Company. He felt dirty, as though he was attempting to see if another person shared a particular fetish. Still, he had to ask.

"So, you like fire?"

Lenoir, continuing to walk with Ray, turned to him and said, "I like it."

The words were bland, but for the first time, Ray saw a gleam in those dark, moody eyes. Ray chose not to pursue it further but ached to do so.

Keep it professional.

They stopped in front of the Royal Albert Hall, the location for the job. They circled the huge, round structure. The streets were empty, so Ray talked more freely.

"This part of the building is where the stage is located. Is it here where you plan to put the device?" asked Ray

"It's already here."

"What?" Ray was surprised. This operation seemed to be going forward without him. "Where?"

"There's a green room behind the stage. Two soda machines are there. Both are now marked 'out of order.'"

"You put them there?" asked Ray.

"I once had a job servicing vending machines. The Company provided a vehicle, uniform, and specially equipped replacements. The rest was easy."

More and more, Ray suspected he'd been sidelined. He understood this was a more traditional job for The Fire Company, and the commission and planning were arranged long before his California job. He still couldn't understand why he was being kept out of the loop.

"How is it rigged?" asked Ray. "What mechanism are you using for setting it off?"

The moody Lenoir suddenly smiled, relishing his telling of details.

248

"It's quite a marvel," said Lenoir. "You see, it is cell phone activated, but the device has an extra level of protection."

"What do you mean?"

"We probably won't need it, but it's protected should a bomb squad show up. You see, most bomb experts tote around a cell phone scrambler. They can scramble all cell phone signals within a small range."

"Rendering it harmless, right?" asked Ray.

"Right." Lenoir's smile widened. "But this beauty has some reverse logic. Once armed, it must have a cell phone signal maintained. If two minutes goes by without one, it detonates."

Ray wasn't sure he got as much enjoyment over this detail as Lenoir was obviously getting, but he had one question. "This is pretty sophisticated stuff. You did all this?"

"I put it all together, but the electronics were supplied by someone else in The Company."

"Who?"

"Don't know. Somebody named Virgil is all I know."

Ray had no idea who this Virgil could be, but he had one last question. "You said this is activated once you arm it. How do you arm it?"

"It's the coin return button," replied Lenoir. "You press it three times and then hold it down for two seconds. You know dot-dot-dot-dah."

"What?"

"It's Beethoven's Fifth. What a hoot."

Ray didn't relish what the famous opening of Beethoven's Fifth represented.

Death knocking at the door.

"What did you get?" asked Paul.

Paul and the agents assisting him stationed themselves at critical points for the Woodward and Lenoir meeting. An agent positioned himself at a bus stop across the street from the bar where the two men met. That man had a directional listening device that could pick up the conversation at the bar. Jennifer Martin, pushing a pram, followed Woodward and Lenoir as they walked down the street. Paul hoped she could stay on the men's tail, but she had to peel off when the crowd on the street diminished around the Royal Albert Hall. They planned backup for such an eventuality. Two men, parked in a UPS van listened in on the conversation at the Hall.

Now, back at their Vauxhall offices, they each reported in turn. The bar conversation was brief and uneventful. Jennifer overheard nothing of consequence. It was the two men in the van who had captured concrete details of what was afoot.

Neither of the men from the van appeared eager to take their turn. At last, one of them said, "We got some information, but most of it was garbled."

Paul wished he had access to all the perfectly engineered gadgets available to James Bond. Reality was far more disappointing.

"So, what did you get?"

"They talked about planning to put 'a device' in the hall. After that they may have said where and when. The people in the lab are still attempting to un-mangle that part. But it was clear they will detonate it with a cell phone."

"So, we *suspect* they will plant some explosive device in the Royal Albert Hall. That may be the case, since these two men were there, at the Hall, when they talked about it. And we *think* this Lenoir fellow will detonate it with a cell phone." Paul looked at the sheepish agents around the table, none of whom could face him. "Is that about it?"

Paul laid out the next steps. "First, we notify the Met to keep a tight guard on Royal Albert Hall, starting tonight. I'll take care of that." He looked at the woman. "Jennifer, tail Lenoir. I want to know where he is every minute of his life."

250

"Yes, sir," responded Jennifer.

"As for me," said Paul, "I'm going to continue keeping tabs on my friendly neighbor, Mr. Woodward."

Chapter 48

London

MI6 Agent Jennifer Martin took the Tube to East London where Lenoir had a flat. She asked around and found the flat was a short-term rental. That made sense since it was in the Spitalfields area in the East End, a hipster location where a young man could blend in unnoticed. Hiding among the Eating London tours sampling one ethnic outlet after another, she spotted Lenoir stepping out of his flat and into the crowd. Jennifer melted into the flow as Lenoir strolled past. She followed him through deserted streets.

Lenoir turned onto Wilkes Street, a lane lined on either side with rows of three-story Victorian townhouses. Long deserted, these houses were now being brought back to life. Save for Lenoir, the street was deserted. Jennifer hid around a corner, peering out carefully. She saw Lenoir enter one of the houses and she went to it.

Despite her instructions to just follow and report, she had to see what Lenoir was up to. The door to the house was standing ajar.

She entered the house to find a wide-open space with a table saw in the middle, some pieces of wood framing waiting to be cut and nailed up, but nothing else. Jennifer heard muffled sounds coming from the second level at the top of newly installed stairs. She crept up the stairs and peeked just above the landing. She saw nothing but an empty room with a fresh wood floor installed. There was a sawhorse in the middle of the room, an old chair, and drop cloths spread over one corner of the room where the ceiling had been patched.

Jennifer entered the room. Everything was silent.

Where could he have gone?

She walked to a front window and looked out into the road. The view of the street was the last thing she remembered before everything went dark.

Her head felt like an elephant had stomped on it. Jennifer struggled to open her eyes as the twilight filtering through dusty windows signaled she had been unconscious for hours. Confused, as though someone had wakened her from her slumber, she shortly realized a snooze in bed would not now have her strapped by the ankles to a chair with her hands tied behind her.

"Hello, sleepyhead," said the dark figure sitting in a chair before her, his face gradually coming into focus.

Lenoir!

Karl Lenoir sat before her with a burning candle in a simple holder on a small table to his left. Her chair, his, and the table were the only furnishings in the room. Lenoir smiled.

"What do you want?"

"I want to show you a trick," said Lenoir.

With that, Lenoir lit a wooden match. It was not a safety match, but an old fashioned one he could set ablaze with a flick of his fingernail, which he did adroitly. He turned the match, studying the flame, and then smiled again. He leaned over to the burning candle and snuffed the flame with a pinch. The smoke rose from the extinguished candle in a thick gray spindle. Lenoir held the lit match in the smoke a foot above the candle. The flame lit the smoke, chased it down to the candle wick, relighting it.

"I love that trick. Fire is such a lovely thing, don't you think?"

Jennifer said nothing.

"Fire," Lenoir said, "cleanses. It provides an opportunity for renewal. It is something so fundamental to humans. No wonder we think it is the first and greatest discovery."

Lenoir stood from his chair and silently walked to a small red canister with a spout that Jennifer had failed to notice. When he removed the spout, Jennifer immediately smelled petrol. Lenoir paced a small circle around her chair, encircling her with a ring of the liquid. The smell made her nauseous. Then Lenoir repeated the process making a wider ring.

Lenoir returned to his seat, the candle still burning to his left. "Now," he said, "Let's play another little game. I'm not expecting you to spill the beans on who you work for, but I'm good at reading people, a human lie detector, if you will. I'm going to ask you questions and read your reactions. Ready?"

Jennifer said nothing and remained as stoic as possible.

"Let's see. Do you work for law enforcement?"

Jennifer remained quiet.

"OK. Let's add some excitement," Lenoir said as he took the candle from the table and flicked the flame with his finger, landing it onto the outer circle of the liquid. The circle quickly completed its route, encircling Jennifer in flames a foot high. Lenoir had left a break in the circle where he sat, so he had an unobstructed view of his victim.

"OK," he said. "Once again, do you work for law enforcement?"

"Yes," Jennifer said, now terrified and cognizant of the center, much closer circle of fuel.

"That's the girl. Now, which part of law enforcement? Scotland Yard?"

"No," said Jennifer.

"Higher?" asked Lenoir.

Jennifer remained silent.

"Well, I do believe MI5 or MI6 is on the case. Am I wrong?"

Jennifer said nothing, but Lenoir could read the answer in her eyes.

"Jennifer, thank you. You've been of big help."

"Release me," pleaded Jennifer.

Lenoir stood. "Ah, my dear girl. I wish I could, but what fun would that be?" Lenoir picked up the candle and threw it onto the inner circle. The flames raced around Jennifer.

"I wish I could stick around, but I think it best I leave before the fire engines get here. It's been a pleasure. Goodbye."

With that, Lenoir left the building.

Chapter 49

London

Tom arrived at Paul's flat late in the day. Paul greeted him, offered food and drink, but Tom declined. Paul laid out everything about the case. He wasted no time in getting to the point.

"No offense, but it's really the Omni I'm after."

"None taken," said Tom, "but I got the feeling you weren't impressed by what she's been able to do."

"Let's just say I'm becoming more of a fan."

"Then," replied Tom, "how can we help?"

Paul spent an uneventful evening listening to dead silence in Ray's place. Recently, Paul's solo surveillance had been expanded to a team of two other men who now shared Paul's flat and who also listened to nothing. No calls. No conversations. Nothing.

"What's Lenoir's status?" asked Paul of the two men. "Has Jennifer checked in?"

"No, not yet," said the man whose job it was to keep tabs on Jennifer's progress.

"I don't like this. I don't like this one bit," snapped Paul.

The door opened, and the team looked up to see Tom join them. Paul had passed Tom off as American intelligence brought in as a data systems specialist. Paul agreed with Tom that too many questions would be raised if Tom were to talk to Omni in their presence; he would communicate with her via text messages.

The agent wearing headphones and eavesdropping on Ray's

telephone, interrupted. "We have a call. I'm putting it on speaker."

The phone rang for a long time. At last, a man with an old crusty voice answered, "Hello?"

"It's Ray."

"Well, hello, Ray. Tonight's the night, eh?"

"I'm not happy about this job."

"Why not?"

"Look, I've thought this over ever since I met with Lenoir."

"Lenoir!" gushed the old man. "The man has done a top-notch job so far, hasn't he?"

"Yeah, yeah. But I don't like being left out of the loop."

"Whatever do you mean?"

Paul and the agents didn't know who Ray was talking to, but it was clear the old man on the line was playing dumb.

"Well, for one thing. The device is already planted. I was not told."

Paul and the men working with him all looked at each other with surprise. Authorities were guarding the Hall round-the-clock against something that had already been placed.

But where?

"You were a busy man," responded the old man. "We had it taken care of."

There was a pause. Ray must have been considering something further to ask.

"Tell me. The detonation will be very late tonight after everyone has cleared the performance. Right?"

Silence from the old man.

"Tell me you're not setting it off during the performance."

"Ray, listen to reason..." pleaded the old man.

Ray's voice grew with rage. "How could you?"

"Ray..."

Ray hung up.

Paul quickly summarized the missing pieces they learned. "So, they talked about a performance. It wasn't a coincidence they were talking at the Royal Albert Hall; it's bound to be there. We know the device is already placed. But we don't know where the triggerman is. Dammit! Where is Jennifer?"

The man charged with keeping tabs on her said, "She last checked in at Spitalfields."

"Get over there. Now! Track her down, or better still, find Lenoir."

"But where's the device?" asked the other man. "The Hall is huge."

Tom reviewed floor plans of the Hall pulled by Omni.

Paul looked at his watch. "We have only three hours before people will gather for the performance. Contact HQ and have someone get over there and stop the concert and evacuate the building."

Paul reached for his jacket and put it on. As he checked his pistol and returned it to its holster, he said, "I'm going to have a chat with my neighbor. Tom, come with me."

The butler must have had the night off. It was Ray who answered the door. "Paul?"

"We need to talk."

"Of course," responded Ray. "Come in."

"This is my friend, Tom Littleton," Paul said.

As Ray closed the door, he said, "What can I do for...?"

Paul cut him off. "We've been listening next door to your phone conversations. We know everything."

Paul saw in Ray's face a mixture of confusion followed by something almost akin to relief — as though relieved of an unbearable burden. Ray no doubt understood Paul was not who he'd pretended to be. The entire realization came crashing down by Paul's simple statement.

"So, you know everything. What organization are you with?"

Paul produced identification. "There are missing pieces, things we didn't hear. We need your help."

"Okay."

"Where is the device?"

"It's in two vending machines near the green room behind the stage."

Paul looked at Tom who gave a quick nod.

"Where's Lenoir?"

"I have no idea. Look, Paul, I never intended to harm anyone. Property damage only."

Paul cut him off. "We'll have time for all that later. We have a bomb to find and a bomber to stop."

Chapter 50

London

On the morning of July 7, 2005, a series of bombs exploded on three London Underground trains. One hour later, a fourth bomb exploded on the upper deck of a bus in Tavistock Square. The attacks were the work of four suicide bombers. It marked the deadliest bombings in London since World War II and the first suicide attacks in modern Western Europe.

Howard Long was an inexperienced, twenty-four-year-old recruit to the London police. Fate placed him in a brand-new uniform that day at Tavistock Square when the bus exploded. He was ill-equipped to deal with the scene and the horror of the victims. But it set him on a new trajectory. He applied to train in the Counter Terrorism Command's Explosive Ordnance Disposal unit — or the EOD for short. That put the young Howard Long on the path to become a leading expert on disarming bombs.

Fifteen years later, Howard Long found himself standing before two vending machines in the Royal Albert Hall. The machines were too large to be transferred to a bomb box where an explosion could be contained. He hesitated to move the machines since they might have a motion trigger. He had to open them up, but would that trigger an explosion?

He explained all of this to Paul Allerton. With Paul was Tom and Ray who'd had to push their way through the crowds and the confused musicians, holding their instruments, to reach Howard.

The evacuation of three-thousand employees and ticket holders already inside the building complicated their work. An announcement that the evening's performance had been cancelled didn't expedite a mass exit. However, when a second announcement mentioned the words 'bomb threat,' people miraculously picked up their pace.

A dark-haired man stood across the street on the edge of Kensington Gardens and watched the crowds leaving the hall on their way back home.

"Do any of you know anything about what we're dealing with?" Howard asked.

"I know it's a fertilizer bomb with napalm," answered Ray.

That shocked Howard. "Napalm? You can't be serious."

"I'm afraid I am," answered Ray. "The people responsible for this are all about fire. Just an explosion won't do."

"Can we open the vending machine door without setting it off?"

"I don't know."

"How is it set off?"

"A cell phone calls it," said Ray.

"Are you sure?"

"Yes."

The Hall's building manager stood by nervously ringing his hands. He implemented the evacuation and had returned here to see if any progress had been made. He stood some distance away, motioning for Paul to come over to him.

"Ray," said Paul, "I've got to talk to the building manager. Come with me. I want to keep you close by."

Paul and Ray walked over to the building manager. From the other side, a bomb squad assistant wheeled in something that appeared to be a large, military grade piece of carry-on luggage.

"What's that?" Tom asked Howard.

"It's a cell phone scrambler."

The Albert Memorial sits directly north of Royal Albert Hall in Kensington

Gardens. It comprises a canopy resembling a 176-foot-tall sandcastle, with a golden statue of the prince beneath it looking toward the Hall named after him.

In front of the gates guarding steps to the memorial, stood Karl Lenoir. Lenoir took out his cell phone. He froze when he felt the cold steel of a revolver against the back of his neck.

"Drop the phone," said Jennifer Martin.

Lenoir held up his hands, one holding the cell phone where Jennifer could see it. "I recognize that voice," he said. "Shouldn't you be toast by now?"

"Escaping Bindings 101. One of the first thing they teach us. Now, I'll take this," she said as she leaned over and grabbed the phone. Lenoir took advantage of her momentarily being off balance, rotated, and knocked her gun out of the way. He took off running. Jennifer aimed her gun at the fleeing man, yelling "Stop!" Seeing crowds scattering in fright, she lowered her weapon and took off chasing Lenoir as he dashed into the park.

Paul finished assuring the building manager that all was under control, although he wasn't sure that was the case. He and Ray walked back to Howard, who now had the cell phone scrambler set up and operating.

"What's that?" asked Ray.

"A cell phone scrambler. Now, we're safe."

"No, we're not!" yelled Ray. "Turn it off! Turn it off!"

"What?" asked the confused Howard.

"Turn it off!"

Paul, trusting Ray, joined in. "Turn it off!" he commanded.

Howard switched it off. "OK. It's off. You mind telling me why?"

"The thing is rigged so that if two minutes goes by without a cell phone signal, it detonates!"

Howard, now wide-eyed, could only say, "Bugger!" He quickly recovered and asked, "Do we know where the person may be that intends to call in tonight?"

"I got a call from one of my agents," Paul responded. "She has spotted the man."

"Well," said Howard, "let's hope she apprehends him before... Well, just let's hope."

Lenoir ran down a wide path with Jennifer far behind. She saw him dart down a smaller path to the right, but lost sight of him behind a grove of trees. As she raced down the path, she spotted Lenoir and another man a few yards ahead of Lenoir talking to someone on a cell phone. She knew what was going to happen next.

Lenoir ran full bore into the man, knocking him to the ground. Lenoir reached down, grabbed the cell phone the man dropped and took off again. Jennifer was too far away to take a clean shot, especially with the man Lenoir knocked down getting up and dusting himself off, blocking the way.

A greenhouse came into view. She saw Lenoir duck inside.

I must get him before he dials!

She entered the greenhouse carefully, her pistol gripped in both hands. Jennifer didn't know if Lenoir had a weapon, but she wasn't taking any chances.

She walked among the trays of plantings, seeing no trace of the man. Then, behind her, she heard Lenoir. "How nice. You found me."

Jennifer swung around, ready to shoot, but stopped. Lenoir was holding the stolen cell phone in one hand with the index finger from the other poised above it.

"I've put in all the numbers save for the last one," announced Lenoir. "Shoot me and it will be the last thing I do. But if you have to shoot, please do it in the body. I would at least have the pleasure of hearing the explosion and perhaps, if I'm lucky, see the glow of the burning Hall before I bleed out."

"You're mad."

"Not mad, my dear. Neurotic, yes. Crazy, no."

Jennifer didn't understand why Lenoir squelched his opportunity to complete his dialing. He was too dramatic for his own good, and Jennifer was a trained marksman. It was no match. Jennifer shot the phone from Lenoir's hand, taking two fingers with it. Lenoir yelled in pain. He reached into his jacket and lobbed a small canister toward her. It exploded just beyond her and hit a small tree that burst into flames.

Lenoir escaped into another part of the greenhouse. Jennifer now needed only to follow a trail of blood. She saw Lenoir duck into a utility room stocked with wheelbarrows and garden tools. Unfortunately, the room contained the only other person in the greenhouse, a frightened man in overalls working late. He had before him a man badly bleeding from a mangled hand demanding he hand over his cell phone. When Jennifer arrived, the worker had passed Lenoir his phone.

Jennifer was taking no chances this time. She yelled, "Lenoir!" When Lenoir turned, she pumped two bullets into his chest.

She carefully walked over to the supine body. "It's OK," Jennifer told the worker. "SIS," she added, flashing her badge.

She kneeled beside Lenoir as blood poured from him. He looked up. "Well," he said as he coughed on blood, "you gave me what I asked for, but you forgot to let me make the call. Now how am I going to enjoy the blaze?"

"There's going to be no blaze tonight," responded Jennifer.

Lenoir coughed a weak laugh. "Ah, but the night is young," he said. "The planets align elsewhere on the globe. There will be flames, glorious flames, I think I can see them."

"What do you mean?" Jennifer demanded. "What planets?"

But Lenoir was dead.

Chapter 51

London

Jennifer called Paul and told him the bomb threat was over. She then left the crime scene to the regular patrols and retraced her steps through Kensington Gardens back to the Royal Albert Hall.

"Now that you've removed the threat of a phone call," said Howard, "we can set about x-raying these beasts and disarming them."

Jennifer said, "Lenoir said something troubling. We may not be out of the woods yet."

"What's that?" asked Paul.

"Before he died, I told him there would be no blaze tonight. He said, 'the night is young, the planets align elsewhere on the globe.'"

"What the devil does that mean?" asked Paul.

Ray looked pale. "Oh, no."

"What?" demanded Paul.

"It all makes sense now," admitted Ray. "A partner told me that an agent of ours would work the planets job in the US."

"But what is the planets job?" asked Paul.

Tom intervened. "Didn't you notice what they were playing tonight?" he asked.

"Gustav Holst," replied Paul.

Jennifer made the connection. "It's Gustav Holst's *The Planets Suite*."

Tom had used Omni as a reference guide during the evening's events; however, Omni had been listening to everything. She took over and sent Tom a text message. Tom read the message to everyone. "Tonight was a celebration of Holst's masterpiece. It will also be performed tonight by the

National Symphony Orchestra."

"Where?"

"The Kennedy Center in Washington, DC."

Jennifer glanced at her watch, "It's already five pm in their time zone. We've got to alert the FBI!"

Tom took out his cell phone. "Come on, come on," Tom said as he impatiently waited for an answer.

"Hello."

"Nick, listen to me. Are you at the Air and Space Museum?"

"Yes. The FBI have their people hidden all around here waiting for Grumman."

"Nick, that's the wrong place."

"What?" exclaimed Nick. "Hold on, Tom. I've got Tanner and Lizzy with me. I'm going to put you on speakerphone."

"It's not about the IMAX movie. 'The Planets' is about Gustav Holst's orchestral suite. The National Symphony Orchestra is performing it tonight. Someone tried to blow up Royal Albert Hall for the same performance."

"Someone has it in for Gustav Holst?" Nick asked incredulously.

"Apparently, but we have it on good authority that The Kennedy Center is targeted tonight."

"OK. I'll tell the FBI agents here. We'll be in touch."

Lizzy was stunned. "Oh, no."

Tanner asked, "What is it?"

"I texted Rachael a couple of days ago, just to see how her trip was going. Didn't hear from her. I just now noticed she returned my message. I responded, but her phone must be off. She's going to be at The Kennedy Center tonight."

Chapter 52
Washington, DC

Rex Richardson gripped his traditional bourbon as he glad-handed the NSO's event planner. The planner gushed over how lucky they were to have him; in return, Rex gulped his bourbon and smiled weakly. Denise sensed his discomfort, aware he didn't relish the role of courted benefactor. She moved quickly toward him. "Rex, you must come with me. I don't believe you've met the NSO's artistic director yet."

Denise walked Rex through the entire process. She thought it was the least she could do. After all, she had twisted his arm to ensure this lunch meeting at The Kennedy Center restaurant. Pete had most of the dealings with Rex; this was the first time Denise had exchanged more than a passing party quip with him. Pete warned Denise that Rex's good-old-boy veneer hid a ruthless businessman. Perhaps in his wheeling-dealing world that was so, but here, Rex acted more the docile house cat than the pouncing mountain lion.

The event planner outlined the running order for the next evening. The NSO director would come on stage first. He would announce the 'Great Composers of the 20th Century' series. This performance would be a celebration of Holst's masterpiece, and it was being performed in London the same evening by the Royal Philharmonic Orchestra. He would announce the generous sponsorship by Rex's company, then wait until the applause subsided. Then Rex would be introduced and come on stage to more applause. Rex would deliver a few words that his people had prepared, and he would leave the stage with the artistic director.

The event planner smiled as she finished. She had done such things a thousand times. Rex looked to Denise as if to say 'help.'

"Don't worry," said Denise. "Pete and I will be there."

Chapter 53
Washington, DC

Rex Richardson reviewed his speech as he waited in the stage wings. Denise Anderson knew he just wanted to get this over with and go home. She hoped that her presence with him backstage at The Concert Hall helped in some small way to calm his nerves.

Denise gazed out into the auditorium with pride. The Kennedy Center Concert Hall was a masterpiece of design, built with wood and brass, materials associated with musical instruments. Crystal chandeliers, a gift from Norway, dripped from the ceiling. An open stage for the orchestra framed pipes at the rear for a multimillion-dollar organ. Rosewood panels, hanging in precise spacing above the stage, ensured excellent acoustics.

The hall was filled to its 2,200-seat capacity for the premier of the NSO season. The orchestra had taken its place on the stage risers and had conducted a preliminary tuning as the audience quieted. The director of the NSO greeted Rex and Denise in the stage right wing ten minutes before the performance. As the orchestra completed its tuning, the director walked on stage to the polite applause of the audience.

"Good evening," said the director as the applause abated. "My name is Robert Logan, and it is my honor to be the director of the National Symphony Orchestra. Tonight, we celebrate the opening of the NSO season with a performance of Gustav Holst's masterpiece, *The Planets.*"

Tucked away on the upper levels of The Kennedy Center sat Jason Young in front of an array of security monitors. Jason had a lonely job as a security guard under contract with The Kennedy Center. A prolific pulp reader and music lover, the job suited him just fine. However, this night, Jason paid special attention to the monitor playing CNN.

One monitor was tied into the stage camera. He loved classical music and watched as the NSO director made his introductions. He, perhaps like much of the public, was unfamiliar with *The Planets* and looked forward to its performance. To one side, a monitor displayed CNN. He saw the screen crawler noting something about *The Planets*. Jason turned up the sound. He caught the reporter in the middle of her report, standing on a dark street in front of a large round building.

"… Authorities are investigating any connection between tonight's performance here at the Royal Albert Hall and the threatened firebombing. Did the perpetrator have some hatred of music, of Gustav Holst's *The Planets*? Or was it just coincidental?"

Jason turned back to the stage camera as he heard the director say, "Tonight, we are celebrating Holst's masterpiece in conjunction with the London Philharmonic which is performing it this evening as well."

Jason needed to know more.

The director continued. "Holst's daughter Imogen recalled that the composer hated incomplete performances of *The Planets*, though frequently he had to agree to conduct three or four movements at Queen's Hall concerts. He particularly disliked having to finish with Jupiter, to make a 'happy ending,' for, as he himself said, 'In the real world the end is not happy at all.'"

Light laughter at Holst's tragic remark sprinkled through the audience as the director continued. "But rest assured, we will perform all movements tonight, just as Holst would have had it. And I think we'll have a happy ending."

"And now, I would like to introduce our sponsor for this season. It is my honor to introduce the Chairman and CEO of Potestas, Mr. Rex Richardson."

A round of perfunctory, polite applause ensued as Rex walked on stage to join the director.

Denise was impressed. Rex waved to the audience and transformed himself. In person, people met a rough, tough, bourbon-swilling cowboy who could alternate between country charm and brutal threats. Tonight, people saw a refined, well-dressed corporate executive devoid of his usual Texas twang. The few words he shared without the aid of written notes were well tuned for an east-coast-big-city audience.

"Hello. Speaking for myself and the team at Potestas, we are pleased to sponsor the National Symphony Orchestra. Music has charms to soothe the savage beast, and some would say I am one who needs a healthy dose of it."

More light laughter.

"At Potestas, we are forward-looking, harnessing clean, green energy for the future. Our medical team is hard at work finding ways to ensure the health and wellbeing of each one of us. All-in-all, Potestas works to make sure *this planet* has a bright tomorrow. Thank you and enjoy the performance."

Rex returned to the wing where Denise waited, applauding. "Rex, very impressive," she said.

Rex returned with a Texas twang, "Just get me to my seat, sweetheart."

As the maestro came on stage, acknowledging applause, Denise guided Rex to their seats on the aisle in the fourth row where Senator Morrison was waiting. The audience quieted, the maestro raised his baton, and the concert began.

Chapter 54
Washington, DC

Two black SUVs raced down Independence Avenue with a Mercedes rental close behind. FBI Agents Newsom and Henderson were in the lead SUV with lights blinking and siren blasting, followed immediately by Agent Lucas and Tanner. Nick and Lizzy brought up the rear in the Mercedes.

Before stepping into their vehicle, Lizzy watched as Newsom called the contact number for security at The Kennedy Center but received no answer.

Henderson turned up Virginia Avenue.

Lizzy asked Nick, "We don't know where the bomb is. Can Omni help?"

"I asked Tom that exact question. He's still in London, but he's at MI6 headquarters and tied into Omni with computers he can program. He's exploring all possibilities. Omni told him she was connecting to surveillance cameras, but she doesn't know who or what she's looking for and for what time period. Tom is working on narrowing things down."

Lizzy kept thinking about Rachael, sitting in the audience. She rang her cell phone, but it was turned off; no doubt because the performance had begun.

Grumman sat on his motorcycle near The Kennedy Center along the curb at the Watergate Hotel. Since a cell phone signal might not reach the bomb, this version was on a timer, and it was now ticking. He intended to pull out at a safe distance at the time of explosion to witness the glory of The Fire Company's handiwork, but for now, he stood guard. If the police had been alerted to what was about to happen, he was ready.

No one on the street could miss the impromptu motorcade coming down Virginia Avenue. Certainly not Grumman, who started his motorcycle.

Time for some fun.

The Saudi Arabian embassy forms an island bifurcating access to The Kennedy Center. The street around to the left of the embassy leads to the front of the Kennedy Center and the one to the right goes to the base of the Center.

The lead SUV made a hard left off Virginia Avenue, and another left past the embassy. The second SUV lagged a few car lengths behind, and Grumman took advantage of that space. He gunned his motorcycle and pulled between the two. The black car, now behind Grumman, slammed on the brakes, but Grumman had already passed to the other side of the street. Grumman was fully equipped with The Fire Company's standard issue. Mini-Molotovs lined the inside of his leather jacket. Before the driver could react, Grumman threw one of them at the car. His aim was perfect. Flames exploded beneath the vehicle from the underside of the engine all the way to the rear.

He looked back over his shoulder as two men leapt clear of the burning car.

Nick saw the explosion but didn't stop. He could see both Lucas and Tanner running after Grumman. Nick made a quick decision and headed to the right. As his Mercedes raced past the abandoned vehicle, the FBI SUV exploded in a fireball, small pieces of debris raining down on the Mercedes.

Nick took a quick left at the base of The Kennedy Center. The force of the turn pushed Lizzy hard against her door, as the Mercedes tires squealed. At the top of the hill, Nick whipped the car to the right and Lizzy exclaimed, "Look!" Ahead of them, they witnessed a repeat of the car firebombing. The motorcyclist had caught up with the lead car, under which he had thrown another mini-Molotov.

Grumman must have assumed the two black SUVs were all he had to worry about. Perhaps he believed Nick's silver Mercedes was a civilian car. He did not see the recklessness of its driver until it was too late. The biker, now in front of The Kennedy Center concourse, gunned his motorcycle forward. Nick pulled alongside and then ahead. He pumped the brakes and slid the Mercedes sideways to block his escape. The motorcycle slammed into the quarter panel of Nick's car and launched the driver airborne over the hood and into a cluster of bushes.

Nick looked up to see Tanner, Lizzy and the three FBI agents running toward the scene. Tanner was first to join Nick. He bolted past Nick and grabbed the dazed fire bomber by his jacket lapels, dragging him out of the bushes. When Tanner jerked the helmet off the biker's head, he saw his face for the first time. It was Grumman. He could barely control his rage. He shook him violently. Lizzy intervened before Nick had a chance to. She put her hand on his shoulder. "Easy, easy," she cautioned Tanner.

The security guard, Jason Young, was wandering the Hall of States when he saw the commotion out front. He left the building to join the men wearing jackets emblazoned with 'FBI.'

Lucas spoke first. "Where's the bomb?" he shouted.

Grumman, still being held by Tanner, smiled, and replied, "Gee, I forget."

Nick's cell phone rang. It was Tom. "Nick, Omni saw the commotion at The Kennedy Center on surveillance cameras. She asked me to show her the face of Francis Grumman."

Tanner freed one hand and drew back to hammer Grumman. Nick blocked the punch with his hand. "Wait, Tanner. I need him."

Nick aimed the cell phone he was holding at Grumman. "Smile," he said, as Grumman looked confused.

"Tom, can Omni narrow her search to surveillance cameras showing this man," said Nick.

Tom replied, "Yes! That's what she needed. She's already narrowing them down. I'm posting to her website."

All of this left the group of FBI agents completely baffled.

"What the hell?" asked Lucas.

"Long story," said Nick. "Get the laptop out of my Mercedes," he told Henderson and Newsom. "Then go to this URL." Nick handed them a card with a series of numbers on it separated by periods.

While Lucas waited, he noticed a security guard standing some distance away, as if debating whether he should get involved.

"Hey," Lucas called out to the security guard. "Who are you?"

"I'm Jason Young. I'm the security guard."

"We've been calling you with no answer," barked Lucas.

"I... uh..." stammered the guard.

"Never mind. You need to evacuate everyone from the building now!"

Chapter 55
Washington, DC

Evacuating over two-thousand people quickly and calmly is no easy task, but the young security guard had help.

Although Nick received surveillance video on his cell phone from Omni, Nick's laptop the FBI agents were using provided a clearer picture. Video portrayed the entire story of Grumman's movements, from his picking up the bomb-ladened vehicle to his driving it to The Kennedy Center.

"I wish we had all of this earlier," exclaimed Agent Lucas.

"I wish we had a photo of Grumman earlier," replied Nick. "My colleague Tom Littleton was trying to make sense of all the surveillance cameras in the city, but that was the missing link."

"Tom Littleton?" said Lucas. "Who's he?"

Nick saw Lucas' puzzled look. "Like I said, long story."

Nick pointed to the screen. The video showed Grumman after he parked the SUV in the parking garage under the center. "Where's that?" Nick asked Grumman, who was now cuffed and securely held by two agents. Grumman said nothing but maintained his indelible smirk.

"I know!" exclaimed Jason Young.

"Take me there!" said Lucas, who turned to the agents holding Grumman. "You keep that guy under control and call in a bomb squad."

"But I have to evacuate the Concert Hall," said Young, who was having to make a choice between two poor alternatives.

"I'll take care of that," said Nick. "Come with me, Lizzy."

Nick knew the FBI would take a dim view of civilians taking on these roles, but Nick and Lizzy were already racing across the plaza to the entrance. Totally against protocol, but he had a bomb to deal with. At least, he had a man who, in a short time, he knew he could count on.

Lucas looked at Tanner. "Come on, Tanner, let's go."

Grumman's SUV stood alone in the parking garage, easy to spot by the three men.

"Why aren't there more cars on this level?" asked Lucas.

"We usually reserve this area for VIP vehicles," answered Young.

"So, if the president came, his limo would be here," said Tanner.

"Were the president here tonight, we wouldn't have a car with a bomb inside. The secret service and their sniffer dogs would have searched every inch of the building. We just have a senator in attendance."

"Just a senator," Tanner sneered.

Lucas peered inside the black SUV. The back of the vehicle was blocked from view by a divider and the tint on the rear glass was too dark to see anything. Lucas pulled from his pocket the key fob he recovered from a search of Grumman's person.

"Wait!" yelled Young.

"What?" asked Lucas.

"What if it's trip-wired and unlocking the car sets off the bomb?"

Lucas now held in his hand a critical decision. Should he wait until the Center was evacuated to press unlock? He didn't know if the bomb had a timer to set it off. Grumman offered nothing on that point.

Should he trust there was no tripwire?

He looked to Tanner for a clue.

Nick and Lizzy raced into The Kennedy Center when Nick realized he didn't know his way around. He didn't even know which way to go to the Concert

Hall. Tom now had Nick talking with Omni directly. He pulled out his cell phone and said, "Omni, can you see where I am?"

"Yes," answered Omni.

"Which way to the Concert Hall?"

"To the end of the hall and to the left."

Lizzy took the lead with Nick behind. They raced down the deserted Hall of Nations and into the Grand Foyer to the Concert Hall. They saw a ramp to their left and took it up to the entrance of The Concert Hall, where they encountered an older woman in a red usher jacket. She gave the out-of-breath late attendees a grandmotherly smile and asked for their tickets.

Lizzy saw that the woman was about her size and said, "Actually, we need to talk to you."

Rachael sat with her friend enjoying the concert, some of which she was familiar with, but not the entire work. She sat in an aisle seat midway up in the center section. Rachael thought it was a perfect location where she could see the entire orchestra. Starting with the second movement, one or two ushers took vacant seats to the side. When the door opened and an usher stepped out, there was another usher standing outside, a redhead who looked just like Lizzy Rodriguez.

Was it well-developed intuition? Was it a reckless guess? Whatever it was, Tanner gave Lucas a simple nod and Lucas pushed the open key on the fob. The locks on the SUV doors clicked open. Security Guard Young nearly fainted, but otherwise, nothing happened.

Lucas and Tanner shared a relieved smile and they walked over to the SUV. Lucas opened the rear door. Large canisters laid sideways on top of each other. No wires were visible. But what bothered them most was the digital display whose bright red digits read 10:00, changing to 9:59. They had less than ten minutes.

Lucas pulled out his walkie talkie connecting to the agents outside. "What's the ETA on that bomb squad?"

The answer came quickly. "They're ten minutes away."

Nick found the stage manager as the orchestra played on and told him why they needed to vacate quickly. Several officials gathered around them talking in hushed tones, asking all the questions one would expect if a stranger had wandered backstage talking about a bomb.

As the men talked among themselves, Lizzy peeked out into the audience and saw someone she recognized. She hatched a plan.

Lizzy walked down to the floor level of the theater and up the aisle to where Denise sat. The audience paid only passing attention to an usher with a message for the man who was sponsoring this event.

"Lizzy!" Denise said in a whisper. "I didn't know you were an usher. But … you were in Wyoming. What—"

Lizzy interrupted the confused Denise. "Listen. I need your help. Are these men with you?"

Denise wasn't sure this newly minted usher had seen the opening, so she explained. "Yes, this is Rex Richardson and that's my husband, Pete."

Lizzy smiled. "Perfect. You all come with me."

Now Rachael was completely mystified by the Lizzy lookalike leading the host of tonight's performance and his people to the exit by the stage.

Lizzy led the senator, Denise, and Rex backstage where Nick was explaining the bomb threat to dubious men backstage. Denise had met Lizzy before, but she didn't know about her connection with Nick Foxe until she arrived backstage. Neither did Nick know that Denise and her husband would be there. It made for an awkward moment as two former lovers discovered each other. That was not lost on the senator who knew about the tryst. It happened many years ago but was not forgotten.

Rex had seen Nicholas Foxe several times and, although Nick didn't know who he was, he had been targeted by the Texan on more than one occasion. Rex listened as Nick recovered quickly from seeing Denise and briefed him on the situation.

Rex set things straight. "Look, I know Nick Foxe. If he says everyone has to vamoose, we got to get to it."

Nick was puzzled by Rex's telling everyone that he knew him, but that could be straightened out later. The NSO director discussed a plan with everyone, and Lizzy added her own element to it.

The second movement concluded and the NSO director walked out with Rex, Pete, and Denise. Lizzy appeared again at floor level.

"Ladies and gentlemen," said the director. "We have a situation in the garage. It is nothing to be alarmed about, but for everyone's safety, we need to ask you to follow the ushers outside. We hope to continue the performance. Please do not enter the garage. Now, if you will all exit as the ushers direct."

The ushers were all perplexed, but they were well-trained. In the unlikely event of an emergency, they knew how to steer a crowd safely out of the building.

The audience began to exit, theories circulating among them about what might be the issue. Fortunately, few mentioned a bomb, and only in terms of a bomb threat, and everyone knows those never have an actual bomb involved.

As Lizzy passed where Rachael and Angie were seated, Rachael said, "Lizzy! It *is* you!"

It confused Angie. "Your friend's an usher?"

"No," replied Rachael, "Or, I don't think so. What's up?"

Lizzy said only, "I'll tell you when we get out of here."

In large red numerals, the bomb's counter now read 05:00.

"The bomb squad's not going to make it in time," said Lucas.

"We've got to drive it out of here," replied Tanner.

"You're right," responded Lucas as he opened the driver's door and hopped in. Tanner ran around to the passenger side. Lucas still had the fob. He started the vehicle and rolled down the window to talk to Young. "Make sure everyone is out front. I'm taking this out the north side."

Young, befuddled, answered, "Yes, sir."

Lucas put the vehicle in drive, and was off, squealing tires toward the exit. He had to slow to go down a ramp to the lower level, wasting precious seconds. Fortunately, the ushers were successful in keeping everyone away from their cars and he had an unobstructed route out of the garage. At last, he reached the exit. Not waiting for the traffic arm to lift, Lucas forged ahead, shattering it. He drove the short distance to the left where he intersected Rock Creek Drive running along the Potomac.

Lucas stopped the vehicle. Tanner didn't understand why. "Are we ditching it here?"

"No," said Lucas. "You're getting out."

"What?"

"Look around you. If we let it explode anywhere around here, we're taking a good chunk of the Watergate and the north side of the Center with it, not to mention cars passing by. There's only one place to put it." Lucas looked straight ahead to the Potomac River.

"I can't let you do that."

"There's no choice, and I'm dying anyway."

Tanner said nothing. His silence told Lucas what he needed to know.

"Yeah, I figured you guys did your homework. You know about that."

"Look..."

Lucas played upon Tanner's army training. "Tanner. I outrank you! Get out!"

Tanner opened the door and got out. Lucas rolled down the window. "Don't worry," he told Tanner. "I'll get out after I dump this in the drink."

With that, Lucas gunned the SUV, tires squealing across the narrow four lanes, across a deserted bike path, hitting the low river wall and launching the bomb-ladened vehicle up and into the river.

Tanner ran across Rock Creek Parkway, horns blasting as he darted between cars, to see the SUV gradually sinking into the water.

"Come on. Come on," he said to no one but himself, looking to see Lucas escape through the door, the window, anything. He saw nothing as the black SUV sank out of sight. Then the bomb detonated.

A huge white pearl of a fireball erupted from the river, its shock waves knocking Tanner backwards to the ground. Cars on the drive screeched to a halt, some striking other cars in the mayhem.

Only half of the audience from The Concert Hall were out front of the Center. They saw the flash to the north side of the building, followed quickly by a deafening boom. Those still inside in The Grand Foyer had a closer view and mass panic was a moment away.

Lizzy, walking out with Rachael and Angie, raced over to an abandoned concession stand and climbed up on it. She yelled out to the crowd, "Don't worry, folks. It's over. Just continue to exit as the other ushers direct."

Lizzy was acting bravely, but she couldn't help thinking.

Where's Tanner?

Grumman, held by the FBI agents, spoke without provocation for the first time. "Beautiful," he said. "Simply beautiful."

Tanner picked himself up and did a quick assessment.

Bad ringing in my ears, but nothing broken.

As the napalm flames burned on the surface of the Potomac, he searched for signs of Lucas. Believing he made it to shore up or down the river, Tanner walked the bike path, hopeful.

Chapter 56
Washington, DC

Nick found Tanner by the river. Professional divers searched for Lucas, but the passage of time with no results dimmed the likelihood that the FBI agent had survived.

Nick put his hand on Tanner's shoulder. "He was a brave man."

"Yeah," Tanner replied. "I guess I've seen my share of brave men. I was the only survivor last time."

Nick knew Tanner meant his last mission in Afghanistan, the one where everyone else was killed in an ambush. It was easy to read Tanner at that moment. Another mission where it was the other guy who died.

News crews gathered under bright lights on the plaza in front of The Kennedy Center interviewing audience members about what they had witnessed. It was clear that the performance tonight would not continue. A camera crew was headed toward the river. Nick knew neither he nor Tanner wanted an interview.

"Let's get out of here," he told Tanner.

Nick and Tanner crossed Rock Creek Parkway where Lizzy, still dressed in her borrowed usher's outfit, met them at the corner of the Watergate complex. She hugged Tanner. "I'm glad you're safe," she said.

"Me, too," responded Tanner.

Just behind her walked Rachael and Angie.

Nick and Rachael's eyes met, but it was Angie that did all the talking.

"Wow," she said. "So, you're Nicholas Foxe." Angie said as she smiled and gave Nick the once over. Angie chatted on, never stopping to catch her breath.

"Rachael told me about the wild things you did, I mean not 'wild' like personal. I mean exciting. Were they all like this? My god, we could have all been killed. You guys must have known what was up. Did they catch the guy? I mean, I thought I saw someone in cuffs…"

Angie rambled on as a young man in a dark suit approached Nick. "Mr. Richardson would like to see you."

"Richardson is the sponsor of the NSO this season," said Rachael for the benefit of those gathered who were taking care of other things. "He said a few things at the beginning of the performance."

"I see," replied Nick. Turning to the young man, he asked, "Who does he want to see?"

"All of you," answered the man. "Please walk this way."

Nick walked beside Rachael, following the young man. He took Rachael's hand. Tanner and Lizzy fell in behind them.

The man led them to a restaurant a short distance away in the south end of the Watergate. Patrons were outside looking at the melee around the Center and barely noticed the short parade as they entered. The man led everyone into the lobby of the restaurant and directly into a private room off to the right. There, sitting in a chair, leaning against a table with a glass of bourbon on the rocks in hand, was the Texan, Rex Richardson.

When the group entered, the Texan stood with a glass raised in his hand as a salute.

"Here we have them," he said. "The heroes of the evening." A woman in a white blouse and black pants passed among the group with a selection of red and white wine in glasses on a tray. Behind her came a man in similar server attire with a tray of hors d'oeuvres. After the evening's events, Nick was confused about now being immersed in a social event.

"You put this together on the spur of the moment?" asked Nick.

The Texan scoffed. "No. This was supposed to be a reception for the folks who put on the concert. Senator Morrison and his wife were supposed to be here, but reporters waylaid them."

"So, we *repurposed* the event you might say," continued the Texan. "Although you all may want something a little stronger than wine." He spotted the server with the wine tray. "My dear, please take drink orders for these fine people."

Nick told the woman he'd like a Johnny Walker Red on the rocks. He asked Rachael what she would like, and Rachael said the white wine was fine for now. Lizzy and Angie were already munching hors d'oeuvres and drinking white wine. Tanner asked for a beer.

The Texan walked up to Nick and thrust his hand out, which Nick shook. "So, you are the illustrious Nicholas Foxe. It's a pleasure to meet you at long last."

Nick took a long look at the man. "It seems like we've met before. I mean, your face seems familiar."

"Likely we've been to the same events, but no, we haven't met. And now, you saved my life, not to mention a whole lot of other folks. I owe you."

"You don't owe me. Let me introduce you to my friends." Nick turned to Rachael. "This is Rachael Friedman."

Rex turned on his Texan charm and told Rachael, "How nice it is to meet you, Rachael."

Nick moved with Rachael and Rex and over to Tanner, who now had a beer in his hand. "This is Tanner, the man who rode the bomb out of the parking garage."

"Pleased to meet you, Tanner," said Rex, who stuck out his hand but received no handshake in return.

Instead, Tanner quickly corrected the telling of the event. "It was FBI Agent Lucas who was the true hero. He rode the bomb into the river. He's likely dead."

Rex changed his celebratory mood to reflect the loss Tanner clearly displayed. "I heard about Agent Lucas. That was quite a sacrifice."

"He was dying of cancer," Tanner said and then looked abashed at his own tactlessness.

"Oh, my," said Rex. "Senator Morrison knows people at the FBI. I'll make sure Lucas' family wants for nothing."

Lizzy had been chatting with Angie, but she left her to join Nick and Tanner when she saw him reliving events of the evening.

"Hi," she said brightly to Rex as she stuck out her hand. "I'm Lizzy."

"So glad to meet the usher who got us out of there," said Rex, shaking her hand.

"Oh," she said, realizing for the first time she was still wearing the uniform. "I borrowed this red jacket. I'm not an usher. In fact, the lady this uniform belongs to may wonder if she's getting it back."

Rex laughed. "I'm sure that after everything that's happened tonight, it might just have slipped her mind."

The senator and his wife Denise entered the room. Denise looked perhaps too long in Nick's direction. Rachael noticed. "Do you know the senator's wife?" she asked Nick.

"Long time ago," he replied, but he could tell that Rachael read everything in his response she needed to know.

Nick's cell phone vibrated in his jacket pocket. He pulled it out and saw that Tom was calling.

"Excuse me," Nick said. "I have to take this."

Nick walked out of the room, thankful that other conversations distracted the senator and his wife. In the hallway, he answered the call.

"Tom, where are you?"

"I'm still at MI6, in something of a war room."

"It's been quite a night."

"I know. We've been watching it all here. They have quite an array of gadgets in this spy shop, but right now everyone in this room has been leaning over my shoulder looking at the surveillance cameras Omni's channeling. I finally put them up on a screen. We saw everything, including the blast in the Potomac. I saw Tanner get out of the SUV. Who drove it into the river?"

"FBI Agent Lucas. You know, Omni gave us the run-down on him."

"Did he survive?" asked Tom.

"It doesn't look good."

"I don't know what to say." Tom paused. "Nick, it's almost morning here, but CNN International has picked up the story. I'm looking at it on a screen now. They just put up a picture of you. I'm reading the closed caption. They say you led the FBI to the scene. You found the bomb. Now there's a photo of Lucas. They say he's a hero."

"Well," replied Nick, "he's getting the credit he deserves."

"Most of the people here are still working the bomb threat at the Royal Albert Hall. Looks like the news outlets haven't yet put together that they're connected." Tom stopped abruptly. "Nick, wait. Paul just arrived, and he's pissed."

Although Nick couldn't make out what was being said, he heard an angry rant from the usually controlled Paul Allerton.

Tom filled Nick in. "Nick, you know Ray Woodward, the guy who helped the authorities at the last minute?"

"Yes."

"He's gone."

Chapter 57

The Cotswolds

Ray's return drive to the Cotswolds was not pleasant.

Grumman eventually folded and told the American authorities all they needed to know. Ray overheard the conversation reported by the FBI to the MI6 officer Paul Allerton. He knew what happened at The Kennedy Center. According to Grumman, when he visited Roland for the details about the Kennedy Center, he was told everything Ray knew, but with one important exception: The bomb would detonate when the building was full of people, not late at night as Roland led him to believe. Apparently, those were the instructions for the Royal Albert Hall as well. Ray knew he had to get away and take matters into his own hands. Paul had turned Ray over to an agent to guard. But when Paul returned, all he would find was an unconscious agent.

Ray was livid. He squeezed the steering wheel tightly as he drove out of London in the early morning darkness. Roland was full of delusional crap about 'the cleansing beauty' of fire. Ray regretted ever becoming entangled with a man who waxed poetically about firebombing Dresden and Tokyo. Ray had managed his love of fire and knew it would never go away. It was a part of him. But he wanted nothing to do with the murder of innocent people.

Ray stopped short of Roland's driveway. He left the car and crept down the country lane to Roland's place. He looked across the garden and saw Roland walking around in his conservatory talking with someone on the phone. It appeared to be an agitated discussion. Ray had no doubt that Roland was talking to a very upset client.

Lloyd Watson was shouting when he called Roland.

"Look," said Roland, "there is a silver lining. *The Planets* was not performed. It is likely it will never be performed again. It carries a jinx."

"Oh, it will be performed again!" shouted Lloyd. "People had to suffer. Suffer like I've suffered. I saw the TV interviews. Everyone was having a gay old time. One man said he looked forward to the rescheduled concert. You've made Holst more popular than ever!"

"Now, now," Roland tried to reason. "I'm sure we can come up with a remedy."

"Oh, I have a remedy. And it has nothing to do with you!" Lloyd said as he hung up.

Lloyd had been tossing down brandies while screaming at Roland and, as he returned to his piano, he poured more. He sat at his baby grand by the window. Bright sunlight poured in, an idyllic day to die.

Lloyd played his masterpiece, the one critics scorned when it premiered. He played the majestic melodies loudly and the refrains soft. His head spun, blurring the composition. Was it the brandy? Was it the additive? The man who sold it to him performed assisted suicides. He assured Lloyd he would have a pleasant departure.

Whatever the reason, his music had never seemed so sweet as it did then. Although, he was beginning to miss a note here and there.

How was that possible?

Lloyd could hear the orchestra come in on queue.

How lovely it was.

He let the imagined orchestra take the lead as he stopped playing and stumbled to his easy chair with the brandy glass in hand. He laid his head back and closed his eyes, enjoying the violins coming into the composition.

Lloyd's brandy glass slipped from his fingers and crashed to the floor. There was a pounding at the door that Lloyd could no longer hear.

"Lloyd Watson, this is the police. Open up!"

More useless pounding.

Ray returned to his car and opened the boot. He fished around until he found a tire iron. He walked up Roland's drive to the shed and used the tire iron to pop the lock off its hinge. He knew what he'd find there.

With the flamethrower on his back, Ray stood before the rear door of Roland's cottage. He pulled the trigger and set that exit on fire. He then walked to the main entrance on the drive and soon set it ablaze. Ray then marched to the front of the house where a plate glass picture window overlooked the garden. Roland stood there, expressionless, smoke entering the room. No fear, no panic, just resignation.

Ray took a long trigger pull and spread flames back and forth across the roof in a defiant demonstration of the fate he intended for his nemesis. Roland sat back in a chair, smiled briefly at Ray, and closed his eyes. Ray spread flames below the picture window. The house was now consumed in an inferno.

Take this for an act of purification!

Ray removed the flamethrower from his back and dropped it to the ground. He returned to his car, started it, and drove away. As he did, two police cars, sirens blaring, blue lights flashing, zoomed past him toward the fire. Ray knew that, had he not intervened, Roland would be arrested. He thought he might have done Roland a favor.

Ray came to the road to London. He drove in the opposite direction.

To: Nicholas Foxe

From: Raymond Woodward

Subject: Farewell

Nick,

By this time, you probably know all about my involvement with recent events. I want you to know that I have terminated my connection with the ancient order. I have burned my bridges if you will.

Several agents of the organization are now dead or captured. I brought an end to one of the principal partners in charge of operations. All of that does not mean the order is no longer a threat. Forgive me for yet another fire analogy, but like the phoenix, it may rise again.

There is one managing partner who remains an unidentified voice on calls. I intend to find him.

Ray

ACKNOWLEDGMENTS

The Fire Starters was a team effort, and the following people were invaluable in its creation.

Thanks go to my beta readers, Ellen Coppley, Walt Curran, Frank Hopkins, Barbara Guzak, Brenda Shaw, Pat Soriano, Laura Maestro, Roger Schreiber, and John Walker. I want to extend a special tribute to beta-reader Bill Kennedy who passed away before the final manuscript was complete. Bill provided much help in getting details right. He will be missed.

On the editorial front, special thanks to Lisa Seabourne who provided invaluable input and helped make me a better writer. To Susan Cleveland whose keen attention to detail smoothed the edges of the final product, and Jessica Gang who performed the final editing of the proof, an essential task in providing the reader with a flawless experience.

And finally, *The Fire Starters* has a great look due to the cover design by Claudia Sperl at Label-Schmiede.

This book is dedicated to my wife Ellen Coppley, my partner in prose.

Read Where It All Began

The Code Hunters

A Nicholas Foxe Adventure

Chapter 1

The Code Hunters
Chapter 1
Afghanistan

They pitched themselves into the dark, cold night, 20,000 feet above the earth.

It was a high altitude, low opening descent, HALO for short. The acronym sounds ethereal, but at odds with a free fall dropping thousands of feet, the air rushing by at gale force. Their mother ship, the C-160 aircraft provided by the German allies, vanished into the night sky. The ground, devoid of the lights of modern civilization, floated below. When altimeters on their wrists read 3,000 feet, they pulled their ripcords. The sliders deployed, slowing and silencing the pop of the ram-air elliptical chutes that provided maximum guidance. The four men drifted about each other in the light of a quarter moon, aiming for the same few square meters of desert at the base of a mountain.

On the ground, they suppressed the air billowing their chutes, made their way to the team leader and huddled in silence. Intel indicated that no enemy would be near this spot, but caution prevailed in making their entry as silent and invisible as possible. Hand signals sufficed.

They were a team of experienced specialists, one that Central Command could direct to capture a key enemy mullah. With the chutes disposed of behind a clump of rocks, they made their way up the mountain. In the chill of morning air, the team waited in a secluded place. As dawn broke, they realized, too late, that the enemy knew they were coming.

In war, leaders make precise plans with well-thought-out contingencies. During the heat of battle, these plans go to hell. So it was with this team as the enemy surrounded them and they were hit by fire from all sides. A young Afghan boy who shouldn't have been there stumbled into the line of fire. No contingency plan for this moment.

A man makes a snap decision that sets in motion events beyond his imagination.

New Mexico – Two Years Later

Experienced cavers formed the team. The moniker 'spelunker' did not apply. Spelunkers once were scientists erudite in geology, but now the term is used for the general unwashed cave explorers. Cavers bring sophisticated equipment to navigate through challenges created by nature. "Cavers rescue spelunkers," say the experts. Tom Littleton, an experienced caver with chambers in the Pyrenees named after him, led the team. Carlsbad Cavern was well explored and tamed to facilitate the paying public. Winding trails bordered by chrome rails lead through limestone openings. Tourists usually were unaware of nearby cave systems much too dangerous for the novice. One, called Lechuguilla, resembled a child's ant farm enlarged a hundred times. It offered long drops where only rappelling experts could descend. Open chambers and lakes were connected by passages barely wide enough to crawl through. Littleton had already explored Lechuguilla's furthest known reaches but believed more remained to discover.

Tom had studied reports of a partially explored area. Cavers rumored the possibility of an undiscovered connection to Carlsbad. Littleton had heard of some half-hearted attempts. A suggestion by a stranger, and Tom's own ego, egged him on. He could do better.

The team winched into the shaft, one-by-one. Previous cavers had hammered and chiseled outcroppings, so that the trip down would be unobstructed. Yet it was laborious to lower equipment for a four-day exploration by means of rope and harness, piece by piece. Littleton and his two teammates worked for hours to get themselves and their gear down and set up a base camp.

The shaft's floor consisted of powdered limestone trampled by cavers before them. The sides of the shaft, jagged layers like rings of a tree, depicted years of sediment from prehistoric seas. It was a rough chimney through which a man could see the last vestiges of daylight. The air inside was cool and still.

Their bodies remained in tune with the sun. They took advantage of fading daylight seeping into the chamber to rest. After tonight, they would move into the depths of the cave where darkness became perpetual. Littleton shared a simple fare of beef jerky and tea with his teammates, Josh Peabody and Jeremy Miller.

Josh served as tactician for the group. He carried maps of previously explored areas and constantly referred to them. He was the man who assembled the gear for this trip and who checked each item to be sure nothing was omitted. In his early thirties and slight of build, Josh had blue eyes seldom seen. They were usually looking down, focused on a map or book, even as he walked along cave paths. It was no mystery why his helmet bore the most dings.

Jeremy was the contrast to Josh. Redheaded, sporting an inch-long matching beard, his fiery hair matching his lively personality. A mid-twenties man with a quick wit and a smart mouth, he was the teammate who constantly looked above and around.

Littleton was not a tall man. Growing up, the boys picked on him since his name fit his stature. But no boy ever picked on him twice. Quick to use his fists from an early age, he pelted his tormentors in an undisciplined series of punches, but they did the job. He had wanted to be an athlete. Baseball or track presented the only way forward for a small, but quick, boy. So, he became a pitcher from little league through high school. Then he discovered caving in his junior year.

Exploring caves was perfect for a man who could squeeze through tight spots. Yet something more made caving right for Littleton. Caves were another world, hidden from the one above. There, in that world, Littleton felt at home.

Littleton possessed a trait he took for granted, but one which his caving teammates assured him was rare. He had a well-developed 'proximity sense.' Many people experience that sense when they feel some unseen person is looking at them. Scientists suspect when we were prehistoric hunters, we had a well-developed proximity sense necessary for our survival. Even today, the blind demonstrate a sense for unseen objects in their path. For Littleton, that sense allowed him to know where the walls of caves were, even in the dark when he couldn't see anything. He sensed his teammates' positions without looking.

"You got everything?" Littleton asked Josh going through the checklist. Of course, Josh had everything. When did he not? Yet Josh, always the self-doubter, hedged with "I believe so." For Josh, 99% signaled failure.

"Well, that was easy," Jeremy quipped at the end of his descent. "This place looks like crowds have been here. Tell me again, why are we here?" He directed the question to Littleton who had convinced the team to come along. "Remind me."

Littleton took time to formulate an answer. How do you rationalize following a random rumor passed along by someone you don't know, mixed with a portion of gut feeling?

300

"It's all about the proximity to Carlsbad. No expert team's been here," Littleton explained, "Until now, that is." A modest boast.

Josh and Jeremy grinned. They were experts, and knew it, even the doubting Josh.

"I suspect there's a connection to Carlsbad," said Tom.

"And no one has found it because...?" Jeremy asked leaving Littleton to complete the statement.

"Because they looked in obvious places," Littleton responded. "Look, most cavers have tried to connect through the shortest distance between two points. That makes sense sometimes, but not always. I think we should try the path less traveled."

"Which means?" Jeremy asked.

"Which means, Carlsbad is to the east," said Littleton, pointing over Josh's shoulder. "So we go west." He smiled as he leaned back, pointing a thumb in the opposite direction.

Josh had done his homework. "Well, it's true the teams before us went east. Few went in the other direction. But in that direction, it peters out. I imagine most thought it was a dead end."

"How far has anyone gone?" Littleton asked Josh, already knowing the answer.

"About 3,000 feet."

"We can do that in a day, maybe two."

"Yeah," sneered Jeremy, "If we have to crawl all the way."

"Some deep knee bends may be necessary," laughed Littleton.

The exertion of lowering gear and setting up camp made sleep come easily; each man cocooned in his sleeping bag to ward off the coolness of the cave.

The next day, Littleton led the team into the "path less traveled." The first 3,000 feet were mapped as Josh pointed out the previous day. The team maneuvered over fallen rock and pits dropping hundreds of feet. It resembled a roadway crumbled by a major earthquake. As they continued, they descended 500 feet below the surface, still short of the 750 feet to the floor of Carlsbad. If successful in connecting to Carlsbad, they would have to find a passage that dropped further.

After hours of arduous climbing over rocks scattered along the way, the channel opened into a room the size of a small cottage. The team sat for a rest as they drank hot tea from their thermoses and considered their next move. Hot tea offered the antidote to both dehydration and the chill they would feel when the sweat evaporated after their climb. Above ground was the dry New Mexico air where perspiration disappeared as fast as it formed. But this was another world and another climate.

The walls of the room were made of limestone with its dusty white surfaces streaked with the browns and reds of iron oxide and occasional blues of carbon deposits. Although the path was cluttered with rock, the entrance to the room contained only a few that had rolled in eons ago. The rest of the room appeared clear. Josh and Jeremy sat on rocks the size of inverted kettledrums sipping tea. Littleton walked the perimeter of the room studying the walls. He examined each crack carefully.

Something is here.

"Well, so much for this idea. No way out," groused Jeremy.

Littleton stayed mute, focused on the cracks in the wall. Josh and Jeremy wondered if Littleton's rumored proximity sense was at work. Then, he announced "Here!"

Jeremy and Josh rushed over to Littleton. "What?" asked Jeremy.

"There's another channel behind this crack."

Littleton stood aside as Josh, then Jeremy, looked into the crack, shining their helmet lamps deep into the darkness. "There's nothing," Jeremy said.

"Look down," smiled Littleton.

Jeremy stood on his toes directing the light downward. Josh followed him, returning Littleton's smile at his discovery.

302

"I see it. There's something there," Josh confirmed.

"Yeah," said Jeremy. "We just need to shrink to ten inches wide to squeeze in."

"Not necessarily," said Littleton as he turned his back to the wall, took out his pick, and struck the wall at knee level near the crack. The soft limestone crumbled into the opening. He looked at his teammates and asked, "Shall we get busy?"

The men took turns hammering away. The first blows pushed through thin limestone at the edges of the crack, but later hammering worked against thicker layers and the progress slowed. Three hours of work provided a fissure just wide enough for each member to squeeze through. Though exhausted, adrenaline motivated each man to push on.

Littleton took a coil of rope and a large piton from his pack. He hammered the piton into the rock outside the fissure, snaked the rope through it and wrapped it under his arms, tying off with a bowline. Josh and Jeremy slipped on their rough cowhide gloves and grabbed the other end of the rope as Littleton lowered himself into the opening. He hammered another piton on the inside of the opening near the top and clicked his rope into it. His teammates would use that one to lower themselves down.

Littleton rappelled down the wall for seventy feet when he reached the floor. "Clear!" he yelled up to Josh and Jeremy as he unknotted the rope. The men each rappelled in turn.

Caves may be wet or dry. Under the surface of the arid New Mexico desert, Littleton had discovered a wet one. His helmet lamp illuminated stalactites and stalagmites surrounding him in a narrow passage, their sweating surfaces reflecting light brought into this chasm for the first time. A small stream flowed on the opposite side. The perfect clarity of the water allowed a view of the bottom only a few inches below. It was a narrow stream in a narrow cave. The water flowed deeper and swifter in another age. The floor of the cave offered a flat path carved by the much larger river parent. Small rocky rubble, falling every century or so, littered the path. Littleton felt like the first man on a secret moon. Josh and Jeremy were soon the second and third man to step foot in this hidden place.

"Wow," the simple exclamation from Josh.

"Yes, wow," responded Littleton. "And look which way it leads. West that way and east this way," pointing behind them and then forward.

"And east leads to Carlsbad," smiled Josh.

"So, we crawled 3,000 feet west to turn around and walk east?" questioned Jeremy.

Littleton grinned. "Well, at least it appears to be an easy walk."

"Yes, but for how long? And 3,000 feet just gets us back to where we started. Carlsbad is beyond that," stated tactician Josh.

"Guess we better rest," said Littleton. "And get our supplies closer."

"Which are up that way," Jeremy grimaced pointing back up the way they came.

"After you," Littleton responded with a wide wave of his hand.

Caving is hard work, but one never wants to be far from supplies. So, the team had no choice but make their way back to base camp. They returned over the same rocky path, exhausted by their efforts and immediately fell asleep. After eight hours of sleep and a dose of hot oatmeal washed down with tea, they returned to the same path, this time taking supplies to last the next extension of their exploration. They set up camp in the limestone room that once appeared to be the end of the line. Each man lowered himself through the crack and down to where they stood the previous day, now armed with food in their bellies and fresh batteries in their helmet lamps.

Once down to the stream bed, they made rapid progress over flat terrain. The team walked cautiously, but easily, along the path. The bright light from their helmet lamps enabled a view of their surroundings. As they walked upstream, seeking the source of the water, they calculated they had passed the 3,000-foot mark. That put them approximately where they started, only far lower.

Forward is Carlsbad!

Without speaking, each man's excitement grew at the prospect they might discover a new connection. They progressed well along the way for another 2,500 feet as the water flow increased. The stream generated a gurgling noise. But as they moved forward, it was joined gradually by the sound of a distant waterfall.

"Listen," said Littleton.

"I hear it," responded Josh, not hiding his exhilaration.

A hundred feet more revealed a shimmering waterfall cascading eighty feet from ceiling to floor. They stopped in silent wonder. Then reality took hold.

"Seems to be the end of the line," observed Jeremy.

No exit appeared. The waterfall covered the back of the chamber. Once again, Littleton refused to accept there was no way out, but back. He walked on a small ledge to the right of the waterfall. "It's not the end. Come on," he yelled over the roar of the water. Then he disappeared behind the fall. Josh and Jeremy rushed to follow.

Emerging from behind the waterfall, wet with a mixture of salty sweat and pristine water, they entered a small chamber. Just large enough to squeeze through, it led from behind the waterfall for a little more than sixty feet, and then opened into a larger area. It was much larger than the limestone room from which they started, and equally dry. As each man entered, their helmet lamps searched the wall surfaces. This time, no way out but back seemed evident. Even Littleton appeared less optimistic. Jeremy put his hand on Littleton's shoulder. "Not bad, my friend. I believe we've discovered a large arm of this cave. Looks like we have naming rights. What do you think? The Jeremy and Friends Cave?" He laughed.

"Wait!' Littleton said. "Look at the floor." Littleton walked across the room, pointing down as he neared a cascade of boulders on the opposite side.

"What about it?" asked Jeremy.

"The floor here is smooth, as if graded, and not by water. There is a place in Carlsbad with the same surface." Littleton's smile expanded as he patted one of the boulders. "I bet Carlsbad is on the other side of these rocks!"

Littleton had walked to the rocks around the left edge of the room. He returned walking directly across the middle. When he took a few steps toward his teammates, the earth gave way beneath him. He fell into an opening and disappeared from sight with only a cloud of dust remaining. Josh and Jeremy rushed over to the hole shouting Tom's name. Then light shown up from the opening. It beamed from Littleton's helmet lamp and bounced in all directions as though reflected from a large mirror.

At last, Littleton spoke. In a slow cadence he reported, "You are not going to believe what I found."

To Learn More About

The Code Hunters

Go to: www.NicholasFoxe.com

ABOUT THE AUTHOR

In addition to *The Nicholas Foxe Adventures*, Jackson Coppley is author of the novel *Leaving Lisa*. His short stories appear in *Beach Life*, *The Apollo Project*, *Bay to Ocean*, and other publications. He writes a daily blog on his website www.JacksonCoppley.com where the entry, *Steve Jobs and Me*, won an award by the Delaware Press Association. A graduate in physics, Coppley's resume includes a career with world communications and technology companies and the launching of what the press called "a revolutionary software program." Now a full-time writer, his work focuses on adventure.

BOOKS BY JACKSON COPPLEY

Nicholas Foxe Adventures

>The Code Hunters

>The Ocean Raiders

>The Fire Starters

Leaving Lisa

Tales From Our Near Future

SHORT STORIES BY JACKSON COPPLEY

>Apollo Summer

>Funland

>Sam Shade

>The Bomber Jacket

>Three Boys and the Moving Pictures

>Women in Cities

>**For more information, go to** www.JacksonCoppley.com

CPSIA information can be obtained
at www.ICGtesting.com
Printed in the USA
LVHW081720191021
700868LV00002B/96